Border City Blues

RIVERSIDE DRIVE

Michael Januska

DUNDURN
TORONTO

Editor: Allister Thompson
Design: Courtney Horner
Printer: Webcom

Library and Archives Canada Cataloguing in Publication

Januska, Michael
        Riverside Drive : border city blues / by Michael Januska.

Issued also in electronic formats.
ISBN 978-1-4597-0674-3

        I. Title.

PS8619.A6784R59 2013   C813'.6   C2012-905803-3

1   2   3   4   5   17   16   15   14   13

We acknowledge the support of the **Canada Council for the Arts** and the **Ontario Arts Council** for our publishing program. We also acknowledge the financial support of the **Government of Canada** through the **Canada Book Fund** and **Livres Canada Books**, and the **Government of Ontario** through the **Ontario Book Publishing Tax Credit** and the **Ontario Media Development Corporation**.

Care has been taken to trace the ownership of copyright material used in this book. The author and the publisher welcome any information enabling them to rectify any references or credits in subsequent editions.

J. Kirk Howard, President

Printed and bound in Canada.

Visit us at
Dundurn.com
Definingcanada.ca
@dundurnpress
Facebook.com/dundurnpress

Dundurn	Gazelle Book Services Limited	Dundurn
3 Church Street, Suite 500	White Cross Mills	2250 Military Road
Toronto, Ontario, Canada	High Town, Lancaster, England	Tonawanda, NY
M5E 1M2	LA1 4XS	U.S.A. 14150

for Laurie

The first policeman I saw needed a shave. The second had a couple
buttons off his shabby uniform. The third stood in the center of
the city's main intersection — Broadway and Union Street —
directing traffic,
with a cigar in one corner of his mouth.
After that I stopped checking them up.

— Dashiell Hammett
from *Red Harvest*

Four and twenty Yankees, feeling very dry,
Went across the border to get a drink of rye,
When the rye was opened, the Yanks began to sing,
God bless America, but God save the King!

— A Prohibition toast

ACKNOWLEDGEMENTS

First I have to thank the Anti-Saloon League's Wayne Wheeler for conceiving and drafting the National Prohibition Act, and Andrew Volstead, chairman of the House Judiciary Committee for helping make it law in 1919. Cheers to them.

Kidding aside, I have to thank Marty Gervais whose writings and tireless enthusiasm for the Border Cities continue to be a source of inspiration. There are other people in my hometown who each endeavour in their own way to preserve and share its rich history. I have them to thank as well (and now we can all be crazy together).

An early version of the chapter "Ojibway" appeared in the *Windsor Review*, and I would like to acknowledge the *Review* for their support and Alex McKay for shepherding that through and for the occasional kick in the pants.

It is such a boost to have one's work recognized. I'd like to thank again the Scene of the Crime Author Festival for twice honouring my work, two short stories, both of which were set in the world of *Riverside Drive*.

Hats off to my editor, Allister Thompson, who was an early champion of *Riverside Drive* and got me to pull it out of the bottom of my desk drawer. And thanks to the rest of the talented individuals at Dundurn for helping putting it between covers, both paper and virtual.

Much thanks and gratitude to family both near and far for their patience and encouragement. I know writers can be such tiresome people.

Lastly I would like to express my gratitude for the teachers I had who never stopped telling me that creative people do indeed have a valuable place in society. I know not all of us get to hear that.

FALSE STARTS

(APRIL 1919–JULY 1922)

Chapter 1

DEMOLITION MAN

April, 1919

Jack McCloskey returned from the war so restless and full of nervous energy he couldn't stand without pacing or walk without running, and whenever he got behind the wheel of his car it was a test of the machine's endurance. While folks in town may have sympathized, they were also getting a little tired of dancing around him like he was an unexploded artillery shell.

The turning point for Jack came one April morning when he set out in his Olds 37 for the post office on the main road and wound up lost in the next county. He pulled over onto the shoulder when he realized he had been driving around blind for close to an hour.

An old farmer mending a fence on the other side of the ditch gave him directions home. When the same thing happened a few days later he didn't pull over or even bother to slow down, not even after he noticed the blood smear on his shirtsleeve. He just kept driving.

He was somewhere on the other side of Wheatley, heading east on the Talbot Road along Erie's north shore. Stealing glances at the stony beach and rough blue water, he wondered if he wasn't somehow trying to drive himself back to his senses. He listened to the tires grind the road and the gravel ping off the fenders. He watched the farms shrink in his rearview mirror before disappearing in the clouds of yellow dust. Putting the last couple of months behind him would be a good start, he thought, a good first step.

He thought about that for a few more miles before deciding to take the long way home around Lake Erie. He suddenly felt a small measure of calm. He told himself he was doing the right thing. He hoped his father would understand. He knew his brother wouldn't. But understanding was never something they expected from each other. What they expected, and got in spades, were rivalries and petty differences that too often blew up into fistfights. Their father tried not to take sides, but there were times when it was the only way to settle a matter.

The road wound away from and then back towards the shore. Sometimes it was level with the beach while other times it traced the edge of a bluff. He felt like he was stitching the land to the lake. At one point the road disappeared into a dense cluster of maples. When it broke through, McCloskey looked out and noticed a couple fishing boats heading into the open water. It occurred to him that he hadn't been stateside since he was a boy, on mysterious journeys with his father that he now knows were rendezvous with other smugglers. That was a lifetime ago.

McCloskey re-examined the blood on his shirtsleeve. It had turned brown. Was it his? He didn't seem to be cut anywhere and wasn't in any kind of pain. He searched his mind but had no recollection of leaving the house, let alone the circumstances under which he did so. He rolled up his shirtsleeve and turned his mind back on the road.

A couple of weeks passed before Frank McCloskey received word from his eldest son that he was working on a construction site in Toledo. Jack had been nearing the end of his 600-mile odyssey when, approaching Michigan, he saw a sign for the Canadian border and hesitated. He wasn't ready to go home quite yet, though that's not exactly what he said in his first postcard home. He simply told his father everything was fine but not to expect him any time soon.

Jack got himself hitched to a team of labourers hired to demolish and excavate a city block. They worked right alongside the tractors and steam shovels with their crowbars and sledgehammers. It was brutal work but he threw himself into it. Having succeeded in driving himself from distraction, he was now set to realign his mind and body. The workers, many of them veterans, were put up in barracks. On the off hours they gambled, drank, and beat on each other. Eventually these three activities were amalgamated into bare-knuckle matches fought in the back room of Buckeye's — the local watering hole.

Although he was passionate about boxing and had won many regimentals, McCloskey wasn't interested in any of this. He figured if he got injured in a fight he could be out of a job as well as out of a purse. And judging by the size of the purse, it wasn't worth the risk. He could be quite pragmatic. That is, until he got inspired.

A few weeks later, under a blazing hot Fourth of July sun, he and several thousand other fight fans sat in a makeshift arena over in Bay View Park and witnessed Jack Dempsey take on Jess Willard for the world heavyweight title. Dempsey looked disciplined, focused as he timed the release of each devastating blow. Willard had at least forty pounds on Dempsey, but Dempsey's skill and ferocious power almost crippled the defending champion before the end of the first round.

Willard staggered about the blood-splattered mat for another six minutes; taking hit after hit, his right eye swollen shut, his face a crimson mess. Before the bell signalled the start of the fourth round, someone from Willard's corner threw in the towel and it landed at Dempsey's feet. Dempsey had battered Willard within an inch of his life. Cheering fans swarmed the ring and carried off their new champion. The next morning McCloskey found a gym and started training.

A fellow from the payroll office who knew a thing or two about keeping a book arranged for McCloskey to go a few rounds with a steelworker from the site. Bets started rolling in and the steelworker quickly became the odds-on favourite. He had a larger-than-life personality with matching shoulders, and when he wasn't dragging his knuckles on the sidewalk he was using them to drive rivets into fastener plates.

The match was held on a hot and humid August night. Everyone came out to witness McCloskey's suicide, filling the back room at Buckeye's with their stench, noise, and cigar smoke. After the initial bell there was about a minute of dancing around that attracted groans and empty beer bottles from the crowd. The steelworker reacted by throwing a few careless swings at McCloskey's head. And then McCloskey came out of nowhere with a barrage of punches culminating in a powerful left hook that crushed the steelworker's cheekbone and sprinkled a few of his teeth across the mat. He went down. His trainer doused him with buckets of cold water, but his lights stayed out for a good long time.

McCloskey stood over his opponent's mangled body and smiled through the blood and sweat trickling down his face. Everyone was amazed at the fury and intensity of McCloskey's blows. He was like a force of nature, moving from unforeseen to unstoppable in a matter of seconds. He surprised even himself. The site foreman lost money on the fight, big money, the kind of money that's hard to forget.

The next day McCloskey was told his services were no longer required and that he should hit the road. That was fine with him. He was confident that he could find work elsewhere by selling himself as both a skilled labourer and a fierce contender, and he did. He became a regular in the factories and shipyards that dotted the western shores of Lake Erie, fighting in bloody, bare-knuckle bouts that re-established his old regimental nickname: Killer McCloskey.

This went on for just over a year until jobs started getting scarce. Recession, labour unrest, and an influenza epidemic were taking their toll on the economy. McCloskey considered going home. He didn't doubt there were opportunities back in the Border Cities; what he was afraid of was relapsing into the twisted wreck of a man he was at the end of the war. At the same time he felt guilty about not keeping in touch with his father and brother. He had written them only two or three times since he left home, and even then it was only a few lines on a postcard.

Days passed between jobs, and the bitter cold sharpened his hunger pangs until they were like a knife in his gut. He rang in the New Year unemployed and without a roof over his head. He was beginning to appreciate how quickly one's fortune could turn. It was a bad spot to be in: even if he could get himself a match, he couldn't fight tired and with no food in his belly. He was running on empty, in every sense.

One morning while on a job hunt he found himself parked on the shoulder of Telegraph Road at the north end of town, staring at the sign that had stopped him from going home once before: CANADA 60 MILES. This time it felt like Toledo was showing him the door. He checked his mirror and saw a truck approaching. He let it pass before merging with the traffic heading into Michigan.

When he reached Monroe he pulled over at a filling station to chisel the ice off his windshield and replenish his cigarette supply. At the counter in the garage there was a conversation going on between the mechanic and a teamster. It had something to do with the local stamping plant. Apparently as of this morning there were a few openings. The driver told McCloskey that if he was interested he should head over there pronto.

For once McCloskey's timing was perfect: he landed himself a job at the plant. He felt saved in more ways than one. With what little money he had left he got himself a hot meal and a room at a run-down hotel near the train station. It would feel good to be working again. He stretched himself out on the bed and listened to the boxcars shunting back and forth until night fell. He closed his eyes and sleep came swiftly.

When he finished his shift the following afternoon and he felt he had a read on the place, he made some noise about being in need of a punching bag. The line workers knew what he was on about. One of them introduced him to a foreman who doubled as the plant's unofficial sports and entertainment director. The foreman immediately paired McCloskey with a regular, a fighter who hailed from Oklahoma and went by the name Kid Okie.

The story was the Kid had been too young to go to war, so he stayed home and pulled his mammy's plow instead. When she couldn't afford to feed him any more because the crops were poor, she sent him into the rustbelt to seek his fortune. He was pocketing the money he made at the plant and sending his ma his meagre winnings. Little did the old lady know.

When the Kid climbed into the ring, McCloskey took a step back. He was about the size of one of the smaller Midwestern states. His short-cropped hair was white, in sharp contrast with his ruddy complexion. His trunks looked like they were tailored from a couple of grain sacks, his fists like clutches of sausages. At the sound of the bell he ambled towards McCloskey. He looked like he meant to do harm.

McCloskey got the Kid to swing first and then weaved to his left, sent a crushing right to his solar plexus and, as the Kid spun, a left to the kidney. The Kid straightened up just in time to receive another combination of furious body blows followed by an uppercut that broke his jaw in three places. He was rolling his wisdom teeth around in his mouth when McCloskey delivered the coup de grace: a solid left hook to the side of his head.

Less than thirty seconds into the fight, Kid Okie was as cold and flat as the prairie in winter. He never knew what hit him. When they pulled him off the mat he was thunderstruck, like a soldier pulled out of the earth after being buried alive by a mortar blast. McCloskey felt sorry for the kid, but only for a minute. He felt sorrier for the Kid's mammy, who wouldn't be getting her accustomed envelope this month.

There was another dry spell and several weeks passed without any fight prospects. Then McCloskey got laid off from the plant. Pretty soon he was idling fast and getting anxious again. He knew what this could lead to, and the choice was clear: either fall apart in the streets of Monroe or take his chances back home in the Border Cities.

McCloskey did his best thinking while eating. He debated the pros and cons of playing the prodigal son over a plate of muskrat, potatoes, and cabbage, washed down with a pint of ale much improved by a shot of rye. When he finished he considered the rat carcass on his plate and the nickel change he had left. Maybe it was time to finally bring things full circle. Ready or not, maybe it was time to take it home.

He jogged through a light spring rain back to his car, where he thought about it some more. Eventually he settled on a compromise: he'd go back to the Border Cities but wait to contact his family. He would get himself a job at Ford's — far from Ojibway but still close to the action — and settle in. Only after he carved a space for himself would he then contact his father and brother.

Satisfied with his decision, he leaned back on the door, stretched his legs across the seat and, listening to the rain gently fall on the roof of the Olds, fell into deep sleep.

Chapter 2

THE SQUARE CIRCLE

April, 1921

McCloskey left Monroe under a pale dawn hoping he had enough gas to get him the thirty or so miles upriver to Detroit. He braked for nothing and no one, coasting through intersections in Trenton, Wyandotte, and Ecorse. It turned into a game to see how far he could get without either stopping or slowing down.

Approaching Zug Island he knew that Ojibway, his hometown and the westernmost Border City, was just over there on the other side of the river. Even if he didn't have Zug to give him bearings, he knew where he was by the angle of the light on the water.

He stayed close to the shoreline, taking Jefferson Avenue all the way into Detroit. He finally had a clear view of the Canadian shore when he came around Fort Wayne, and where the river bends at its narrowest point he could make out the spire of Assumption Church amid the budding trees and the cars moving along Riverside Drive. Those were his people over there; that was home. He hadn't realized how lonely he was until now.

He had been wandering the desert, trying to heal, and learning more about the world along the way. His mind rolled back two years to when he originally set out on his journey. It was a clear April morning not unlike this one, but his head was in a fog. He felt he was a different person now, better equipped for life. He had crossed paths with a lot of veterans in his travels. Some had found their way while others were still pulling themselves out of a mental foxhole. He could tell when one of them wasn't going to make it. He could see it in their eyes. He wondered what others saw in his.

There was a lot of a commotion around Union Depot, and he had to stop for a train crossing Jefferson and heading into the station. Taxis and luggage wagons were jockeying for position around the departures area so he dropped down to Atwater. He could have taken the ferry across at Woodward Avenue, but when he saw the crush of people at the docks he was convinced he was doing the smart thing by taking the side-door entrance into the Border Cities upriver. Ford City was his objective anyway.

Fortunately, there were enough fumes in the engine and quiet in the streets that he was able to just make it through the downtown. He let his dilapidated Olds roll to a stop near the corner of Dubois. He abandoned the vehicle and its contents, resisting the impulse to take a match to it. Instead he hoofed the last few blocks to the bottom of Joseph Campau Street. The air was cool, but he could feel the sweat on his brow and the anticipation stirring in his belly. *We're going to take things one step at a time*, he reminded himself, *one step at a time*.

It was early morning and commuters were gathering at the dock: drab pencil pushers from the distillery scanning the business columns of the *Free Press* and talking export duty, and a couple middle-management types from Ford's discussing productivity. McCloskey walked up to the kiosk where he exchanged his life savings — a nickel — for a ticket to Walkerville.

The ship's whistle blew once and then a second time.

He boarded and climbed the stairs to the top deck as the little wooden ferry pushed off. To his left the sun was peaking over Belle Isle, burning off the thin fog that was clinging to its beaches. Straight ahead was the Canadian shore. He watched the perspective enlarge from a postcard to life-size view. When he could clearly read the "Distillery of Canadian Club — Walkerville" sign he got a lump in his throat. It was like seeing the dome of St. Paul's after spending months adrift at sea. Only a local could get this sentimental over rye.

The water was blue-black and smooth as glass. Near the imaginary line running down the middle he glanced back and forth between Detroit and the Border Cities. A mile of water separated them but these two communities seemed worlds apart. On the American side was a sprawling metropolis, factories that were putting the world on wheels, buildings that poked the sky; hustle and bustle, challenge and ambition.

In contrast, the Canadian side was still very green in places. Cottages and clapboard houses stood alongside the small factories along the shore; church steeples watched over tree-lined streets. The downtown still had an old-world feel and the pace was slower. There was still less horsepower than horse power.

The ferry docked and McCloskey was the last one to disembark. When he entered Canada Customs he was greeted by a portrait of King George V in full regalia, eyes bulging and beard sharpened to a point. He would have preferred a greeting by a barmaid pouring shots of homemade peach brandy, but he knew that would come later. The official asked the usual questions and McCloskey, penniless and jobless, returning home with little more than the shirt on his back, answered politely and played the veteran card. The official waved him through and once outside, he took a deep breath.

Devonshire Road looked the same as it did before the war — the Peabody Building, the train station, Crown Inn. He resisted the temptation to drop to his knees and kiss the cobblestone and instead started picking his feet up and putting them down again until they got him all the way over to Ford's, about a half-dozen blocks up Riverside Drive.

He wandered around and then fell in with some workers sharing a cigarette around a smouldering scrap heap. They exchanged stories about France and then McCloskey told them about his post-war life on the other side of the border. When he felt he had their trust, he told them he was willing to wager that after putting in a day's work on the assembly line, he could step into a ring and demolish any challenger.

He did a good job of selling himself. Word quickly got around, and by the end of the day he got himself a job at the engine plant and an invitation from an old comrade from the 99th Battalion to stay with him until he got a place of his own. The soldier and his young wife kept an apartment above a store on Drouillard Road. It wasn't much, but after all the nights he'd spent sleeping in his car, McCloskey was more than happy for a warm spot on the chesterfield. Fortune seemed to be smiling at him again. It felt good to be home.

It was a few days before McCloskey got a match. His opponent, Vito "the Volcano" Tarantino, worked in casting. McCloskey checked him out at shift change. He was a mountain of a man with a bald head and hairy shoulders, and the word at the plant was that he could bend and twist automobile parts with his bare hands like he was making balloon animals at a kid's birthday party. McCloskey smiled to himself; he was back in the game.

The fight was set for the third Saturday of the month, a couple of days before a big referendum on Prohibition in Ontario. The bookies had a field day with it. The short money was on a victory for the *wets* and the Volcano. If you wanted to hedge, you saw a potential victory for the *drys* since the rest of the province never seemed to go along with what the Border Cities wanted.

McCloskey was the long shot. People weren't familiar with his fighting skills, and when they saw him he didn't exactly inspire a whole lot of confidence. He was six feet but not that big, weighing in at 180 pounds. And despite the broken nose and scar over one eye, he seemed too well-preserved to have had the experience needed to flatten the Volcano. With his jet-black hair and sculpted features, he didn't look like a fighter so much as a Hollywood actor playing one in a movie.

When the bell rang McCloskey got right to work on the Volcano, driving blow after blow into his face and torso. The Volcano stood his ground. His massive body and granite-like head absorbed every hit. The timekeeper's bell was mounted on a board perched on his lap. After three minutes he gave the string a yank and the bell went *ding*. McCloskey walked back to his corner, surveyed the audience and saw a bunch of yolks with stupid grins on their faces. He wondered if he hadn't been suckered into something. He glanced down at his weapons: fingers and hands wrapped in a thin layer of cheesecloth begged off a butcher at the local delicatessen, already bloodied. It would be a bad thing to lose his first fight in the Border Cities.

The bell opened the second round. McCloskey immediately decided to open things up a bit and offered the Volcano a few golden opportunities, but they were ignored. It became clear his opponent's strategy was to lie dormant while McCloskey tired himself out, and then erupt.

But McCloskey wasn't going to let it come to that. He started circling the Volcano, all the while winding up a punch from the tips of his toes. When he felt the power surge into his upper body he stopped dancing, planted his feet on the mat and pointed his right foot at the Volcano. His right arm then swung naturally, like a lightning bolt discharged from a storm cloud. It made sharp contact with the side of the Volcano's head and nearly knocked it off his shoulders. He went down hard and the boys standing along that side of the ring took two steps back.

A cloud of dust billowed up from the mat and there was a big empty space where the Volcano used to be. The audience was in shock at first, then the shouting started between attendees and between Volcano and his trainer. His trainer, who also happened to be his brother, started crying into his towel. Over in a dark corner of the room serious money was changing hands.

McCloskey just stood there, surprised that he still had that much fire in him. He had thought he would have mellowed a bit. He took another look around the room, half-expecting to see his father and brother in the crowd for some reason. If word had not already made its way out to Ojibway that he was back in town, it would very shortly.

At the end of the day it turned out to be a bittersweet victory. While McCloskey won the fight and Windsor voted against Prohibition, the majority in the province supported it. So for anyone who happened to miss the war to end all wars, they needn't worry, Prohibition would be their chance to see some action.

DRYS LEAD BY 140,000 read the headline in Monday's paper in big, bold letters. It was like the world had finally come to an end. Technically speaking, though, the world wasn't scheduled to end for another three months. July 19, 1921 — that's when the new legislation would come into effect. From that day forward, not only would it be illegal to manufacture liquor for sale within Ontario, it would be illegal to import it as well. There was still time to stock up.

McCloskey was in a downtown pool hall going through the mechanics of his left hook with his new friends from the plant when someone came in with the afternoon edition of the *Border Cities Star* and began reading bits out loud. McCloskey remembered being in Cleveland when Prohibition hit the States. The general feeling then was that folks would just have to get their booze from across the lake. Now both sides would be more or less dry and a solution would require a little creative thinking.

Further reading revealed the date for the upcoming Dempsey-Carpentier championship fight. The focus of the conversation immediately shifted back to boxing, with brief asides on the seating capacity of a Studebaker Big Six and the best route to Jersey City.

Then the room fell silent. McCloskey noticed everyone suddenly looking past him and some then retreating into the shadows.

"You like Dempsey?"

There were a few, especially among American veterans, who still thought of his hero as a slacker. McCloskey turned slowly, expecting a challenge. It was a suit. The man filling it out was not as tall as McCloskey, but broader. His nose was pressed against his face and a scar intersected his left eyebrow. His jaw resembled a truck fender. McCloskey figured the guy had to have been a fighter, probably twenty years and as many pounds ago.

"You're Killer McCloskey, aren't you?"

"I might be."

The man smiled and under the brim of his hat his squinty, deep-set eyes twinkled like diamonds at the bottom of a mineshaft.

"That was something the other night," he said. "I mean the floor shook when that dago hit the mat."

McCloskey wondered what he was after. Judging by the reaction of the boys in the pool hall, it wasn't an autograph. McCloskey played it down.

"It was no big deal."

Actually, it was a big deal. Little did McCloskey know, but his win had made the man in the suit a tidy sum of money and had nearly ruined a number of his rival bookies in Detroit.

"C'mon. I'll buy you a drink. Not here — I've got a little place around the corner."

Apparently, the man had come to talk business. He said his name was Green. Later on McCloskey heard some other fellows refer to him as the Lieutenant.

— *Chapter 3* —

THE LIEUTENANT

It was getting late and the stragglers were heading home to flop. Green walked McCloskey around the corner to a diner on Pitt Street next to the Department of Soldiers' Civil Re-establishment. Green picked through his key ring while McCloskey pressed his nose against the window. What he saw didn't look like much.

"No — over here."

Green was unlocking a plain-looking door to the right of the diner entrance. On the door was a small plaque that said "International Billiards — MEMBERS ONLY."

The door opened to a narrow stairwell lit by a bare bulb hanging over the landing. McCloskey walked in Green's shadow all the way up. On the landing and to the right they were confronted with an even heavier door that had a covered peephole the height and width of a pair of eyes. Green jangled his keys again, poked the locks, and swung it open.

The room was pitch black except for a bit of light in the windows overlooking the street below. Before stepping inside, Green reached around the doorframe and finger-punched a couple switches on the wall.

From the copper ceiling hung globe lights that illuminated a bunch of tables and cane chairs arranged haphazardly between the entrance and the bar. To the right were five billiard tables standing side by side. A big skylight punctured the ceiling above the centre table. Blinds covered every window except the ones along back that faced a brick wall in the alleyway.

It was first-class but not fancy, all oak and polished brass with spittoons on the floor instead of sawdust. Green could tell McCloskey was impressed. He let McCloskey take it all in and then pointed with his chin towards a room jutting out from the far corner.

"My office," said Green.

He went in ahead of McCloskey and pulled the chain on a desk lamp. He shuffled some papers into a pile, removed his bowler hat and set it on top.

"Take a load off."

McCloskey lowered himself into one of the matching wooden armchairs that faced the desk. Green offered him a cigar from a humidor that looked like a small treasure chest.

"Thanks."

On a little table that stood between the two chairs was a metal contraption for snipping off one end of a cigar and lighting the other. It looked like it had been made in a machine shop out of spare engine parts. McCloskey put it to work and got the tip of the Cuban glowing. It was nice. Green poured some brown liquid into tumblers while McCloskey surveyed the room. Trophies lined a mantle and photos of boxers in their fighting stance hung on the wall. One of the pugilists was unmistakably Green.

"That was a long time ago."

He handed McCloskey one of the tumblers and then settled into his chair. The leather groaned beneath him and he stole a puff from his cigar.

"If you don't mind my asking, how much money you make last year dropping palookas like the Volcano?"

McCloskey told him.

Green gave a gravelly laugh then paused for dramatic effect. "How'd you like to make that in one fight?"

McCloskey nearly swallowed his cigar.

"Seriously — I've got money and connections. As far as I can tell that's all you need to take a fighter to the next level."

"You a promoter?" asked McCloskey.

Green leaned forward. "Not exactly. But I got what it takes, and so do you."

He was trying to grab the wheel from McCloskey, and it made McCloskey a little uncomfortable.

"Whoa, I like money just as much as the next guy, but let's be honest here — I'm no boxer. I'm just a fighter, and if you're looking for someone to go the long haul with you're a few years too late with me."

"How old are you?"

"Twenty-six."

Green waved a dismissive hand. "Forget about that."

He got up and perched on the edge of his desk. His movements were always slow and deliberate. He was a man that didn't hurry for anyone.

"You got fire in you," he said, pointing at McCloskey with his cigar. "I can see that. All it needs is a little refinement."

What Green also saw in McCloskey was his second, albeit vicarious, chance at achieving boxing greatness. He had missed his first opportunity after getting shot up in the Transvaal. He had come limping home from South Africa with no prospects and ended up doing time in the streets or the jails of Montreal. Another war came along, but this time the army wouldn't have him, so he started looking for the big payoff, a caper that would set him up really nice. As luck would have it Prohibition arrived in the States and created a world of opportunities. He signed on with a smuggling syndicate and got shipped down to Windsor to secure a territory along the border opposite Detroit. Green was the Montreal boss's first lieutenant. He'd done well for himself but his heart was still in the ring. Seeing McCloskey drop the Volcano was like rekindling an old flame.

He got down to brass tacks. More chit-chat followed, but before long Green was through talking and there was one last dramatic pause.

"So what do you say?" He extended a meaty paw. "We got a deal?"

Okay, McCloskey thought, *okay: I make some money, he gets his thrill, and then right before I get crippled by the next big thing to come along, we both go back to our day jobs.*

"And if it doesn't work out," said McCloskey, "we both walk away with no hard feelings?"

Green rested his hand on his knee. "You telling me you won't be committed, Killer? A fighter's got to be committed."

"I'll be committed, all right. But I got my limits, just like any man. I know that now."

Green shifted his cigar from one corner of his mouth to the other and studied McCloskey through the smoky cloud that hung between them.

"Don't think I'm not grateful for the opportunity," continued McCloskey. "It's just that I've had a bit of a rough time since I got back from overseas. I found my feet but I still need to set a few things right."

Green squinted at him, like squeezing his eyes would squeeze the truth out of McCloskey. "You in any kind of trouble, Killer?"

McCloskey straightened in his chair and, thinking of his father and brother, said, "I have some debts to pay."

"Well, what better way to do it? So, do we have ourselves a deal?"

Green extended his hand again and the expression on his face told McCloskey that this time he had better take it. Green was a compelling figure and the slightest change in his body language or tone of voice would convince anyone he meant business.

"Yes, sir — deal."

"Good. Now let's drink a toast."

Chapter 4

REDEPLOYMENT

McCloskey got himself a room in a boarding house on Cadillac Street, a couple blocks up from the Drive, behind Our Lady of the Lake church. His landlady was a tough old bird who lost both her sons in the war and so doted on McCloskey, keeping him well fed and under strict curfew. It wasn't necessary, but Green slipped her a few notes every now and then as a token of his appreciation.

When he wasn't loading engine blocks into vehicles on the assembly line, McCloskey was training in the local gym or running laps alongside the Lieutenant's Packard around the park on Belle Isle. It was a cobalt blue, twin-six roadster and its every line was ingrained in McCloskey's mind. It was a beautiful car and McCloskey often thought the Lieutenant was baiting him with it.

One day, son, you could own a car like this.

Needless to say, McCloskey never made it to Jersey City for the Dempsey fight. He remained in the Border Cities all summer long, making good money going the distance with middleweight, sometimes heavyweight, contenders from up and down both sides of the Detroit River.

All of this activity and all of these distractions made it easy for him to ignore the fact that he still hadn't made contact with his father or brother. What was the compromise he had made with himself? He would get a job and settle in, then play the prodigal son. They had to know by now that he was back in the Border Cities. Was he making things worse for himself by putting it off? Probably. But whenever it weighed heavily on his mind, he noticed how he worked that much harder, ran that much faster, and threw a punch that much more forcefully.

On Labour Day weekend he fought in a match downriver in a warehouse adjacent to where Ford was building another blast furnace for his River Rouge plant. The street felt hotter than the surface of Mercury that day, but McCloskey was as ready as ever. And so was his opponent. "Eagle" Eckhardt got his nickname building Eagle Boats at Rouge during the war. The patrol boats were steel-plated with a cement-filled bow made for ramming and sinking vessels, and Eckhardt had since sunk more than his share of enemy craft.

They beat on each other for a solid four rounds before they started staggering around the floor, suffering from heat exhaustion and looking for the opening that might mercifully bring it to an end. Off in a corner Green fanned himself with his straw hat while watching his fighter wither under the strain. The audience took pity on the two but held on tightly to their betting slips.

McCloskey was hallucinating. He was looking down at him and his father, just as they were that fateful morning. He was in another one of his blind rages, and his father was trying to calm him. Billy entered the room, pulled him off his father, and pinned him against the wall.

Eckhardt noticed McCloskey was slowing up and letting his guard down. The golden opportunity was presenting itself and Eckhardt responded with a series of quick blows to McCloskey's torso, sending him stumbling into the ropes. Then Eckhardt moved in for the kill. Green clenched down hard on his cigar, almost biting it in half, and shouted something at the referee.

McCloskey wasn't in the ring anymore; he was in the front room back at the house. And he was ready to take a crack at Billy. He shook the sweat off his face and in an explosion of energy sent his brother tumbling back over the low table.

Eckhardt didn't know what hit him. McCloskey shook the sweat off his face and was swinging hard at him. McCloskey grazed his face and then drilled a hard left into his gut. Eckhardt was already sore from dehydration and instinctively tried to protect his belly. He handed McCloskey the opportunity to hammer his skull with a series of lightning-fast hooks. Red, amber, and then black.

Eckhardt's eyes rolled back and then he folded onto the floor. McCloskey stood over him, cursing Billy and blathering nonsense about the war, their dead mother, Mary, who had died of influenza while they were en route home from the war. Frank told his boys as soon as they got in the door and that was what finally pushed them both over the edge. Billy retreated into a bottle and Jack flew into a blind rage. He spent some nights literally bouncing off the walls. It got so bad his father had to hold him down to keep him from hurting himself.

McCloskey saw himself turn and move towards his weakling father who had failed them. He remembered swinging, and then the sound of an ambulance and men in white taking Eckhardt away on a stretcher. He came face to face with the fire deep inside him, and in this sweltering furnace it gave him chills.

By the middle of September, McCloskey had fought nine times in fifteen weeks and suffered only one loss — his first to date. He lost that match only because to win it he would have had to kill his opponent. McCloskey had become a fighting machine. Green himself quietly wondered what the eventual toll might be.

On the surface McCloskey remained cautious. He saved his winnings and kept his job at the factory. Fighters had short careers, and the ones who didn't have anything to fall back on had proportionately shorter lives. All the same, he threw himself headlong into the fight world that Green had opened to him.

But Green's world was starting to change. The bootleg business was gathering momentum and required his undivided attention. He began to regret starting something with McCloskey he probably knew all along he couldn't finish. He felt he either had to find McCloskey a real manager or something equally as challenging and lucrative. It occurred to him that there might be a place for McCloskey in the outfit. McCloskey had grit and character; he also knew what it took to get a job done. He had talents that were being wasted in the ring, and Green could see that now.

"You're smart," said Green to McCloskey one day. "You could really go places if you wanted."

They were standing on a street corner trading racing tips with a newsboy. It was the middle of September and an unseasonably warm day, what some folks call an Indian summer.

"C'mon. I'll buy you a drink."

It was time to talk business again. They walked over to the pool hall.

"I'm not telling you to leave the ring. You do what your gut tells you. All I'm saying is there's work here for you if you want it."

McCloskey was sort of relieved. He felt that he had turned a corner with the fight down at Rouge and was now stuck in a dead end. He wasn't getting anything out of it anymore. He didn't really care about the money, or about taking his fight skills to another level and pursuing a title. He had been looking for a way to break it to Green, but now he didn't have to. Green continued.

"I feel sort of responsible, like I talked you into something. I hope you don't have any regrets. I know I don't."

Green had believed in him from the start and helped save McCloskey from himself. And McCloskey not only wanted to pay him back, he wanted to do him proud.

"A guy should take advantage of every opening that presents itself, both in and out of the ring. If there's a place for me in the outfit, I'll give it everything I got."

Green smiled and pulled his best bottle and a couple glasses from a desk drawer. He filled them and then passed one to McCloskey.

"To Wheeler."

"To Volstead."

Green explained how business had been building steadily since the referendum.

"I'm telling you, kid, as long as people are drinking we'll be selling. Dry? What a fucking joke that is. Queen's Park and the Methodists ought to go into vaudeville together."

Green leaned back in his chair and took a drag on his cigar. He punctuated every sentence with a big blue smoke ring.

"We're fortunate to be living here in the Border Cities, Killer. It represents an incredible opportunity for us. All these towns are lined up like kegs behind a bar, just waiting to quench the thirst of each and every American between here and Chicago." He leaned back in his chair. "And then there are the peripheral activities — gambling, money-lending, women, you name it. We play our cards right and by the end of the year we'll have turned this place into an oasis — *our* oasis."

McCloskey was well aware of how quickly folks were developing a taste for the money, not to mention the thrill that came from bootlegging. Almost overnight the pond had become full of little fish — little fish that were only going to get chewed up by the first big one to come along. Now here was McCloskey, sitting across from that big fish and being asked to be its teeth. An hour and several whiskies later he found himself a sworn member of the outfit, Green's new Big Six.

Green took McCloskey's hand and looked into his eyes. "I know you won't let me down, Killer."

"Thanks, Green."

Green held his grip. "I'm your Lieutenant now. You're one of my soldiers."

McCloskey stood firm. "Yes, sir."

He had never met anyone like the Lieutenant. He had encountered street fighters, hardened criminals, mercenaries, and business types before, but never someone who was all of these things put together. The only person who even came close was his father. But his father didn't have the style and the worldliness. He didn't have a platoon of soldiers behind him, either.

Chapter 5

COLLISION COURSE

The referendum results had a sobering effect on Billy McCloskey. When at the end of the summer there began to be supply issues at his local roadhouse and his liver finally got a day off, he took the opportunity to ask the proprietor what all the fuss was about.

Pierre explained it to him, and Billy, being fairly lucid, took it pretty hard, like he was just handed a prison sentence. He asked Pierre how he planned to remedy the situation. Pierre told Billy not to worry — everything would be taken care of. He was in good with Windsor's biggest bootlegger.

This took Billy by surprise. There were plenty of smugglers out here on the Ojibway shores, and lots of folks making moonshine, including his pa. He told Pierre he didn't have to go to Windsor to get his liquor. Pierre saw it a little differently.

"I didn't have any choice, Billy."

The barfly smelled a rat. "Oh yeah? Who was it set you up?"

Pierre hesitated. He should have kept his big mouth shut. He braced himself before uttering the words. "Your brother."

After Billy climbed back on his barstool he started with the questions. "When did my brother get back? Who is he working for? Why didn't anyone tell me?"

"We tried," said Pierre, "but you've been drunk since Armistice."

This news didn't sit well with Billy. As far as he was concerned, Jack had deserted his friends and family a long time ago and had no right coming back like this only to put the screws on the local citizenry. It just wasn't right.

"Does my pa know about this?"

There was no point in holding back now.

"Yep."

Billy gave that one a think while Pierre riffled through the icebox below the bar.

"There's one legal beer left and it's got your name on it."

"Keep it for a souvenir."

"You feeling okay? Hey — where you going?"

Billy was going to fight fire with fire. The first thing he did was bring a telephone into the house.

"Welcome to the modern age," he said to his pa, "now you can call ahead to Chappell House so they have your suds ready when you get there."

"They'll have the cops ready for me too."

Then he invested in a better boat for ferrying his product — a 28-footer with 180 horses. It was low-slung and lightweight, making it easy to hide among the bulrushes and manoeuvre through the canals. Billy christened her *River Rat* with a jar of his pa's moonshine.

Actually, it was weak lemonade; Billy never let a drop go to waste.

Next he developed partnerships that would save him work and buy him a few allies. Some folks in the area had connections in Quebec distilleries, and Billy arranged either to act as their local wholesaler or to broker deals for them into the States.

Lastly he cleared some space for surplus liquor in the old cabin that stood between the house and the shore. Newlyweds Frank and Mary McCloskey had lived here while the house was being built. It later became Frank's fishing cabin, his "home away from home," and where he kept his still. More recently it was where Billy spent his lost weekends. And when those weekends turned into weeks, his pa would have to drag him out and leave him in the sun to dry. Now the cabin had a new purpose.

"Yer not getting rid of my still, are you, boy?"

"No, Pa," said Billy. "We're gonna need it."

It was all about supply and demand, and Billy was ideally situated. Several weeks later — by the end of October — Billy became the leader of a smuggling outfit that served a small but potentially lucrative territory just downriver from Detroit, mainly around Ecorse and the Rouge. Part of him thought it was a nice little cottage industry. Another part of him thought it was only the beginning.

It was at a ceremony at the Armouries for Great War Veterans where Jack first heard about his brother's ambitions.

"I thought he was working for you, Jack," said an old comrade from the 99th.

McCloskey tried not to look surprised. "No, no he's not."

"But you knew about it, right?"

The fellow was goading him on, and he knew it.

"Sure. We have an agreement."

"Whatever you say, Jack."

"*Goddamnit,*" McCloskey muttered under his breath as the soldier walked away. If this yolk knew the score, the Lieutenant probably did too. Life was suddenly very complicated again. It was just like when they were kids; Billy had to have the same as what Jack had, and all the better if it took a little away from Jack in the bargain.

There was that, and then there was the Lieutenant. If he knew that Billy and some ragtag outfit were encroaching on his territory, and by territory that meant everything within a hundred miles outside of Detroit, there would be serious hell to pay.

Once again McCloskey made a compromise. In an effort to save his father from getting tangled in any of this, he would deal only with Billy. He telephoned Pierre at Chappell House and asked him to keep tabs on his pa's movements. When Pierre called back a few days later, he informed Jack that his father had gone fishing up in Michigan. Jack then took the opportunity to drive out to Ojibway to have a word with his brother. It promised to be an interesting conversation.

"Long time no see," said Jack.

"Yeah, long time."

They were standing on the stretch of property between the house and Front Road. Billy was tying up a young peach tree. He looked like a new man, Jack thought.

"You know why I'm here?"

"Yeah, you come to fix the hole in the roof."

"You're not going to give me a hard time about this, are you?"

"Give you a hard time? Jack, I'm just a small-time businessman trying to make a buck."

"I want you to quit your bootlegging before my boss asks me to do something I really don't want to do."

"Like what?"

Billy took a step closer to his brother. He was lean, muscular, all springs and coils. He was prepared for a fight but Jack wasn't going to give him the satisfaction.

"I'm telling you, Billy, if it weren't for Pa —"

"If it weren't for Pa what?"

"Just leave him out of this," said Jack and walked away. Billy followed him to his car.

"Gosh, Jack, I didn't know you cared. He'll ask about you, you know. What should I tell him? That you had dinner reservations in Detroit? That you had to go harass our neighbours?"

Jack turned. "I mean it — leave him out of this."

"He's in it, Jack, like he always has been."

"What the hell are you trying to prove, Billy?"

"That like your boss, you're just a bum in a fancy suit. I'm the one out here on the homestead, looking out for my own. You're a long way from Ojibway now, aren't you, Jack?"

"You're so full of shit you'd embarrass an outhouse."

Jack climbed back into his Studebaker. He had wanted to ask Billy about Clara, his sister-in-law, but he was all out of polite talk.

"Shut down your little lemonade stand, Billy, before I have to come back and shut it down for you."

Jack's car kicked dust all the way up the path to the road. After regaining control of himself and the Studebaker, he got to thinking. Sure, what Billy said was true: smuggling was the family business and their pa was a player. But Billy was such a schemer, a sloppy one at that, and their pa could get caught in his undertow. Jack knew that unless he could get Billy to cease and desist, they were all headed for a heap of trouble.

Meanwhile, all fired up by the exchange with his brother, Billy decided to step up his operation and get his father even more involved. Locals started taking him more seriously. Eventually, a neighbour, Moe Lesperance, said he had a relative in Belle River who wanted in on the action. Billy was intrigued but played hard to get.

"Let me think about it."

Belle River was centrally located at the top of Essex County — a rectangular peninsula framed by Lake St. Clair to the north, the Detroit River to the north and west, and Lake Erie to the south. On a map it resembled a fist delivering an uppercut to Michigan's jaw. Where Lake St. Clair flows into the Detroit River, strip farms give way to a string of municipalities known as the Border Cities: Riverside, Ford City, and Walkerville, where the river narrows until it's a mile wide at Windsor and you'd swear you can hear the factory whistles in Detroit. Next is Sandwich, and at the point where the river runs due south is Ojibway, a tiny farming community. Heading out of the Border Cities and then east along Erie's north shore, you eventually hit Kingsville. If you travelled north as the crow flies, from there you'd wind up back in Belle River. Billy saw Ojibway and Belle River as strategic locations, providing easy access to waterways, Windsor and Detroit, and the interior of Essex County.

"You know, Belle River just might work," he said to his father one day out of the blue. They were chopping wood in the yard. It was early December and their shoulders and arms were powdered with the season's first snowfall. "We could set up a route along the back roads of the county. If we take Maidstone Crossing, we might even be able to pick up some extra business along the way."

His father saw an opportunity to control the overland supply routes into the Border Cities. The neck of the peninsula was less than twenty-five miles of flat farmland with only a few passable roads and a couple of railway lines connecting it to the rest of the province. If they controlled that frontier, it would only leave the river, and the river was a fast-moving no man's land.

"Tell you what," Frank McCloskey said, "I've done a bit of business out there before. I'll make the trip."

Billy smiled. This is just what he wanted to hear. Plans were drawn up for an annex operation in Belle River. Boats would be refurbished over the winter, materials ordered for new docks, and stills fired up along the county roads.

Less than a week later, Lesperance got a call from his cousin Bernie. The deal was off. What Lesperance and McCloskey & Son were unaware of was that the Lieutenant's boys were also knocking on doors in Belle River. Any operation that impacted negatively on their business had to be either assimilated or eliminated. They were finished making overtures; now they were delivering ultimatums. Frank McCloskey took Lesperance out to investigate, but now no one would even give them the time of day.

The Lieutenant called Jack into his office to explain this business with his family. Before stepping across the threshold, McCloskey asked himself which would be worse: to lie and say he knew nothing, or to tell the Lieutenant the truth and say he knew but hadn't come clean. McCloskey lied. He owed it to blood being thicker than whisky. He swore to the Lieutenant that he knew nothing about their activities and in fact hadn't had words with them in years. The Lieutenant wasn't interested in the family history. He just wanted the matter resolved.

"Listen, Killer, the boys'll take care of those frogs in the county, but I want you to lean on your father and brother."

McCloskey said he would deal with it.

One of Billy's overland suppliers was scheduled to make a delivery the next day. A provincial policeman being paid by Billy to keep the way clear reported this to Jack. The lesson to be learned here is that while good money might buy you information, better money will buy you a snitch. McCloskey headed the supplier off at Maidstone and relieved him of his whisky, his gun and, as an added touch, his pants.

"Next time you want to do business in the Border Cities, get in touch with the Lieutenant first."

Billy phoned his contact the next morning and demanded an explanation. The contact told Billy what happened and said word was out that the Lieutenant was running things between Lake Erie and Lake St. Clair.

"I'm telling you kid, you're finished."

The man hung up before Billy had a chance to form a reply. Billy tore the phone off the wall and hurled it through the kitchen window.

Chapter 6

THE INSURGENT

By the end of the year the Lieutenant had accomplished everything he had set out to, so he threw himself a New Year's party fit for a king. The guest list included not only the brash young bootleggers who helped him seize the day but also the police, lawyers, and city councilmen he enlisted along the way to ensure things continued to run smoothly.

The soirée was held at his palatial new digs on Richmond Street in Walkerville. He had purchased two side-by-side properties and levelled them both to make room for it. The classically-inspired pile took over a year to build and was an architectural assault on the *dry* establishment's cozy Queen Anne manses. The guests arrived around eight o'clock, rolling into the semi-circular drive in their brand new Lincolns and Cadillacs. The men looked sleek and refined in their tuxes. The girls made their entrance in full-length furs that, once inside, they peeled off to reveal slinky shift dresses that barely reached to the tops of their stockings.

The main hall was done in Italian marble. Staircases curved to the left and right and between them stood the centrepiece to this enormous space: a sculpture of a winged goddess that stood over a shallow reflecting pool that tonight was filled with whisky. At the front of the reflecting pool was an ice dam, already melting, and below the dam was a model of an American city that by midnight would be awash in Canadian Club.

Guests were led to a great ballroom forming the north side of the house's quadrangle. Rose-coloured walls were complemented by a wooden floor stained a rich amber hue. Sumptuous curtains with a striking Oriental pattern framed the floor-to-ceiling windows overlooking the garden, and the vaulted ceiling was adorned with a gold-and-turquoise mosaic reminiscent of a sunset over the river.

A band from Detroit had been hired for the party and they played all-out jazz, the real thing, not the fluff that Paul Whiteman was churning out for the masses. There were six musicians and a singer the boys called Queenie. Together they were the Royal Seven, and they got things rolling right away with a hot little number called "Jazzin' Babies Blues." Queenie sang about jazz blues causing her to scream and moan and make her think of all the good things that her *sweet daddy's done*. It was liberating, frenetic, and fun.

Mesmerized by the performance, the crowd didn't actually start dancing until the second or third number, and then they hammered away at the Anvil Trot until dawn. Everything glittered; whisky was gold. If 1921 was the test drive for the Lieutenant and his gang, 1922 was going to be the Grand Prix.

Billy McCloskey spent most of the winter sitting in a rocking chair in the back room of the house, watching the river ice over then break up, ice over, and then break up again. Out of the corner of his eye was always the cabin, empty now except for his pa's old still. It mocked him, as did *River Rat*, which was dry-docked in the yard.

After their well had finally run dry, Frank McCloskey somehow managed to acquire a crate of English ale. He figured it had been traded a few too many times and finally fell into the hands of someone who simply didn't have a taste for it. It was packed with pages of newsprint. Frank passed the pages to his son.

Not having anything else to do, Billy read them. They happened to contain articles about the labour movement in Great Britain, and about strikes and political unrest. He wanted to know how the folks in Belle River enjoyed being the Lieutenant's wage slaves. He was suddenly inspired.

On a spring-like day in February, he went out to Belle River and managed to sell a few yolks on the idea of solidarity among bootleggers and still operators.

Word got back to the Lieutenant, who told McCloskey to resolve the matter once and for all, or he would have to get personally involved.

"This ain't baseball, Killer. You don't get three chances. The only reason I let it get this far is because these people are your family."

Jack found Billy sitting alone at the bar in the Crawford Hotel downtown on Riverside Drive. He grabbed Billy by the shoulders and dragged him back towards the kitchen.

"Let's you and me have a conversation."

They interrupted a group standing around a chopping block discussing odds on horses. A fat, sweaty man holding a fistful of betting slips shot Jack a look as he hustled Billy around the corner into the pantry.

"I swear the Hun was the only thing that kept those two from killing each other in France."

No one laughed. Too much money was on the table. Suddenly there was a commotion out front.

"Jee-zuss!"

Two Mounties brandishing Colts burst into the hotel and ran up the stairs to the rooms. The dozen or so folks drinking liquor at the tables guzzled what was left in their coffee cups while the bartender dropped his bottle under a floorboard and kicked sawdust over the joints.

Assuming there were more police out front and the alley was covered, no one knew which way to run. When the police could be heard making their way back down the stairs, it was decided the alley might be worth the risk. Like rats in a sinking ship, the bar patrons scurried towards the rear exit.

Meanwhile, the bookie was stuffing the slips into his socks and the gamblers were pocketing their folding money. The lookout pulled his face out of the porthole in the kitchen door and went over to the pantry to warn the McCloskeys. What he saw nearly made him choke on his tobacco. Jack had his left arm tight across his brother's neck and was jabbing a revolver into his ribs. Billy's face was bloodied but still defiant.

In their haste the gamblers knocked over a stack of dirty pots and pans. The noise startled Jack, and in a split second he had the revolver aimed at the lookout's face. The lookout grabbed some air.

"Whoa, fella!"

An inebriate came stumbling through the door between the bar and the kitchen area, and a stampede followed. Jack finally snapped out of it and lowered his revolver. The brothers looked around the corner to see what the ruckus was about and got caught in the current of bodies flowing out the back door.

Snow was falling and it was bitterly cold. Two uniforms were making their way up the alley. They had been sent by the Mounties to cover the back door and hadn't bargained on any of this. They were quickly trying to assess who in the mob would come quietly and who would put up a fight.

"They all look game," said one, and he blew his whistle.

"Up against the wall!" shouted the other.

The McCloskeys were at it again, rolling around in the trash that was piled up behind the hotel. Then Billy threw his brother off and managed to get to his feet.

A bottle struck the policeman with the whistle. He pulled his revolver out of its holster. The other cop was receiving complaints, blow by blow, from a couple of frustrated old barflies. The gamblers fought with the bookie, bar patrons fought with the bartender, and everyone wanted a crack at the cops, who were overwhelmed.

It was a lethal cocktail of anger, distrust, and 110-proof whisky. Somebody swung a piece of two-by-four and knocked Jack's revolver out of his hand. When he bent down to pick it up, Billy tried to tackle him. Jack deflected him onto a cop. Billy stood up and tried to take another run at his brother, but the cop grabbed him. Billy freed himself and as he turned to strike, a shot rang out and echoed between the buildings.

All eyes fell on Billy lying on the ground with a red stain blooming on his shoulder, and then on Jack who was standing a short distance away with his revolver. Everything seemed to stop for a moment except for the blowing snow.

Then an arm reached out of nowhere, grabbed Jack, and pulled him down the alleyway. The cops didn't know which way to turn: chase down Jack McCloskey or try and save his brother's life? Either way they still had to defend themselves against a drunken mob that needed to be brought to heel.

A vehicle was waiting with its engine running for McCloskey and his rescuer at the end of the alleyway on Ferry Street.

"Get in the car."

They took a sharp left onto Riverside Drive. McCloskey recognized the driver but didn't know his name. Sitting in the passenger seat was the fellow that had pulled him out of the alley, Shorty Morand. Seated next to McCloskey was Jigsaw, the Lieutenant's deadliest soldier.

McCloskey remembered Jigsaw earning his nickname during the war. At first it had to do with his tall, angular frame and jagged yellow teeth. Then, after he had been shot, cut, blown apart, and sewn back together a few times, it became even more a propos. He came home with a scar that undulated around his face, head, and neck. When he passed people in the street they looked away; women's faces turned white with horror. He played on the name by making a serrated bayonet his weapon of choice.

"That was a close one," said Shorty.

"Here — let's get rid of that," said Jigsaw.

He pried the revolver out of McCloskey's hand and passed it up to Shorty.

"You can have the honours."

Jigsaw told the driver to pull over. Shorty looked around then jumped out and darted across the street. Railroad tracks were directly below and beyond the tracks was the river. Holding the gun by the barrel, Shorty hurled it towards an ice floe, ran back, and climbed into the car.

"There's nothing like a Colt for settling an argument."

"Or a blade, eh, Jigsaw?"

"Wipe your nose, Morand."

McCloskey glanced out the window. He was still in shock. Snow squalls blew up from the river and big white flakes swirled in the headlight beams like sparks in a foundry. The car rumbled a little further along the Drive before turning up a side street.

"Where are we?"

"A friend's house," answered Jigsaw. "Shorty, go to the door and make sure everything's copasetic."

The house looked abandoned. The windows were boarded up and some of the clapboard was falling away. McCloskey watched Shorty ascend to the veranda, knock on the door, and mouth some words into a small opening. Shorty then turned and gave them the signal. McCloskey followed Jigsaw out and the driver disappeared with the car.

Inside, the place had all the charm of a bus station lavatory and was just this side of derelict with its crumbling plaster and rotten floorboards. McCloskey was led upstairs. Two men stood like sentries outside a closed door. One of them gave a knock and a voice from the other side said to come.

McCloskey caught his jaw before it dropped. The Lieutenant was sitting behind a mahogany desk, listening to a telephone receiver and nodding. The room was fancier than the office in the pool hall and better outfitted. It reminded McCloskey of those British officers stationed in the far reaches of the empire with their liquor cabinets, phonograph players, and portraits of the king — all the comforts of home. The Lieutenant hung up.

"It was a drug bust, opium and cocaine. A couple dope runners from Montreal had been operating out of one of the rooms. Two dagos got pinched. There was a Chinese too. He was probably the fence. The mess in the alley was a different kettle of fish, something the cops hadn't anticipated."

The Lieutenant leaned forward and rolled his cigar from one corner of his mouth to the other.

"You surprise me, Killer. I knew you had the instinct, but this is a little different. Your own brother. Damn."

McCloskey just stood there, silent. The last thing he was going to do was spill about having not even fired his revolver. He was trying to think of all the angles. He studied the Lieutenant and could tell that his wheels were turning.

"This looks good on you, McCloskey. It looks good on all of us. It says we know how to hold a position."

The Lieutenant kept shifting his cigar in his mouth. He took only furtive glances at McCloskey now. He made another dramatic pause before continuing.

"Looks like you're going to have to disappear for a while. The cops have more witnesses than they can handle and the drug bust complicates things. We're going to leave the investigators to do their job — unless they get too close, and then we might have to close the file for them."

The Lieutenant rose from his chair and started pacing around the room. He finally lit on the edge of his desk and sat there quietly for a moment, arms folded. McCloskey couldn't read him, though he had a sense that something was wrong.

"So while the cops are sniffing around, trying to look like they know what they're doing, you'll be in Hamilton."

"Hamilton?"

The Lieutenant brushed come ashes off his knee. "Yeah, Hamilton. Brown could use your talents for a while. When things settle down we'll call you back."

McCloskey looked over at Jigsaw, who seemed surprised, perhaps even a little disappointed. Maybe Jigsaw was hoping the Lieutenant would throw him to the cops, make a scapegoat out of him in order to take the heat off. Jigsaw never liked McCloskey; he had made that clear from the beginning. He said McCloskey was only good for providing entertainment for the crew. McCloskey always watched his back when he was alone with him.

"Our driver will take you part way. He'll make sure you don't get into any trouble. You'll rendezvous with one of Brown's boys and he'll take you into Hamilton."

When McCloskey finally managed to get the Lieutenant's undivided attention, he looked into his eyes and saw something he had never seen before. He didn't recognize it at first. Then he realized what it was. It was fear.

"They're expecting you, Killer. Now scram."

Chapter 7

JUST LUCKY, I GUESS

McCloskey woke from a deep sleep when the engine stopped. He rubbed his eyes and looked out the window. An illuminated sign in the near distance blinked.

ALL DAY BREAKFAST

They were parked at a roadhouse. He slid his cuff away from his wristwatch and then attempted some simple math, but his mind was still somewhere back down the road.

"Where are we?"

"Brantford."

The driver flashed his headlights. Another vehicle parked

several car lengths away flashed back.

"Wait here."

McCloskey watched the drivers exchanging words for a minute or two before he was gestured to come forward. The blast of cold air woke him fully.

"You're in good hands, Killer. We'll see you when you're finished your tour."

The other driver told McCloskey to get in and then they pulled away slowly through the drifting snow. He introduced himself as Slip and briefed McCloskey on the situation in Hamilton.

The story went something like this: not too long ago, Brown got into a routine of absorbing members of rival gangs they had subdued. He envisioned a sort of Grand Army of the local underworld, with himself as its Napoleon. This scheme worked well enough at first, but lately Brown had to question the loyalty of some of these soldiers. There were too many unfortunate coincidences, and a pattern of double-crossing was developing. It had come down to Brown struggling to maintain control of his outfit while simultaneously trying to keep resurgent gangs at bay. Drastic measures had to be taken before the Montreal boss was forced to intervene. A couple of days before, Brown turned to Green for help. After the incident involving the McCloskeys in Windsor, Green was looking for help as well. The lieutenants came to an agreement that was mutually beneficial.

The driver parked at a warehouse down on the waterfront. He led McCloskey inside and through a maze of massive containers that eventually opened up to an arrangement of crates that seemed to suggest an office. A bare bulb hung in the middle of the space. Either this was all Brown needed to run his operation, or it was all he had left. Brown smiled and extended a hand.

"Killer McCloskey."

McCloskey nodded and gripped the hand firmly. "Lieutenant Brown."

Brown was a small man but not insubstantial. There was tension in his body, but he wasn't nervous or agitated. He was taut, precise, and lean.

He filled three small glasses then handed one to Slip and one to McCloskey.

"Slip paint a picture for you?"

"Yeah."

"You've got your work cut out."

"I can handle it."

"That's all I wanted to hear."

They drained their glasses and set them back down on the battered wooded crates in front of them.

"There's a flophouse in the east end being used by some of the more questionable members of the outfit. You and Slip are going to put a match to it and shoot anyone that tries to escape. Catch my drift?"

This guy doesn't mince words or waste any time, McCloskey thought.

"Yes, sir."

"You're going to be hitting fast and hitting hard. That's how we're going to get through this. Slip will tell you who's who and what's what. You carrying?"

McCloskey suddenly remembered that his gun was at the bottom of the Detroit River. "No, sir."

Brown snapped his fingers and a tall man in a big coat appeared out of nowhere. This was Brown's shadow, a walking arsenal who went by the name of Lynch. He pulled two British service revolvers out of his coat, .455 Webley Mark VI's. McCloskey was familiar with them. They were like hand-held artillery and could do serious damage.

"One for each hand."

McCloskey took them.

"When you're done, I want you both back at the Connaught Hotel."

Less than thirty minutes later, McCloskey was taking aim at a fellow trying to negotiate a leap from the window of a burning building. The fool probably figured if he played it right, he could slide down the roof of the veranda and land on a pile of snow. McCloskey put a bullet in his hip and watched him tumble off the roof and land on the frozen pavement, missing the snow by inches.

A shot rang from the house and a bullet hit the car adjacent to where McCloskey was standing. He remained focused, spotting a figure in another window. He threw some lead in its direction and the figure fell backwards into the flames. More shots followed, but they were coming from the other side of the house. Slip reappeared.

"I got one," he said. Glancing over his shoulder to the pavement he remarked, "I see you were busy." There were sirens in the distance and McCloskey tucked away his revolver. "Let's get out of here."

The next morning there was some unexpected news from Windsor: Billy McCloskey was alive and recovering nicely from his bullet wound. According to the doctor, if he had been standing at a slightly different angle or if the cold had not slowed the bleeding, he'd be dead right now. Of course Jack was relieved, but then came a raft of questions.

Was Billy under the impression that his brother was the shooter? Did Billy actually see the shooter? Who could it have been? Was it an accident or did someone in that mob actually want Billy dead? And what was Billy telling the investigators right now? McCloskey's moment of relief suddenly evaporated. He had no choice but to wait and see how things played out.

McCloskey expected to be called back home, figuring Billy's survival must have taken some of the heat off. That may have been the case, but there were new developments in Hamilton as well. The mandate now for Brown's outfit was to extend their influence to the tips of the Golden Horseshoe — the region stretching west from the Niagara River along the peninsula, around Lake Ontario, and then back east to Toronto's borders. To that end, Brown was told by the boss in Montreal that he could retain McCloskey's services indefinitely. Apparently Green had no say in the matter.

Lieutenant Brown was unrelenting in his campaign, and McCloskey became the go-to guy in virtually every operation.

It looked like it was going to be a long winter, but then spring arrived early in the form of a fresh-faced girl sporting a sleek blonde bob. McCloskey was waiting for Slip in the mezzanine of the hotel when he spotted her sprinting up the stairs from the lobby. Her knees played peek-a-boo with the hem of her dress, and she jiggled in all the right places. When she passed McCloskey, she glanced at him with eyes like blue saucers.

"Down, boy," said Slip. "That's the boss's girl."

"The boss's girl? How come I never seen her? Does she live here in the hotel?"

"Yeah, but you didn't hear it from me. She's his best-kept secret. Now forget you ever saw her."

She looked young, sweet and, according to McCloskey, had no business hanging around guys like Brown.

Slip just smiled and shook his head. "Just remember what I told you," he said. "Now c'mon. We gotta be somewhere."

A few days later McCloskey saw her having breakfast downstairs. *That's twice in one week*, he thought. *It must be a sign.*

"Mind if I join you?" he said. "My name's —"

She looked up at McCloskey's devilish grin. "I know who you are."

Her tone was playful, like she knew the score.

"Call me Jack."

"Nice to meet you, Jack. I'm Sophie."

He gently took her hand.

"Sophie." McCloskey said it a few more times in his head. "I like that."

"It's kind of grown on me. Do you like eggs, Jack?"

Sophie pointed out the waiter hovering impatiently.

"I'll have whatever she's having."

They got to talking about this and that, and eventually McCloskey got around to asking her how she got mixed up with a guy like Brown.

"Just lucky, I guess."

"No, really."

She told him the story of how Brown pulled her out of a chorus line in Montreal. Rescued her was what he liked to say. Now she was sitting on the shelf in his trophy room.

"So why stick around?"

"The money's good and I like the hours."

McCloskey tried to guess her age. Sure, she was young, but she had a worldly air about her, so he guessed older.

"I turned eighteen the first of April. That makes me an April fool."

McCloskey almost choked on his scrambled eggs. It made her laugh and she had a great laugh.

Slip happened to be walking through the dining room at the time and spotted the two of them playing footsy. He made a beeline for McCloskey and grabbed his arm.

"What did I tell you?" said Slip.

Slip gave Sophie a look, as if to say *Leave my boy alone.*

"What? We're just —"

"I know what you're doing. C'mon, let's go."

"Don't tell me — *we gotta be somewhere.*"

McCloskey looked back at Sophie and shrugged. Sophie just smiled and waved goodbye.

Regarding his brother Billy and the incident in the alleyway, McCloskey was still waiting for the other shoe to drop. Was it possible that everyone was still under the impression that he pulled the trigger? Did Billy know the truth? Was he just waiting to play that card?

And then his mind would invariably turn to their father. What could Billy have told him? McCloskey was tempted on a number of occasions to jump in his car and drive home so that he could settle the matter once and for all.

It felt like he had already been down this road: trying to get home, wanting to find his place, and hoping to set things right. But something always came along to make it all that much more complicated. He admitted to himself that sometimes it was himself, but most times it just seemed like fate was working against him.

A couple weeks after Jack's aborted breakfast with Sophie, Brown called McCloskey to his suite, and McCloskey arrived at the door the same time she did. She appeared quite agitated but he kept his distance. When the maid opened the door, Sophie stormed in. McCloskey cautiously followed.

She proceeded to make what is commonly known as a scene. Evidently Brown had just sent her a message cancelling their plans for the evening, and this wasn't the first time. It was all a bit awkward and McCloskey had the distinct feeling that Sophie was taking advantage of his being in the room.

Desperate for a quick resolution, Brown glanced over at McCloskey. If he could trust this guy to get him out of a tight spot in the streets, he should be able to trust him to get him out of one at home.

"Listen, if I let Killer here take you dancing tonight, will you shut up?"

Sophie had Brown right where she wanted him. She managed to conceal her delight and looked McCloskey over like he was applying for a job in the kitchen.

"Sure, he'll do."

"You bring Alice and Fay with you too."

"Sure, sure."

Brown took McCloskey aside and laid down some ground rules: no other man was to speak to Sophie, and Sophie was not to speak to any other man. McCloskey was to keep his hands and his ideas to himself, and Sophie was to go nowhere without Alice or Fay.

"Got it."

In the weeks that followed, Jack and Sophie recruited not only Alice and Fay but any bellhop and chambermaid they could trust in order to be able to rendezvous at a safe destination: out of the way diners, neighbourhood dance halls, and movie houses. They also took these opportunities to share stories and discovered how much they really had in common. Sophie called her and Jack orphans in a storm.

Early in June, McCloskey was sent out on a reconnaissance to a narrow strip of land that stretched from Hamilton's North End to Burlington on the other side of the lake. A channel broke the strip, and on the marsh side, the lakeside as well as on the inside of channel were several dozen boathouses, many nothing more than tarpaper shacks. He had been sent out by Brown to secure the territory, which was ideal for smuggling.

There were a couple watering holes and clubhouses. People came for the duck hunting and fishing mostly, and to get away from the city and the factories. It reminded McCloskey of Ojibway. It quickly became a sort of retreat for him, and eventually he started bringing Sophie along with him. It became their place.

But the more time they spent together, the more potential he could see for her to get drawn deeper into the world of guns and bootleg liquor. He knew the best thing would be to get her out of Hamilton and back home to her family. But to steal her away would also mean deserting his post, and after that it was anyone's guess what his fate might be. For all he knew he could end up with a bounty on his head.

But the more McCloskey thought about it, the more he thought it might be another turning point for him, a chance to re-invent himself yet again. After he got Sophie out of Hamilton he could go back to Windsor, explain everything to Green, reconcile with his father and brother and maybe even broker a deal between them and Green. Once that was done he could join Sophie in Montreal. But before McCloskey could get the wheels in motion, the wheels started falling off.

Green was receiving reports that McCloskey wasn't pulling his weight in Hamilton, was getting careless, and — worst of all — was rumoured to be carousing with Brown's girl. Then word reached Brown from Windsor that not only was Billy McCloskey recovered from his bullet wound, he was also back to his old tricks with McCloskey Sr.

Green and Brown knew that if their boss found out about any of this, it wouldn't just be Jack McCloskey's head on a pike. Something had to be done.

Saturday, July 22

Though Sophie had her own suite just down the hall, every once in a while she spent the night at Brown's. Last night was one of those nights.

It was early morning, and Brown was in his office. The door between the office and the bedroom was slightly ajar, and in a waking state Sophie could hear Brown on the phone. That wasn't unusual, but when she heard McCloskey's name, her ears pricked up.

It quickly became obvious that Brown was talking to Green. She sat up quietly and tiptoed over to the door.

She heard Brown say that McCloskey's recent carelessness was threatening to undo all the work that had been done, and he didn't have any choice in the matter. He would let Green "know by Monday."

Sophie didn't know what that meant exactly, but she knew it couldn't be good.

Later in the afternoon, she was standing outside the fifth floor beauty salon waiting with Fay for an elevator. When the car finally arrived, it was packed with people. Sophie spotted McCloskey in the back and jumped in before the doors closed, leaving Fay behind.

When the elevator reached the lobby, Sophie got out and walked straight out the front door and into a waiting taxi.

McCloskey's car was parked as usual right outside. He jumped into his vehicle and followed the taxi as it drove out of town.

He had no idea where she could be instructing the driver to take her, but it was obvious to him that he was meant to follow. It had to be some place where they could be alone.

The taxi eventually pulled into a motel somewhere along the peninsula east of Hamilton.

McCloskey watched Sophie step out of the taxi and then waited for it to drive away. McCloskey parked away from the road. He met up with her in the office, where they got themselves a cabin near the lake. The manager took one look at McCloskey and knew better than to ask any questions.

It was a relief to get out of the heat of the city. The two stripped down and collapsed on the bed, tired but not sleepy, listening to the cicadas in the trees.

"What are we going to do?" asked Sophie.

McCloskey's head was full of dead-end ideas and questions he didn't have answers to. He had become so tired of his life, and while he could see the possibility of a new one with Sophie, he knew that people like him ultimately ruined people like her. He had never felt this way for any other girl. Was it love? He wasn't sure. His heart had always been a stranger to him, something he couldn't quite fathom, though not for lack of trying. All he knew was he had to get Sophie out of harm's way.

"Let's not think about that right now," he said.

They grabbed some towels and headed down to the beach for a moonlight dip. McCloskey got a fire going and waded out into the water. Sophie couldn't swim so McCloskey gave her a piggyback. She panicked when the water came up to his neck and he laughed. When he wouldn't turn around, she screamed and threw her legs over his shoulders. He relented and waded back to shore.

When he dropped to his knees Sophie rolled onto the sand, just a few feet from the fire. McCloskey climbed on top of her. She looked golden. He leaned over her and gazed into her eyes, searching for answers, clues even. What he saw was a life just as complicated as his.

Sophie spent the night at Brown's again and was awakened this time by shouting in his suite. The door was closed, so she couldn't make out all the words. She got up, grabbed a glass off the bureau, and put it to the wall. The other voice sounded like it belonged to Slip. Brown was telling him about a telephone conversation he just had with Green. Apparently, there was a confrontation back in Windsor between Billy McCloskey and one of Green's men, and the gang member got himself shot up. And then Brown said something about her and Jack. It sounded like Slip had shadowed them to the motel. The conversation ended with Brown clearly saying that if they did away with the McCloskeys, it would resolve a number of issues and cut their losses.

Sophie got a message to Jack via a chambermaid, and within the hour he was running with Sophie down the platform at the train station. *This is it*, he thought. This was the moment that he had been more or less waiting for, though it wasn't the way he had imagined it would play out. No matter.

"Kiss me, Jack!"

For the first time in his short, violent life, Jack McCloskey had a sense of his own mortality. He watched Sophie take her seat in the car then followed her on foot as it rolled down the track. He was able to keep up until a fence at the end of the platform blocked his path.

There was a commotion behind him. He turned to see a group of Brown's men running his way. He threw himself through the nearest doors of the station and once inside zigzagged through benches and luggage carts. Out front there were other vehicles parked around his, so he had a few seconds of cover. When he pulled away, shots were fired and a couple hit his door panel. He raced out of the parking lot and headed west out of the city.

Was it only a year ago that he had left Monroe? It had been a tough decision. He remembered coming to it after a series of compromises: *first a job, then a match or two, and a life on my own terms*. Then and only then would he make peace with his father and brother.

So where did things sit now?

He had become a mercenary for another gang in the syndicate, fallen in love with the gang leader's girl, stolen her away, and deserted his post. It seemed like his life was forever spiralling out of control. Had it always been like this? He was heading home yet again. Would it be different this time? Had Sophie awakened something in him? Possibly.

The sun was setting. He hit the accelerator and passed every vehicle he came upon. It occurred to him that Brown now knew Sophie's whereabouts and destination and could intercept her at any station between Hamilton and Montreal. Jack had left her completely exposed.

FIRST GEAR

(SUNDAY, JULY 23, 1922)

Chapter 8

A LITTLE STRAGGLING HAMLET

… to behold on one side a city, with its towers and spires and animated population, with villas and handsome houses stretching along the shore, and a hundred vessels or more, gigantic steamers, brigs, schooners, crowding the port, loading and unloading; all the bustle, in short, of prosperity and commerce; — and, on the other side, a little straggling hamlet, one schooner, one little wretched steam-boat, some windmills, a catholic chapel or two, a

supine ignorant peasantry, all the symptoms
of apathy, indolence, mistrust, hopelessness!
— can I, can any one, help wondering at
the difference, and asking whence it arises?
There must be a cause for it surely — but
what is it? Does it lie in past or present —
in natural or accidental circumstances? — in
the institutions of the government, or the
character of the people? Is it remediable? is it
a necessity? is it a mystery? what and whence
is it? — Can you tell? or can you send some
of our colonial officials across the Atlantic to
behold and solve the difficulty?

Anna Brownell Jameson wrote these words the summer
prior to the Rebellion in '37, and in Vera Maude's opinion things
hadn't changed all that much. Sure, the little straggling hamlet
grew up to become the City of Windsor, but there was still a huge
difference in size and scope between it and Detroit, its American
cousin on the other side of the river.

What really struck Vera Maude, though, was the last
sentence in this particular passage. In it Mrs. Jameson exposes an
attitude that Vera Maude felt might be at the heart of the matter:
let us commission a gaggle of bureaucrats, a handful of Mother
England's privileged sons, to force an artificial solution on the
problem, whatever it is, rather than try to tackle it ourselves.

Winter Studies and Summer Rambles in Canada. She snapped
the book shut and stuffed it into her canvas bag. The next book she
pulled down off the shelf was a volume of Shakespeare's sonnets
given to her by an admirer in her senior year of high school.

Tom would steal glances at Vera Maude when it was his
turn to stand up in front of the class and read from it. He was
an original and Vera Maude liked him. But something wasn't
right with Tom; a dark cloud hung over him at times. There was

talk of an illness, and not of the physical variety. He found joy in Shakespeare, however, and filled the book's margins with his own verses.

He had approached her once on Shakespeare's birthday. Vera Maude said she wasn't interested in going with anyone at the moment, which was true. She had just recently concluded her first romance and was feeling emotionally exhausted. Tom was very sweet and didn't push himself on her. At the end of the school year he presented her with the book, asking if she would accept it as a token. Flipping through it, she realized the verses Tom had written were about her. For the first time in her life Vera Maude was speechless.

Part of her refused to believe she could have inspired such heartfelt tributes. She didn't want the responsibility. She told herself it all came from somewhere in Tom's imagination. His last few sonnets trailed off unfinished.

> *To say that you are always in my thoughts*
> *Suggests I also think of other things.*
> *Truth is if you entirely I forgot,*
> *My mind would be cleared of all its musings.*

And the final entry was a single line: *My love for you is nature's cruelest gift.*

Vera Maude had struggled with that one for a long time. Eventually she had moved on. Had Tom? There were rumours he had been shipped off to a sanitarium, where his mind was presumably cleared forever of all its musings. She couldn't believe that was five years ago already.

Poor Tom.

She remembered reasoning with herself that unrequited love was not actually love at all. For it to be true love, it had to be shared by two people. Otherwise it was just madness. She placed the volume in her bag then pulled the last book off the shelf: a copy of Bulfinch's *Age of Fable* her father had given her for Christmas last year. She would try to remember to read up on Aphrodite tonight before bed. The gods still had a lot of explaining to do.

Every Sunday Vera Maude would come home for dinner and take something else away with her. This was the last of it. The room was bare now except for her mother's needlework hanging on the wall. Her father had been trying to get Vera Maude to take a few of her mother's things, but Vera Maude always refused. She never knew her mother, who had died shortly after she was born. Vera Maude believed these things should go to her older siblings. Her father said they wouldn't appreciate them.

The old man was preparing to sell the house and move in with his brother, Uncle Fred. Some of the Maguire children had hoped Vera Maude would remain to watch over their father and help keep the house in the family. She wondered which one of them thought they were going to get it in the end. The rest resented her for what they saw as a betrayal. Vera Maude was clearly the favourite, so how could she abandon him like this? None of them should have been surprised, though. Vera Maude was the black sheep of the family. She had different ideas, different ways of doing things. She even looked different than the other children.

To answer the folks who liked to joke about her being the milkman's daughter, her father pointed out the fact that she resembled his Irish mother, a woman of Spanish heritage. Vera Maude had chestnut hair, green-brown eyes, and in the summertime she was the first to have any colour. The rest of the family was tall and fair with red hair, like their mother. Vera Maude called herself a throwback, a remembrance of things past.

This would be the last Sunday dinner in the old house. She knew it saddened her father, but she also knew he didn't want to make a big deal about it. *He'll sit at the head of the table*, she thought, *quiz them about their week and then make sure they are caught up on current events*. Her father loved debate and enjoyed playing the devil's advocate.

She could hear the plates clattering on the table downstairs. Over the years more chairs were added to accommodate girlfriends, boyfriends, and spouses. Soon there would be grandchildren. The very idea of being an auntie made her want to jump out the window.

"Maudie! Dinner!"

"Coming!"

It had become increasingly difficult for her to behave herself at these gatherings, to hold her tongue and not rock the boat too much. But her father enjoyed seeing her in action. She held her ground and countered her brothers' volleys.

She could pretty much predict what the dinner conversation would be like: her father would back the idea of using martial law in Michigan to get the coal moving again. Joe won't like that. He'd be applauding the Red influence among the rail unions.

Bob would cut in with a comment about hydroelectricity being the wave of the future. He spent his days at McNaughton's store selling electric toasters, vacuum cleaners, curling tongs, and gawd knows what else.

Dorothy and her husband would try to steer the conversation towards temperance, pointing out the Mounties' successful raid on the Meyers house in Ford City last week. They'd picked up his still, a quantity of mash, and a few jars of third rail whisky.

Jennie's tastes bordered on the sensational. She'd likely bring up the brutal murder of a watchman at a factory in Hamilton and ask what the world was coming to.

Gavin was the aspiring real estate tycoon. He'd have noticed that the Labadie farm sold and that would lead to talk of planning and the Border Cities and then the amalgamation hot potato would get tossed around until the eldest, Austin, cooled things off with the latest news on the Old Boys festivities kicking off in a couple weeks.

Vera Maude grabbed her book bag and headed down the narrow stairs. When she got to the bottom she had to wiggle around the table, which was so long it stretched from the dining room into the parlour. Vera Maude dropped her book bag in the foyer and looked for a seat.

"Maudie, I want you sitting here next to me," said her father as he pulled out the chair to his left.

The older boys looked at each other but didn't say a word. The wives and girlfriends started bringing food out of the kitchen. It was typical Essex County fare: a pork roast, sweet corn on the cob, fresh tomatoes, radishes and cucumbers, warm biscuits, and a potato salad tossed with green beans and mayonnaise. Austin said Grace.

> Bless us, O Lord, and these thy gifts,
> Which we are about to receive from thy bounty
> Through Christ Our Lord.

Vera Maude mumbled her own made-up words and her father nudged her under the table.

"Ah, men," she concluded.

Everyone grabbed one of the dishes and her father cut into the roast. Plates were passed around. Vera Maude's came back with a radish on it.

"Gee, thanks a bunch."

Chapter 9

THE THIRD PAGE

RIDING WITH THE BORDER CITY BLUES

THIS WEEK:

A DULL ROAR

Prohibition means there will always be more battles than there will be men to fight them, and the police in the Border Cities know that. Sometimes the best they can do is just keep things down to a dull roar. They do this first by picking off the low-hanging fruit.

Last Thursday a fellow

burst into the station claiming his car had been stolen. While he was giving his statement a call came in about an abandoned vehicle: a patrolman had found a car with its front bumper joined to a telephone pole. He also found a trunk full of illegal beer. The fellow tried to pin it on the alleged car thieves but after the police applied the right pressure the fellow confessed to being in the 'transport business.' He had jumped the curb trying to avoid a child in the street and rather than get caught with wet goods, he decided to report the car stolen. He was charged and given a court date.

Trying to stop the flow of liquor in the Border Cities can be a bit like trying to hold back the tide with a mop and pail. There are a number of hotel bars and roadhouses that the police watch in a random rotation. Last Friday night the Dominion Tavern's number came up. Undercover police discovered strong beer on the premises and the owner was fined $200. He put it down to the cost of doing business.

That was an easy one. However, simple exercises like this can easily turn violent. One night last week Officer Allan Corbishdale was patrolling the alley behind the streetcar waiting room at Ferry Street when he heard an engine fire up and pull away. He suspected foul play. When they refused to halt the officer broke into a sprint and jumped onto the running board. Corbishdale later told the *Star* that the driver, Clayton Pastorius, then 'stepped on the gas.'

Corbishdale climbed into the rear of the vehicle where he discovered the reason for the driver's anxiety: six cases of illegal beer. When Mr. Pastorius's accomplice, Alex Renaud, reached back and started getting rough with Corbishdale, the officer struck him over the head with his nightstick. Renaud, the officer said, then wrested the club from his hand and returned the favour. Frustrated, Corbishdale drew his revolver and fired a warning shot through the roof of the car.

Renaud remained aggressive, Corbishdale said, and the officer was eventually forced to strike him over the head with the butt of his revolver, rendering him unconscious. With the vehicle approaching the Prince Edward Hotel, Corbishdale knew he had to put the brakes on this caper.

He fired another shot that shattered the windshield and caused Pastorius to briefly lose control as he turned onto Park Street. The vehicle finally came to a stop at the front steps of St. Alphonsus School. The next day the Sisters had a few things to say about the broken glass and skid marks on the front lawn.

There is this black and white world of thieves and smugglers and then there is the shadier world of the confidence men. This afternoon Mr. Karl Schwab of Janette Avenue reported to police that a bogus raid had been made on his home and the fraudulent officials hauled off three cases of legitimately-obtained whisky.

Watch for this space in next Saturday's *Star* to discover how it all played out.

"Hold on to this," Montroy said to Corbishdale as he folded the newspaper and tossed it onto the dashboard. "Your mother might want it for her scrapbook."

They were sitting in the new police flyer, a sleek, sprawling Studebaker Six. Corbishdale was behind the wheel and Montroy was sitting next to him, going over the events of the past thirty-six hours, bringing the rookie up to speed.

"Yeah, and so Schwab arrived at the station with his tongue wagging like a setter's. He collapsed in the chair by my desk, mopping his forehead with a damp handkerchief and clutching his documents. He told me two men — he noticed a third waiting in the car running outside — came knocking on his door. They said they were licensing department officials, flashed some ID, and then proceeded to frisk the place. When they found the whisky, Schwab protested. He told them it was legal."

"Why didn't he just show them his papers?" asked Corbishdale.

"Said he got flustered and forgot where he kept them. Wouldn't have done any good anyway. A few minutes into their search he knew that they weren't real inspectors."

"How?"

"The cut of their suits and the make of the car. He was smart not to call them on it. He could have got hurt. Anyway, what he kept telling me was that he had nothing to hide. He said he shared some of his whisky with a couple of his neighbours. When he happened to mention that one of them, a man by the name of Walters, had recently moved down from Hamilton, a bell went off. I showed him a photo of a goon from up that way I been keeping tabs on. He recognized the face, said he saw the man leaving Walters' house once or twice."

"So it was Walters?"

"Wait, it gets better. Me and Bickerstaff raided Walters' place this afternoon and turned up a case of wine, a case of beer, and a few bottles of Schwab's whisky. We brought Walters in for questioning. He admitted the guy in the photo, the Pole, was an acquaintance of his. He said he used to lay bets on the Pole's book in Hamilton. Walters managed to win just enough to keep him in the game but never enough to pay his debts."

Montroy started fanning himself with his hat before continuing with his story.

"Things got interesting when a rival bookie started spreading rumours about the Pole's books being fixed. Suddenly the Pole had more enemies than even he could handle, and so he blew. Walters figured he was off the hook. That was until the Pole darkened his door one day looking for money. Walters scraped together just enough to buy himself the kind of time that gets measured on a stopwatch, not a calendar. When the Pole came back for more, Walters got cocky and told the Pole to scram or he'd rat him out.

"The Pole just laughed. He told Walters he knew he was in deep with the other bookie and that he could fix it for him. Next thing Walters knew he was reading in the papers about some low-life found floating in Hamilton Harbour. The description matched the bookie. The Pole went to Walters' house to brag about it and tell him that he wouldn't hesitate to pin it on him if he needed to. Walters was indebted for life now and every week the Pole came to collect."

Montroy noticed Corbishdale becoming a little slack-jawed in disbelief.

"After a while Walters had had enough and quietly slipped down here. It only took the Pole a few days to track him down. He made Walters give him the lay of the land and then put him to work on Schwab. The whole thing made Walters sick. Walters said when we came knocking on his door he realized the only way to get rid of this phantom for good would be to finger him and suffer any consequences."

Montroy turned and set his gaze back on the building across the way. He and Corbishdale were watching the Pole's apartment on Tuscarora from a position across the street on Marentette. Montroy's plan was to follow the Pole to his target, watch him execute his raid, and then find out where he took his liquor. He finished his story, talking out the side of his mouth at Corbishdale.

"This morning we brought back Schwab to corroborate Walters' statement, and I spent the day gathering more evidence. The Pole's a bottom feeder, son, picking up bottles wherever he can, the hard stuff mostly — whisky, bourbon, that sort of thing."

Corbishdale couldn't understand the lengths people went to make, traffic, and drink liquor. Temperance had always been the theme in his home. Looking back, he remembered his family being stable and content, not to mention loyal and God-fearing. He couldn't understand why anyone would want it any other way.

Montroy peeled the cigarette butt off his lower lip, crushed it under his shoe, and got another one going.

"He's just a big ugly bohunk who's picked the wrong town to do his business."

Corbishdale was unfamiliar with that term. He guessed it had something to do with the Pole being a foreigner.

"We've got all the excitement we can handle here; we don't need any outsiders upsetting the balance."

Corbishdale's mind drifted back to when his father would rail against the followers of the Roman Church — mainly the Irish and Italians. The French became the focus of his anxiety when Quebec made conscription an issue. When the province refused to stay dry, it sent him right over the edge. "*Freedom of the human conscience* ... pah." He'd roll his eyes and shovel another helping of roast beef into his mouth. "It's the alcohol," he'd say, "it retards the brain."

Montroy slumped down in his seat. "Light's out."

The apartment had gone dark. Corbishdale swallowed hard. He imagined the Pole making his way down the stairs of the building, his bulging eyes and long, mustachioed face in the dim light of the hall, his silhouette moving towards the doorway, and a flash of gun metal in his belt. He would step outside then check the shadows around the building and the adjacent street corners. Maybe he'd spot the police flyer. Maybe he was already on to them. Corbishdale adjusted his grip on the wheel.

"Steady, son. You don't want to jump from the Third Page to the obituaries, now do you?"

Three figures climbed into a yellow Maxwell just on the other side of Tuscarora. The Pole was in the driver's seat.

"All right, let's go," said Montroy, "but not too close."

They followed it up Marentette. Montroy hadn't told Corbishdale everything that was in the Pole's file. He didn't want to scare the boy shitless. At the same time he felt Corbishdale needed the experience, despite his recent adventure. The city was changing and he, along with the other young officers on the force, needed to be better prepared.

The Pole had been a loose cannon on the deck of Hamilton's biggest outfit. When he got caught in a double-cross, the gang leader made an example of him. The Pole didn't like that, so he made some threats. After that the gang leader wanted him dead. He sent his heavies over to the Pole's safe house to burn it to the ground. Somehow the Pole managed to escape.

The Maxwell slowed to a stop then turned left onto Ellis. Montroy grabbed his pack of Macdonalds off the dashboard and shook one loose. He fired it up and took a long, soothing drag. The Maxwell hung a left onto Pierre and finally came to a stop in front of a house just south of Ottawa Street.

"Pull in here," said Montroy.

He was pointing to some cars parked on the opposite side of the street. Montroy surveyed the block.

"Go knock on that door — where the light's on — see if they have a telephone. Call the station and tell Yoakum to get down here."

They slipped out curbside and split up. Montroy used the parked cars for cover as he moved closer to the Pole's target. The moment the gang entered the house, Montroy did a duck-and-run across the street and took up a position below the veranda. There was some shouting inside and then the Pole's boys came out, each carrying a case of liquor. The Pole followed presently and helped arrange the crates in the trunk of the car. As soon as they pulled away Montroy ran back and joined Corbishdale in the flyer.

"Don't take your eyes off them."

The Maxwell zigzagged through the city, cutting through neighbourhoods and skirting the downtown before finally slowing in front of a small building on the west end of Park Street. It was Windsor City Dairy.

"Let's go see what's curdling their milk."

They found a window at the side of the garage. Montroy wiped the grease and soot from the glass with his sleeve. The Pole's boys and a fellow from the dairy were unloading the Maxwell. When they finished the milkman disappeared and then returned with bottles of milk. The Pole's boys cracked open the cases of liquor while the milkman arranged the bottles on a table. One of the Pole's boys started pouring liquor into them. Montroy and Corbishdale looked at each other. The whisky wasn't displacing the milk.

"I've seen enough. Stay here and cover the front while I go around back and try and find another way in."

"Yes, sir."

Montroy found a rear entrance in the alleyway, but it was locked. He pulled out his Colt, took a deep breath and kicked the door open.

"Hands up, boys — where I can see 'em."

The milkman dove for cover. One of the Pole's boys drew his pistol and Montroy fired, hitting him in the shoulder. The other fellow grabbed some air. Montroy cocked his revolver and aimed it at the Pole. The Pole laughed, pulled what appeared to be a butcher knife out of a sheath hanging from his belt, and started inching towards Montroy.

With his lanky black hair, white flesh, and big round eyes, there was something dark and weirdly medieval about this man. Montroy took a step back. That was a mistake. Now the Pole knew he had him.

There was a noise at the front door. The Pole didn't turn around at first. He just kept grinning, and as he moved into the light he threw a dense, cold shadow that seemed to bleed into every corner of the room.

"Sergeant Montroy?"

It was Corbishdale. He was standing there with his pistol drawn. The Pole turned and was a breath away from throwing the knife at Corbishdale when Montroy put a bullet in his back. The Pole froze for a moment, then his legs twisted under him and he dropped to the floor.

"Goddamn," said Montroy and ran over to the Pole. "Call an ambulance."

"Sir … I heard a shot … I …"

"That's all right, son. Just get us that ambulance."

Montroy looked up at the table and saw the milk bottles. He grabbed one. They were empty but painted to look full. When you held one in your hand it was pretty obvious, but on your porch at 5:30 in the morning no one could possibly tell the difference.

The Pole and his injured partner were loaded into the ambulance. Montroy rode with them and took the opportunity to ask the accomplice a few questions. When Montroy didn't like the answers, he poked the man in the shoulder with his nightstick. Every so often he would glance over at the Pole lying unconscious on the stretcher. He had this creepy grin on his face, like he was listening to everything they were saying.

Ugly bohunk.

Chapter 10

OJIBWAY

McCloskey watched the sun drop behind the horizon like a penny in a slot, gently triggering the astromechanics of nightfall. By the time he reached Essex County everything was black around his headlight beams.

At Maidstone he switched over to Talbot Road. When he reached the Huron Line he hung a left and continued west to Ojibway. Cottages and small farms began to appear, and then finally the river. He turned up Front Road.

He saw a bonfire in the distance and recognized some landmarks in the firelight: a row of poplars, an old oak tree — his father's old truck.

"Shit."

Anxiety gripped his body as his mind accelerated with the car. He turned sharply, nearly missing the bridge that spanned the ditch and then skidded to a stop near the house. Just as he was about to step down onto the running board an explosion threw him back into his seat. The windows and part of the roof were blown out of the cabin, showering the yard with burning debris.

McCloskey pulled himself up. Through the cloud of smoke he could make out his nearest neighbour, Lesperance, running towards him with a bucket. Taking his cue from the old man, McCloskey raced to the well and started pumping water into the bucket that hung from the spout. Lesperance arrived, breathless, just in time to exchange his empty one for McCloskey's overflowing one.

The old man shuffled over to the cabin and tossed the water through a broken window. Steam, smoke, and sparks billowed out in a thick, noxious mixture. He shouted over the roar of the flames, "Let it burn, Jack."

"No," he replied, "might be kegs under the floor."

Or money, McCloskey was thinking. He ran to the cabin and doused a section of shingles curling in the flames. The walls shuddered and the roof collapsed. He jumped back and turned away as a geyser of sparks shot up into the night sky. It got dark quickly after that, quiet too. McCloskey ran inside the house to fetch a lantern.

The place was a wreck. Chairs were overturned and cabinet drawers were spilled out onto the floor. He found the lantern and then gave a holler up the stairs.

"Pa? Billy?"

Nothing. He switched a light that hung outside the kitchen door and stepped back into the yard. His eyes fell on a set of drag marks in the loose dirt and gravel. They appeared to run in the direction of the cabin. He turned to Lesperance.

"Did you see anyone here tonight?"

The old man shook his head. "I just got home."

McCloskey started fiddling with the lantern. Lesperance approached him tentatively.

"You back for good, Jack?"

McCloskey looked at the old man sideways. He was a cagey fellow and McCloskey was never sure how far he could trust him.

"You know, Jack ... it might be dangerous here for you."

McCloskey got the lantern going and went over to the cabin. He could see parts of a whisky still poking through the glowing rubble, as well as various tools, jars, and jugs.

"Hold this."

He handed Lesperance the lantern then ran over to the garden and grabbed a shovel. He pulled down what was left of the cabin walls then stepped carefully into the smouldering ruin. He couldn't remember exactly where the trap door was. He used the shovel to leverage larger pieces of the cabin off the floor then kicked the rubble aside.

He saw something. Boots, two pair pointing up at different angles.

"Shine it over here."

McCloskey moved faster, trying to gently lift the brittle framework and then ... overalls, burned flesh, a lifeless hand, and a face still expressing what must have been the body's last agonizing moments. McCloskey went numb and the shovel dropped from his hands.

He became acutely aware of the darkness surrounding him, penetrating everything. It was in his father's and brother's dead eyes, the inky blackness of the river, and the farmland that stretched beyond the fading glow of the lantern. His knees felt weak. He was teetering at the edge of an abyss buried deep inside him, the same one he had fallen into after the war.

And then something snapped and he was like a machine kicked into overdrive.

"Did you call anyone before you left the house?"

"No, Jack, no one."

McCloskey couldn't tell if he was lying. "Make the call after I've left," he said. "Tell the police I hit the road while you were walking back to your house. And you have no idea where I could've gone to."

"It won't look good, Jack."

"I have to get to Clara before anyone else does."

He looked down and noticed his torn pants and burnt shoes.

"Wait here a minute."

He ran into the house. Upstairs he found some of his old clothes in a heap. He picked up a brown suit, a shirt, and a pair of heavy shoes. There was some soap and water on a table in his father's room. He quickly scrubbed the black off his face and hands, dressed, and ran back downstairs.

Lesperance had his head cocked towards the road. "A motor," he said.

"Cops?"

"I can't tell."

McCloskey ran to his vehicle. "Don't mention Clara," he said and started the engine. "Understand me?"

"Who did this, Jack?"

McCloskey ignored the old man. He dropped the clutch, shifted into reverse, and did a half-circle around him. Lesperance ran up to McCloskey and grabbed his arm.

"They were expecting you, you know."

The approaching car could be heard clearly now.

"Tell Clara what you got to tell her then get out of town."

McCloskey yanked his arm away, shifted out of reverse, and headed up the path. When he turned onto Front Road he could see the headlights of the other vehicle in his mirror. He kept glancing up until he saw it turn onto the property.

He couldn't get away from the image of their faces in the charred rubble. He twisted his hands around the steering wheel until it nearly snapped apart.

At the highway junction he continued north along the river road. Wanting to avoid the downtown he took the Huron Line to Tecumseh Road, the back door into the Border Cities.

Several cars were parked outside the Elliott Hotel and a couple of guys were keeping watch by the road. McCloskey turned his face as he drove past.

Thoughts began to ricochet inside his head. Who was behind this? If he had gotten to Ojibway sooner, could he have saved them? Was Sophie still safely on her way to Montreal? The bell of a locomotive engine got him focused again. He slowed down while crossing the tracks and then kept an eye on the side streets along Tecumseh.

There was a box of cigars on the seat next to him. He fumbled one out, bit off the end, and spat it onto the road. He found a match in the box as well, struck it on the dashboard, held the flame to the tip of the cigar, and took a few quick drags until it had a nice orange glow. The aroma filled the car. It helped calm his nerves.

Years ago on summer nights like this, he and his father would sit on the porch after Billy went to bed and just talk. Sometimes all Jack could see was the orange glow of his father's cigar floating back and forth as he rocked in his chair. The conversation would start with Jack telling his father what trouble he had gotten into that day. Then his father would start with his own stories.

He wanted to avoid the Avenue so he turned left up McDougall instead, rumbling over the train tracks at Hanna and then gliding passed the rows of idle factories. He slowed at Giles Boulevard, where these factories gave way to little wooden bungalows. He was thinking he shouldn't leave the car anywhere near Clara's, so at Erie Street he pulled in behind City Garage. McCloskey hoped Orval wouldn't sell it or use it for parts before he got back to him.

Erie was quiet; most of the dwellings above the shops were dark. McCloskey moved swiftly through the shadows. He darted across the Avenue and when he reached Pelissier Street he ducked in the doorway of the building opposite Clara's apartment.

On hot, humid nights like this, one could almost hear people sighing in their beds. McCloskey took one last drag on his cigar, walked up to the front door, and found the name on the register. He pushed the buzzer — three times fast then once. The door clicked open.

He slowly climbed the stairs to the second floor and paused in the dim light of the hall before knocking. He heard the clunk of the deadbolt inside the lock and then the door slowly swung open. When she recognized who it was, she threw her weight behind the door. McCloskey stopped it with his foot.

"What do you want?" she hissed.

"It's about Billy." He inched closer to the door. "Can I come in?"

She couldn't see around him into the hall.

"You alone?" she asked.

"Yeah."

Clara gave McCloskey another once over, relaxed her grip on the door, then stood back. He moved right past her and straight to the window in the front room, turned off a nearby table lamp, and peeked through the curtain.

"So, what's this about Billy?"

She was standing in the middle of the room, wrapped in a silk robe embroidered with a Chinese design. Her arms were folded across her chest and McCloskey could tell she was trying not to lose her temper. He pulled his eyes away from the street below only long enough to tell her very matter-of-factly that Billy was dead.

Clara closed her eyes for a moment and took a deep breath. When she opened them again the tension was gone from her body. There were no tears; this was the news she had been anticipating for the last six years. A long, sad chapter in her life had finally come to an end.

When the reports from the war were particularly bad, she would lie in bed wondering if he was still alive. When he came home a shattered man and drank until he couldn't drink anymore, she wondered how long it would take for him to kill himself with booze. When he left her and became a notorious bootlegger, she wondered where she'd find out about his death first: in the newspaper, from an overheard conversation in a streetcar, or from a cop. She thought she would have been more upset about it but she wasn't. She had mourned the loss of her husband too many times now to be shocked by his actual death.

"What happened?"

McCloskey told her what he came home to in Ojibway, leaving out the gruesome details. Clara was saddened about her father-in-law. She always had a soft spot for him. He was such a larger-than-life character.

"Drink?"

McCloskey was still at the window. "Yeah."

Clara came back from the kitchen with a couple of ryes, hers with ginger. She handed McCloskey his then dropped into a big, cushioned chair near the window.

McCloskey sat across from her on the chesterfield. He liked how her robe parted over one of her thighs and the small electric fan nearby was tousling her hair. He took a sip from his glass.

"Who were you expecting tonight?"

Clara pushed her eyebrows together.

"Not everyone knows the buzz," he said, "and you wouldn't open the door for just anybody, not dressed like that."

Clara rolled her eyes. "It could only have been you or Billy, and last I heard you were still in Hamilton."

McCloskey wasn't entirely satisfied with that but let it drift. They sat silently in the dark for a while. Clara could tell something else was up and McCloskey's mind felt like a cloud of exploded shell fragments. He had left Hamilton with such purpose and determination. Now where was he? Maybe his journey wasn't over yet.

And then someone started speaking. It took McCloskey a moment to realize it was himself. "I want you to fix it so I can see Henry tonight."

Clara sat up. "What for? He'll arrest you before you say boo, Jack."

McCloskey finished his drink. "Smooth him out for me first. Tell him what I told you. Tell him anything. But it has to be tonight."

"You're serious, aren't you?"

She got up and, doing away with the gingery pretense, refilled McCloskey's glass as well as her own. McCloskey poured it down his throat. He could still taste the cedar from the burned-out cabin.

"I want to know who was behind it — before the police have a chance to cover it up or try to hang it on me."

"Why don't you cut your losses and just get out of town, Jack? Don't you realize you're probably next on their list, whoever it was?"

"Don't you care who did this?"

"No, Jack, I don't. As far as I'm concerned it's over, it's finally over. Now maybe we can get on with what's left of our pathetic lives."

That was harsh. It came straight from the bottle.

"Not until I find out who's responsible."

"What's the mystery, Jack? Wasn't it the same sons of bitches you work for?"

"Used to work for. I don't know. Something tells me it's more complicated than that."

"It's never more complicated than that."

Clara got up, fetched her pack of cigarettes off the windowsill, and got one going with the little Ronson striker she had in her pocket. She took a puff before replying.

"Okay, I'll talk to Henry. I'll do it for your father. I always thought he deserved better than you two."

He let that one drift too. He figured he should probably start getting used to it.

"Tell him to meet me at the British-American in half an hour."

"You have to promise me one thing."

He stood up and set his glass down on the coffee table. "What's that?"

"If you don't get anywhere with Henry, don't come running back to me. I never want to see you again."

"We'll talk tomorrow."

"Don't bet on it," she said and she pulled her robe tight across her chest. "I'll take care of the funeral arrangements."

Jack reached in his pocket and pulled out a roll of bills. He peeled off a couple layers and tossed them onto the table next to his glass.

"This place still got a back door?"

"You know where it is."

Clara followed McCloskey down the hall past the bedrooms.

"Put the latch on and don't open the door for anybody," he said. "I wasn't here."

Chapter 11

THE BOILING POINT
OF ALCOHOL

Young Bertie Monaghan and his father Jacob were sharing a pitcher of lemonade under the silver maple in their backyard. Mrs. Monaghan was visiting her mother.

'In the old days we'd hide it in the bush where it wouldn't draw attention or cause any damage, but in our case,' Jacob gestured with his thumb, 'I think the garden shed will do just fine.'

Bertie nodded and tipped his glass to his mouth for another sip. The ice sloshed back and some lemonade dribbled down his chin. He wiped it with the back of his hand. While other boys were getting driving lessons from their dads, Bertie was learning how to make moonshine. It was an old family tradition.

'We'll need an oversized kettle for fermenting. It sits on a rack a couple feet off the ground, and the gas burner goes underneath. Gas is the best. Oh — and we'll need a good thermometer.'

Monaghan took another look over his shoulder to make sure none of his neighbours were about.

'Now, from a hole at the side of the kettle, right near the bottom, we run a rigid, narrow tube and close it off with a valve. The still is smaller than the kettle and positioned an arm's length from the rack. Its neck should taper to an opening just large enough to accommodate an end of narrow, flexible pipe. Running out the side of the neck, just above where it connects to the still, is another rigid tube like the one coming out the side of the kettle. Connect the end of this tube to the valve. Together, these tubes should form a straight line parallel to the ground. The pressure of the gases in the kettle will push the liquid along this connection, letting it drip smooth and regular into the still.'

It was difficult to tell who was more excited, Monaghan, who was describing it like it was a magical invention he saw in a dream, or his son, who was taking it all in, agog.

'Back to the flexible pipe: first, keep in mind that its length will affect the distillation process — the longer the pipe, the weaker the product. Bend the pipe so it points down at a 45-degree angle. Connect a short length of much wider, rigid pipe to the end. This is your condenser. Connect a much smaller tube to the open end of it and run it to whatever vessel you're using to collect the alcohol, say a good size jug. And we can't make this tube too short: if the jug is too close to the burner the alcohol will evaporate or explode.'

'But what do we make the spirits with, dad?'

'Basically, corn. We pour it into the kettle and then top it with just enough lukewarm water to cover it. Let it breathe for two weeks. After a few days the ferment will start to bubble and stink like shit in a frying pan, so we'll have to keep the shed well-ventilated.

'The thermometer is so we can keep the heat at a steady 180 degrees — just above the boiling point of alcohol and below the boiling point of water. When the pressure starts building in the kettle, open the valve until you have a slow drip into the still. Make sure the amount of ferment getting forced into the still is equal to the amount of steam going up the pipe — you don't want the still to either fill up or boil dry. The steam will condense and then run down the tube into the jug. What we've got now is 198-proof ethyl alcohol. It's filtered through charcoal, and then diluted three parts alcohol to five parts distilled water. If we mess it up, we just keep trying. Every still has its own personality, and you just have to take the time to get to know her.'

That was about ten days ago. Right now Bertie was lying awake in bed like he was waiting for Christmas. He could smell the ferment from his window. He wondered if any of his neighbours on this hot summer night could as well. His dad said that anyone who did could get bought off with a jar.

Mrs. Ferguson had noticed the odour a few days ago when she sat down to her tea. It came wafting in through the dining room window and seemed to be coming from across the alley. She asked her son to confirm her suspicions for her and he did just that.

'I guess you just never noticed it before, ma.'

'I know what that smell is. Why hasn't anyone done anything about it?'

'Because this family makes good whisky. Now mind your own business, okay?'

Mrs. Ferguson was beside herself. It was a nightmare come true. Could a person really distill whisky in their own backyard without fear of consequence?

'What is the world coming to, Stannie?'

'About a buck a quart,' he cracked.

He was twice her size but that never stopped her from

slapping him around a bit for his 'insolence and sinful behaviour.' She fetched her rolling pin and started chasing Stannie around the dining room table with it.

'All right, all right, ma. I won't be buying any of his stuff. Just please do us both a favour and don't go to the police.'

That wouldn't be a problem. Mrs. Ferguson had made her rather poor opinion of the chief constable and his force known to several officers, and they were no longer returning any of her calls. No, Mrs. Ferguson was going to take a different route. She had recently heard of a young officer who was not afraid to do right and uphold the law. And it just so happened she knew a woman, a certain Mrs. Scofield, who was friendly with this boy's mother. Mrs. Ferguson had made sure she crossed paths with Mrs. Scofield at the Avenue Market earlier this morning.

'Have I got something to tell you!'

'You have something to tell me?'

'Isn't that what I just said?'

'Don't ask me what you said. I'm the one that's hard of hearing, Mrs. Ferguson. Besides, if you're not going to pay attention to what you're saying yourself,' said Mrs. Scofield, waving an impatient hand, 'then I'm off.'

'Oh, Thelma, don't be like that.' Mrs. Ferguson touched Mrs. Scofield's shoulder. 'I've got a neighbour making spirits on his property.'

'Whisky?'

Mrs. Scofield's hearing was improving.

'I'm not sure. It was Stannie told me.'

'Oh, Stan.'

Mrs. Scofield didn't care for Stan. She still blamed him for the death of Goldie, her golden retriever. Stan used to take Goldie to the river to swim. She was a good swimmer but one time Goldie dove in and never came back up. Mrs. Scofield said she knew the law. She said Stan should have been charged with negligent canicide.

'Corn?'

'How would I know?' said Mrs. Ferguson as she adjusted the bag hanging from her shoulder. 'All I do know is we have to put a stop to it.'

'Yes, we do,' agreed Mrs. Scofield. '"How do we do that?'

'Why, your friend Mrs. Locke, of course.'

'I don't follow.'

'Walk with me, dear.'

Mrs. Ferguson hooked Mrs. Scofield's arm in hers and dragged her towards the streetcar stop.

'Are you not an intimate of Mrs. Locke's?'

'Yes.'

'And is not Mrs. Locke the proud mother of Officer Tom Locke of the Windsor Police Department?'

Mrs. Ferguson gave Mrs. Scofield a minute to catch up.

'You want me to tell Mrs. Locke about Stan?'

Mrs. Scofield's streetcar pulled up. 'No, Thelma, I want you to tell her about Mr. Monaghan. He's the villain making moonshine in his backyard and he's going to get the whole block inebriated.'

'Well, then,' said Mrs. Scofield, 'you should report it to the police.'

Mrs. Ferguson gave a sigh. 'You know what a rotten bunch they are. It would be useless. That's why I want you to talk to Mrs. Locke. I've heard good things about her boy. He's an honest one. And he respects his mother.'

The two ladies eyed the passengers stepping off the streetcar. Mrs. Scofield climbed aboard then turned and said she'd mention it to Mrs. Locke at church.

'Bless you, Thelma! Our cause is a noble one, dear.'

Walking alongside the streetcar, Mrs. Ferguson followed Mrs. Scofield to her seat.

'For Goldie!' cried Mrs. Scofield.

The streetcar was pulling away.

'What, dear?'

At church this morning Mrs. Scofield elbowed her way

through the crowd and got a seat next to Mrs. Locke. When they sat down Mrs. Scofield gave her pitch. Mrs. Locke kept her eye on the minister but listened to Mrs. Scofield. Every once in a while she nodded her long, sour face. The Reverend's sermon, coincidentally, was on the evils of strong drink. He had the congregation all fired up. Mrs. Locke raised the issue with her son over dinner.

Tom Locke knew the neighbourhood. He parked around the corner from Mrs. Ferguson's place and made his way silently up the alleyway armed with his trademark baseball bat. No uniform, no badge, and no gun. He recognized the smell right away and honed in on the Monaghan property. In the moonlight he could see that the one window in the shed was recently boarded up and part of the roof was cut away, no doubt for ventilation purposes. He found a shovel in the garden and pried open the flimsy door.

Jacob Monaghan arrived just in time to see a shadowy figure smashing the components to his whisky still, which the assassin had dragged out into the alleyway. The reek of the ferment filled the air and made Monaghan gag.

Locke turned upon hearing his protests. Monaghan was prepared to confront him until he saw the baseball bat and the mad gleam in the swinger's eye. Monaghan had heard about this fellow, and the word on the street was that he was actually a cop. Locke stopped swinging and pointed his weapon directly at Monaghan. His eyes were blazing and sweat was streaming down his face. To Monaghan, he looked like a man possessed.

"You want some, mister? I've got plenty left."

Monaghan backed off. "No, sir."

Locke looked around. Lights were coming on in some of the windows facing the alley. There were silhouettes in a few of them. He hoped they all got a good look. Bertie Monaghan sure did. He had his face pressed against his bedroom window, watching. So much for family tradition.

— *Chapter 12* —

THE BRITISH-AMERICAN

The British-American Hotel stood at Windsor's main intersection — the Avenue and Riverside Drive, just a stone's throw from the ferry dock. It was built on the site originally occupied by Pierre St. Amour's tavern and ferry. St. Amour was among the first to operate a regular service between the south shore and Detroit. That was in 1820 and the ferry was a dugout canoe.

Hirons House came to occupy the site towards the middle of the century and saw the arrival of the Great Western Railway, completing the link between the Atlantic and the Mississippi. Hirons survived the Great Fire of 1871, was expanded and renamed American House.

A decade later, the mayor of the town persuaded Mrs. Lucetta Medbury of Detroit, owner of the property the hotel was situated on, to allow the block to be opened up to the water's edge and make possible the construction of a new ferry landing and customs house. The dock quickly became the main junction for people travelling not just between Windsor and Detroit but Canada and the United States. The owners of the hotel, overtaken by a fit of patriotism, soon after renamed it the British-American.

Today, the British-American represented a sort of neutral territory. There was no bootleg liquor behind the bar, no gambling, no needles in the washrooms, and no guns or badges. When parties from opposite sides of the law met here, it was usually for diplomatic reasons.

Fields entered and looked around uncomfortably. He stood out like a sore thumb and he knew it. His blue suit and brown shoes said *honest* and *sensible*. His handlebar moustaches said *cop*. He walked over to the bar where McCloskey was drinking what these days passed for beer. He took up a defensive position, leaving a stool between him and his brother-in-law.

"Thanks for coming, Henry."

"I'm only here because Clara asked me."

"Can I get you anything?"

"Let's get to the point."

McCloskey swallowed a big piece of his pride and got right to it. "I need your help."

That seemed to tickle Fields. He let out a snort, the Henry Fields equivalent of a belly laugh. "McCloskey, I only tolerated you and your family because of Clara. Now that Billy is dead, that connection is gone and as far as I'm concerned you're fair game."

McCloskey looked at himself in the mirror behind the bar. Part of him was already regretting this. "My pa and Billy were murdered."

"That's rich. I made a few telephone calls. There was a fire in the cabin that housed your father's still. The still exploded, the cabin caught fire, and they were killed trying to save their liquor. End of story."

"That's not true, at least not entirely. There were obvious

signs of a struggle in the house. They were dragged into the cabin. For all we know they may even have been burned alive."

"Maybe they had it coming."

Under normal circumstances McCloskey would have beaten Fields within an inch of his life for a remark like that. He swallowed a bit more of his pride and continued. "If the people who did it think I'm going to take this lying down, they're wrong."

McCloskey could sense patrons turning an ear towards the bar. And then the murmuring started. For anyone interested in the social climate in the Border Cities, the British-American was the barometer and right now the barometer was suggesting a storm was on the way.

"Clara said I should cut my losses, but seeing as I've got nothing left, I think that puts me at a distinct advantage."

"I can't be a party to your vigilantism, McCloskey. Give me one good reason why I shouldn't just lock you up and throw away the key."

McCloskey was getting tired of this dance, but he wasn't going to let go of Fields until he had what he wanted.

"Listen, Henry, this is bigger than a family of bootleggers operating out of a farmhouse at the edge of town and you know it. If you really want to fight the good fight you'll forget about chumps like me and start going after the crooked cops, gang leaders, and political bagmen because they're the ones running this burg, not the mayor, not the chief of police, and not the president of Ford or Walker's. You talk a good talk, Henry, but they've got you right where they want you. Can't you see that? You're window dressing, a straight and narrow poster boy for a police force that's as dirty as any whore on Pitt Street. You'll live and die in the dead end that they've steered you into unless you make your move right now."

It was Fields' turn to study his reflection in the mirror. McCloskey finished with a twist.

"The Lieutenant was probably told to make an example of my father and Billy. Wouldn't you like to take the opportunity of making an example out of him?"

There was a barely perceptible slackening in Henry

Fields' shoulders.

"It's not like it was before you left, Jack." And the tone of his voice changed. "The Lieutenant's boss is working out of the Border Cities now."

"Then all the more reason to strike." McCloskey lowered his own voice. "Where are you going to be a month from now, Henry? Walking a beat? And who's going to watch your back when you're sent alone into those dark alleys?"

Their eyes met in the mirror behind the bar. McCloskey could tell he had him.

"You'll leave town when it's all over?" asked Fields.

McCloskey was prepared to say anything at this point. "You won't have to tell me twice."

"I'm not just clearing a path for you to take over the Border Cities?"

"I don't want the job. I want out and I want my freedom."

It was Fields' turn to swallow his pride. "All right," he said, "what are you looking for from me?"

McCloskey shifted over to the stool next to Fields. "I want to know who was involved. Go nosing around Ojibway; talk to the old man next door — Lesperance. I want to know what the cops know and I want to know where the Lieutenant figures in all of this."

Fields had conditions.

"Okay, but we don't meet in person again until this thing gets sorted out. We communicate by telephone — and you don't call me, I call you."

Everything was coming together again. There was a purpose to his being here. "Deal."

Fields stood up and replaced his hat. "This isn't a *deal*, McCloskey. I don't bargain with thugs and bootleggers. If there's been some wrongdoing here, I intend to get to the bottom of it."

McCloskey figured that was for the benefit of their audience. He watched Fields pass through the doors of the hotel and then turned around to face the crowd.

"I'll be in my room if anyone needs me."

SECOND GEAR

(MONDAY, JULY 24)

Chapter 13

BOXCAR BLUES

Despite the heavy shelling, the line was preparing to advance. The bridge had been blown, barbed wire cut, and an artillery barrage was creeping ahead of them. The plan was to take back the trenches they were forced out of a week ago and hold that position until reinforcements arrived.

The whistle blew.

Jack McCloskey was the first one over the top. He didn't get far, though: less than five yards out he was knocked down by a series of explosions that seemed more timed and deliberate than the shelling.

Intelligence had failed. The enemy was well equipped and on the move, cutting in from the left and right underneath the barrage and preparing to steamroll across the Allied defences. Thick, acrid smoke blanketed the field. Jack lost sight of Billy.

As the mortar eased up the artillery grew heavier, pulverizing the battlefield, churning up a gruesome sea of rubble, mud, and broken bodies. It became impossible to make heads or tails of anything. When the artillery became sporadic again, Jack could hear the injured soldiers' shouts for help. He located the trench he had leapt out of, or what was left of it. The walls had collapsed and there was water streaming into it. He saw limbs. Some were still attached. He moved a piece of wood frame and saw an arm. When he pulled it the body followed. It was Billy, semi-conscious and badly bruised.

Jack pulled his brother's arm across his shoulders and dragged him back through the gunfire to a foxhole behind the line. He made Billy as comfortable as possible and then looked around for help. He saw a paramedic wasting time trying to revive something that looked like it should have been hanging from a meat hook in a butcher shop. Jack gave a shout and waved him over. While the medic tended to Billy, Jack tried to catch his breath.

His moment's peace was shattered by an unearthly cry. He peaked over the edge of the foxhole and saw a shadow zigzag across the field. It vanished in a cloud of smoke and then reappeared just a few yards away. It was Jigsaw. His uniform was scorched and tattered. He jumped into a foxhole. There was a terrible noise and a German soldier crawled out holding his belly. Another one of the Kaiser's boys feebly threw himself over the edge. Jigsaw dragged him back down, finished him off, and then climbed out to survey the chaos. He was like an angel of death, terrifying to behold. Jack instinctively ducked back into his foxhole, even though he knew he had nothing to fear. After all, Jigsaw was on his side.

'He's gonna make it.'

The medic stabilized Billy and was bringing him to.

Billy blinked. 'Am I dead?'

'You should be so lucky.'

'Now what?' asked the medic. They were pinned.

McCloskey looked down at the stinking pool of filth and human remains they were standing in. Cold, wet death seeped into the cracks of his boots and chilled him to the bone.

'We get the fuck out of here.'

'What about the reinforcements?'

'There won't be any. We're going find out who's left and we're going head back to where we blew up that bridge.'

'You gotta be kidding,' said the medic.

'We'll wade across the river at sundown.'

Monday, 4:50 a.m.

McCloskey was lying on his bed thinking, remembering, and blowing smoke rings at the ceiling when a set of knuckles came rapping on his door. He grabbed his revolver and pressed himself against the adjacent wall.

"Jack? Jack McCloskey — you in there?"

"Yeah."

"Telephone."

He eased the door open. One of the porters was standing outside.

"I didn't know you was back in town, Jack."

"Then you're not reading the society columns."

McCloskey tucked his revolver in his belt, threw on his jacket, and walked with the porter down the stairs. The desk clerk was holding out the telephone.

"Hello?"

"It's Fields."

"You got anything?"

"A little while ago we brought in a drunk that was found staggering down Tecumseh near Crawford."

"And?"

"To make a long story short, he was the driver."

"What?"

"He drove the car to Ojibway last night."

"I'll be right over."

"Don't bother. He's speaking Italian with a thick Scotch accent. So far all we've been able to get out of him is that his gangland friends are hanging out at the Elliott and they owe him money."

"That's it? That's all you've got?"

"Calm down, McCloskey. There are a couple uniforms and a detective at the Elliott right now. I'll let you know if —"

Fields heard the line disconnect. "Damn."

After he hung up a call came into the station. The police at the Elliott needed reinforcements. One of the constables was down and the detective was being taken to hospital. Fields immediately headed out with another officer.

Meanwhile McCloskey ran out into the street and spotted a Yellow Cab turning around at the ferry dock. He jumped in before the driver came to a full stop.

"Elliott Hotel — fast."

They climbed the hill then turned right onto Riverside Drive. When McCloskey looked over and saw the Detroit skyline in the pre-dawn light, it made him think of Montreal. He imagined Sophie asleep in her own bed, her cheek pressed against her pillow. Was she thinking of him? Part of him hoped that he was the furthest thing from her mind right now, or at most a bit player in a bad dream. Her life was hers again, uncomplicated with guys like him or Brown. He on the other hand had just spent a sleepless night in a hotel room, and while he may have been unencumbered, he still didn't feel his life belonged to him. Maybe today would be the day he'd finally win it back.

As they approached Crawford, the cabbie slowed for the left-hand turn.

"No," said McCloskey, "not the front door. I'd like to keep a low profile."

"Gotcha."

The cabbie continued past Crawford and the railway ferry terminal, turning up McKay instead. A few minutes later they were pulling into the Michigan Central station, where gunshots could be heard coming from the direction of the hotel, which was just on the other side of the tracks.

"Thanks."

McCloskey got out and tossed a note through the passenger window. As soon it touched the front seat the cabbie mashed the pedal and tore through the parking lot. This was obviously more excitement than he was looking for this morning.

McCloskey started towards the hotel. Boxcars were passing back and forth between him and the hotel, and he used them for cover as he made his way across the tracks. He could see police shooting from behind a vehicle parked to the left up on Wellington Street, and to the right, near Tecumseh Road, two motorcycles were parked.

A metal fire escape zigzagged down the back of the hotel. McCloskey pulled down the ladder and climbed up to the second-storey window, where he saw a man in a suit sitting with his back against a blood-splattered wall and a constable face-down on the floor. As soon as he stepped through the window a shot echoed through the building. It sounded like it came from the stairwell at the front of the hall. McCloskey wasn't anticipating a shoot-out. He checked the Webley; it held six rounds.

He heard more shots upstairs as he crept along the hall. McCloskey paused for a moment to think about not just what side he was on, but what side everyone else might think he was on. And then he stopped thinking. He sprinted down the hall and slid shoulder-first across the floor. A gunman positioned on the landing below turned and fired where he expected someone would be standing while McCloskey buried a round in his shoulder, sending him tumbling backwards down the stairs and into the lobby. Maybe now the way was clear for the cops.

McCloskey ran up to the next floor. The door to the corner room was slightly ajar. He was easing it open further when he heard the clatter of the fire escape.

Shit.

He ran down the hall to the window and spotted what had to be the second gunman now hoofing it towards the tracks. McCloskey went bounding down the fire escape and made his way back among the boxcars.

Finding himself standing between trains moving in opposite directions, he spotted the gunman running towards the river. McCloskey chased after him until he vanished between the cars on the left, which were moving in the same direction. McCloskey grabbed the ladder on the next car and climbed over the hitch. The gunman was still running towards the river, but he was even further away now.

McCloskey had heard stories of fugitives clinging to the underside of boxcars through the tunnel to Detroit. He paused to take a wasted shot with his Webley and then resumed his sprint. When he caught up, the gunman switched to the opposite track.

The two men exchanged shots every time there was a gap between the moving cars. Pretty soon McCloskey was out of ammo. He climbed over the next hitch and quickly caught up. He finally got a good look at the gunman's face. Now he imagined him at Ojibway.

It was you.

The gunman jumped at the ladder on the back of the boxcar he was chasing. His feet dragged over a several railroad ties before he managed to pull himself up.

McCloskey made a leap for the same ladder and got his hands stomped on. He was regaining his grip when he looked up and saw the gunman reach into his jacket. McCloskey yanked one of the gunman's feet off the ladder, and while he struggled to regain his balance, McCloskey hoisted himself up. They were face to face on the ladder now. With his free right hand, McCloskey delivered a lightning-quick blow to the gunman's ribs.

The gunman fumbled his pistol and while he looked down in disbelief McCloskey delivered another blow. This time the man let go and rolled into the shallow gully between the tracks.

McCloskey followed. When he got to his feet he saw the man disappear behind a row of boxcars standing back near the road. Crouching down he could see the man's legs running in the direction of the tunnel again.

There was one track in the tunnel and a string of boxcars presently moving along it. McCloskey threw some coal on his own fire. He caught up with the train but still couldn't see the gunman. He heard a whistle. Two cops and a railway worker were running towards him. The cops were brandishing Colts.

"Hold it! Hold it right there, mister!"

McCloskey kept running. Then he saw the gunman way up ahead, cradled under a boxcar, waving at him — going, going, gone.

The cops started firing shots in the air so McCloskey stopped running. He looked up and saw the sun peeking over the trees at the edge of the yard. There wasn't a cloud in the sky.

"I'll take that piece," said one of the cops.

McCloskey handed it over.

"You Jack McCloskey?" asked the other.

McCloskey was bent over now, trying to catch his breath. "Yeah."

The older cop waved his Colt up the tracks towards the hotel. "That way."

McCloskey started walking and the cops followed. Rail workers were appearing on the scene and residents from Wellington Road were gathering on the grassy slope, trying to get a good look. A couple boys held their hands like guns and made "bang bang" noises until a young woman in a faded housecoat gave them each the back of her hand.

McCloskey felt like he was being escorted to the gallows. He listened to the gravel underfoot and the gulls overhead and tried to imagine he was somewhere, anywhere else. When they reached the hotel the tracks were level with the road again and they walked around to the front entrance. Cops were standing at the curb holding back a small crowd.

Inside, McCloskey gauged the hotel guests assembled in the bar. They looked like the type always looking for stories to tell, other people's stories. He stepped over the bloodstain on the floor at the bottom of the stairs and wondered if the guy was dead. The cops didn't say a word and neither did McCloskey; they just continued silently all the way up to the third floor.

At the end of the hall was a cop loaded with attitude standing outside a guestroom. The room was empty except for a single wooden chair. The older of the two cops gestured McCloskey to go in and sit down, and then closed the door behind him.

Even with his back turned McCloskey recognized Detective Samuel Morrison. He was a big man, fat with bribes and secrets. Light filled the room when he moved away from the window that overlooked the rail yard. A few uncomfortable minutes passed while he stared down McCloskey. He had the look of a man tired of manoeuvring through the political minefield that was the Border Cities. *Murder is easy,* he often said; *Prohibition's the devil.*

Morrison started off by repeating what Fields had told him earlier, that the guy they already had in custody, Gears Gabrese, was the driver last night. The rest went something like this: the two mugs that were killed in the hotel — the one McCloskey found dead in the hall and the one he shot in the stairwell — were Ace McTavish and Red Williams. Witnesses put these two at a card game in the hotel bar at the time of the events in Ojibway. These same witnesses said Gabrese and Mutt Melvin — the guy McCloskey was chasing down in the rail yard — joined the card game around 10 p.m. A few hands and several whiskies later Gabrese was ranting about Mutt being a cheat. Everything degenerated after that and Gabrese said if he couldn't claim the pot, he at least wanted his fee for driving to Ojibway. He was hammered. He tried to start something with Mutt but then the bartender finally threw him out. Good thing, too. Mutt Melvin, having already tasted blood once that night, was looking for more. Morrison told McCloskey it was Mutt that killed his father and brother and he suspected a certain bootlegger in Detroit was behind it all. And that was all Morrison had to say. The cops were still waiting for Gabrese to come to his senses so they could question him proper.

Morrison took a puff from his cigar and blew smoke at the window. McCloskey wondered how Morrison could possibly know what truth was any more, he carried around so many versions of it in his head.

"You need anything else from me?"

"No. We're through here."

"That's it?"

"Yeah, that's it. Sorry, no door prizes today."

His speech was very nice but something told McCloskey that he was either dead wrong or lying. If he was wrong, that was one thing, but if he was lying it was for a reason. McCloskey could only guess it was to get him to stop nosing around. But why would Morrison want him to drop it? Could the Lieutenant be behind this? He had to be. It was interesting that Morrison didn't even mention him. Maybe Gabrese could provide some clues. McCloskey felt he had to talk to him. The best way to get to Gabrese was through Fields, and the only way to get to Fields was through Clara.

"You can have your piece back," said Morrison. "If I take it from you, you'd just go get yourself another one. Now beat it."

Chapter 14

THE LIBRARIAN, THE LODGER, AND THE LANDLADY

Vera Maude was peeking through the curtains in the vestibule. "Well, well, well," she muttered to herself, "you're running a little early today."

She watched him trot down the front steps and waited until he advanced a little up the block before following him down Tecumseh Road.

The man's name was Braverman. He had moved into the spare room at Mrs. Cousineau's back in May and he'd been a source of curiosity to Vera Maude ever since. At first it was the garb, sort of rustbelt bohemian. Then it was the paint-splattered briefcase: it always appeared to be heavier when he was leaving than when he was arriving. She thought about asking her own landlady if she knew anything about him but was afraid of getting tangled up in the Clothesline — Mrs. Richardson's network of neighbourhood gossips.

As the commuters converged on the waiting streetcar Vera Maude stuck close to Braverman. He sat himself street-side near the exit. Vera Maude sat on the bench at the rear and examined the homes along the tree-lined Avenue as they sprung to life. People were taking in the milk and the paper, pushing their kids out the door, and generally cranking their piston-driven lives into action.

"Ha-a-a-NUH."

The conductor hollered street names like he was calling plays at a ball game. Two chatty, smartly dressed women boarded at Hanna Street. Vera Maude recognized them from Smith's department store, the ladies' undergarments to be exact, or the girls' bait & tackle counter.

She had considered bringing up the subject of Mrs. Cousineau's mystery man with her in the course of conversation by saying something like "oh, and I happened to notice" or "I haven't seen your lodger lately," but Vera Maude nixed that idea because she didn't want to appear to be looking for an introduction. The Misses Cousineau and Richardson were always asking if there was a special man in Vera Maude's life, and Vera Maude was always saying yes, even if that wasn't the case. The absolute last thing she needed was the Clothesline playing matchmaker. She'd wind up with somebody's idiot nephew, or worse, some yolk with a face like an elevated railway.

"SHE-E-E-P-herd."

When Vera Maude found out that Braverman actually lived in Detroit, she became even more suspicious. It made her wonder if Mrs. Cousineau's lodger wasn't a bootlegger. That was when she decided to turn detective and try to gather some more facts.

Traffic was light and the streetcar continued to make good time. Half the city seemed to be on vacation. Vera Maude once considered going on one of those weekend excursions to Colchester Beach, but she needed someone to go with and couldn't bear the thought of tripping with any of her co-workers getting paired with some loathsome, giggling girl who had a crush on her cousin and wore a nightgown to bed.

Wait — why hasn't Mrs. Cousineau tried to set me up with Braverman? Does she know something?

"E-e-e-llis."

The streetcar was starting to fill up. Vera Maude watched the long faces pile aboard, the folks that already used up their vacation time, the folks without an electric fan, the folks that couldn't stand the heat and were staring down the short end of what was going to be a long week. In a few months these same people would be complaining about the cold. Last winter, when Mrs. Cousineau took ill and was practically bed-ridden, Vera Maude brought her magazines from the library. It became a habit, and now Mrs. Cousineau was used to her regular rotation of *American Cookery*, *Ladies' Home Journal*, *House Beautiful*, and *Chatterbox*.

A few weeks ago Vera Maude decided to use one of these visits to try and learn more about her lodger. She found Mrs. Cousineau turning soil in the flowerbed. She was wearing her enormous, straw sunhat and oversized garden gloves, and they made her look like a little girl playing in the dirt. Vera Maude was feeling reckless. She asked her if there was anything she might bring the gentleman in her next parcel.

— Do you know what sorts of things he likes to read?
— I couldn't say, dear. I don't think I've ever seen him with a book.
— His work probably keeps him very busy. What line did you say he was in?

Well, that got Mrs. Cousineau's gums flapping, and that's how Vera Maude learned that the man's name was Braverman, worked as a commercial artist somewhere downtown, and though he resided in Detroit, he had taken this room in Windsor in case he worked late or felt like spending the weekend.

—   Why doesn't he just move here?
—   He says his situation is only temporary. He's planning to move abroad.
—   How interesting. Did he say where?
—   No, but if I were to guess I would have to say Paris.
—   Paris!
—   Mm-hm. A few days after he took the room he got a giant carton from Paris. Had to be delivered by truck. Supplies for work, he said. And he gets letters all the time.
—   Supplies?
—   That's right. Paints and varnishes. It looked heavy. Nice fellow. Always pays his rent on time.
—   Does he ever —
—   Have any plans for the long weekend, Maudie? I know a young man who —
—   Oh — got to run, Mrs. Cousineau. I hear Mrs. Richardson calling me for supper.

Since then Vera Maude had made several attempts at trying to find out where Braverman works. All she knew for certain was that his office was nearer the river than the library because she always got off the streetcar before he did. Today, however, with the extra time she was determined to go through with her investigation and see where it took her.

"Gi-i-i-i-iles."

Some professional-types got on, the new midtown crowd. They kept their noses wedged in their morning papers, counting the days until they saved up enough for this year's Cadillac and they could be rescued from public transit.

Cadillac: What a Wealth of Satisfaction.

A milk wagon halted on the tracks. The horse was either harbouring a grudge against the modern age or coping with a belly full of bad grass. People were pulling at both ends of the horse. Vera Maude suddenly imagined the word "Vexed!" on a movie dialogue card in her head. If her plans were foiled by this old nag, she would have to start advocating a prohibition on milk.

She looked over at Braverman. He was gazing out the window and drumming his briefcase lying flat on his lap with his fingertips. He had a far-away look in his eyes, like he was imagining elegant cafes, romantic cul-de-sacs, and ancient bridges; artists, lovers, and ex-soldiers walking the streets, basking in the glow of the city of light. Vera Maude had never noticed before how handsome Braverman was. There was something vaguely aristocratic about him. Surely he was one who could move comfortably through a range of social circles.

From saloon to salon.

Vera Maude liked the sound of that. She thought it would make a good title for her memoir. The horse was finally coaxed off the tracks and the way was clear.

"E-E-E-E-rie."

The stop outside St. Joe's Hospital seemed to last an eternity, and it cost Vera Maude a bit of her surplus time. She started working on her lateness excuses for Miss Lancefield.

I overslept. The streetcar derailed. There were these sailors on leave, drunk, vandalizing public property. They wouldn't quit. Let's just say I made the ultimate sacrifice.

She studied Braverman some more. She thought about his hands holding a brush, and then she looked at her own small hands. She had been biting her nails again.

"Wy-y-y-yn-DOTTE."

The blocks were shorter now. This was the city in one of its earliest incarnations. On the older maps the river was the main street with little lanes running off it into farmers' fields. On the newer maps the streets intersected the Avenue like steps up a ladder towards the river. In a little over a decade, streetcars and the automobile had completely shifted the axis of the city.

Some uniformed schoolgirls were skipping down the Avenue towards the sound of a bell. St. Mary's Academy was coming up after Maiden Lane. Had her great-grandfather, a Catholic farmer, not decided to re-invent himself as a Methodist linen merchant, Vera Maude might very well have found herself a graduate of St. Mary's.

And got me to a nunnery.

She wondered how the other branches in her family tree were managing their inheritance, especially those still in Ireland now living through a violent revolution. Maybe some wished they had remained Catholic. Perhaps some had even converted back. To Vera Maude, it was all a bit like those people jumping on the Giants bandwagon at the beginning of the World Series.

Some old codger was looking her over, and she made a face at him. He kept staring so she looked away. She would much rather have belted him one.

"Pa-a-a-rk Street."

On any normal day, this was her stop. She could still potentially make the library on time, provided Braverman wasn't going all the way to the ferry dock. Vera Maude stood up and grabbed one of the leather straps that hung in the aisle. She needed to be able to bale out as soon as Braverman made his move.

The streetcar driver was trying to motivate some of the taxicabs that were congregating in front of the Prince Edward Hotel. Insurance agents, dentists, physicians, and barristers, a host of characters Vera Maude preferred to avoid like the plague, were marching into the King Building. Next door the girls at the Laura Secord Candy Shop were putting the finishing touches on today's window display. A fellow on a ladder was straightening the letters on the marquee at the Allen. At first glance Vera Maude thought it said *The Man for Me*. It actually said *The Man From Home*. It boasted "American millions, European titles, Mediterranean beauty, and smashing romance!"

Not to mention air-conditioning. I feel a double feature coming on.

"Lo-o-o-on-DUN."

Braverman stood up as they approached the Bank of Montreal building at the corner. The streetcar came to an abrupt halt just as Vera Maude was letting go of the hand strap. She fell into a man standing in front of her.

"Pardon me, I'm sure."

He helped her regain her balance. It was his pleasure. She made a beeline for the door and managed to wiggle through before it closed.

She spotted Braverman walking in front of the streetcar and followed him down Chatham Street. A couple people went into Wesley Radio, some went into the Chinese laundry. Others continued around the corner down Pelissier. The clock was ticking. Vera Maude stopped at Dougall and watched Braverman cross. She was about to give up hope when she saw him enter a building just up the block. She hustled over and checked it out.

CURTIS PRINTERS

She stared at the building for a moment. She was a little disappointed, though she wasn't sure exactly why. What was she expecting?

A big sign saying Braverman & Co.: Bootleggers, Con-artists, and Petty Criminals?

She made a few mental notes then double-backed and turned up Victoria. She noticed the time and got going as fast as she could in heels. She slowed at London Street just long enough to let a streetcar pass and then almost got knocked down by a bicycle when she ran across Park without looking.

"Jeepers, fella!"

When she got to the top of the steps of the library, the janitor greeted her at the door.

"Don't rush yourself, Maudie. They're a little preoccupied this morning. And Miss Lancefield's at another one of her meetings."

"Thanks, Joe."

Vera Maude strolled in and sure enough they were all huddled around Daphne, gasping and whistling like so many kettles on the boil. Daphne was telling them about the gunshots she heard early this morning from the direction of the rail yards. Mavis said she heard something that sounded like gunshots too, though she had thought it was just a truck backfiring.

"But, come to think of it, it did sound more like a gun."

Yeah, like you know what a gun sounds like.

Vera Maude started sorting the daily papers. She was grateful no one noticed she was over a quarter of an hour late. Unless they were saving it for Miss Lancefield. Some of the girls were like that — walking around with an ace up their sleeve, waiting for just the right moment to slap it on the table. Vera Maude knew Miss Lancefield was getting tired of her excuses and apologies. One wrong move and Vera Maude would be facing a life sentence behind a counter at Smith's department store.

There was another conversation wrapping up at one of the reading tables. Several members of the Music, Literature, and Art Club were discussing topics for the fall season. They were recalling a meeting held earlier in the year. It was an open meeting, Vera Maude's introduction to the club.

She had to attend. Among the members were Miss Lancefield, a couple of assistant librarians, several schoolteachers, and representatives of the city's cultural elite — the Merry Wives of Windsor. It was held up the street at the Bowlby house. The guest of honour was an associate of the Royal Academy of Music. He gave a talk and then later in the evening he and Margaret Bowlby played an arrangement of Beethoven's 5th. In Reverend Paulin's wife's report on current events she touched on the so-called Art War being waged over a modernist exhibit at the Metropolitan Museum in New York. Vera Maude had to bite her tongue through the discussion that followed. The meeting closed with the singing of the national anthem.

It was all very pleasant and very civilized and done with the utmost taste and decorum. But it was quite different from the new world of music, literature, and art that Vera Maude was reading about in the journals from London and New York.

Veddy different indeed.

She tried to picture Braverman in the audience, dressed as he was today and with his paint-splattered briefcase on his lap. Part bohemian, part gentleman, and part gangster.

Gunshots from the direction of the rail yards?

Chapter 15

ALL BETS ARE OFF

McCloskey was sitting at the bar at the British-American having his first meal since leaving Hamilton: a plate of chicken and frog legs with a near-beer chaser. The beer, Cincinnati Cream Lager, tasted like the punch line to a joke that no one was getting.

He needed to clear his head after the police had finished with him, so he walked the short mile back to City Garage on Erie Street, where he reclaimed the Light Six and topped up its fuel tank. His plan had been to head down to the British-American to trade information, but arriving on the scene he found everyone tongue-tied and with their fingers in their ears. Getting nowhere, he pulled up a stool at the bar and ordered breakfast.

"That sounds more like dinner," Eddie said.

"I'm catching up."

He was cleaning off the last of the chicken bones when a boy came in with copies of the morning edition of the *Border Cities Star* draped over his arm. McCloskey peeled one off the top and pressed a coin in the boy's palm. The boy continued to work the room, alternately offering a shine with the gear slung over his shoulder, but met with little success.

McCloskey turned to the sports pages and noticed the *Star* was still carrying "Fanning with Farrell."

"Wills thinks he can take Dempsey," he said to no one in particular.

Eddie returned with clusters of empty glasses dangling from the fingers of each hand like dirty chandeliers. He set the glasses down below the bar and immediately got to rinsing and polishing them.

"That so?" he said.

He was a bear of a man with a gentle touch, just the kind of diplomat the British-American needed. McCloskey continued his digest of Farrell's column.

"Rickard says Wills'll fight for less than a hundred thousand. He must be figuring he can take the purse. And listen to this: 'Every time the champion fights, thousands will go just in the hope of seeing him knocked out and their presence adds to the house and the fighters' purse.' How do you like that?"

"They set them up for the pleasure of watching them fall."

"Is this you waxing philosophical, Eddie?"

"I wouldn't say it if it weren't true."

"I should've gone to see him fight Carpentier. Who knows, maybe things would've turned out different." McCloskey sighed.

"Now who's the philosopher?"

"The fight of the century. That's what they all said."

"You know he was here on the weekend, don't you?"

"I know, I know."

McCloskey turned the page. Eddie was referring to Dempsey's exhibition fights down at the Devonshire track on Saturday. Dempsey got a grand for putting pillows on his mitts and going two rounds each with Billy Wells and Bert Snyder. It was pretty light stuff. All the same, McCloskey wouldn't have minded the chance of meeting his hero. But he had his hands full with Sophie at the time. Every time he thought of her a little tremor went through his body. Her image played like one of those short films at the arcade, the ones in the little machines with the hand-crank. A penny for a few minutes of flickering light and magic.

It suddenly became very still and very quiet in the room. The tension that McCloskey had felt when he first sat down was quickly being replaced by something more tangible, like a chill in the air or a charge of electricity. He glanced up at the mirror behind the bar and saw a familiar face. Jigsaw was making his way towards him. He pulled up a stool, leaving one between him and McCloskey. Tilting his hat back, he exposed part of the scar that the Lieutenant said made him look like a goddamn autopsy.

"I've been wondering when I'd see you," said McCloskey. "Then I thought if I just stayed still long enough you'd probably come to me."

"Yeah. You attract trouble, don't you, Killer?"

Jigsaw hadn't lost his patronizing tone.

"Actually, I just got tired of talking to myself. You and your boys have this town sewn up pretty good, don't you?"

Jigsaw's grin looked more like a gash in his face.

"Well, you haven't bumped me, and I know if you really wanted to you would have by now, so you must be here to —"

"I'm here to tell you to blow."

McCloskey took a gulp of his beer before replying. "Maybe I'm not finished my business here yet."

"Really? I understand you chased the guy that done your father and brother all the way to the border. The trail's still hot; you should think about —"

"I'm not interested in him anymore. I don't want the serpent's tail; I want its head." McCloskey paused. "C'mon, it was you who gave the order, wasn't it?"

Jigsaw put his hands up in mock defence. "Now don't go jumping to conclusions, Killer."

"I didn't buy the line the cops were selling about the gangster from Detroit. That's the one they use whenever they need to blame the Yanks something." McCloskey paused. "So who gave the order?"

"You know who."

"No, I don't. That's why I'm asking."

"Green."

"I don't believe you."

"It's true. You were naïve to think that Green wasn't all business, because he is. You and your family were costing him."

"So he's still running things?"

"Of course he is."

"That's not what I heard."

"Is that what this is about? The Captain isn't bothering himself with our little skirmishes. He's busy fighting a war. The Lieutenant's in command of this front. He's the reason you're not locked up or at the bottom of the river right now."

"Yeah, feel like I owe him a debt."

McCloskey finished his beer.

"He gave you too much credit," said Jigsaw. "You're a meathead and you belong back in the ring. There you're actually worth something. In the real world you get too confused and you lose focus. You need the bell, the ropes, and somebody standing over you with a bucket of ice water."

Eddie reappeared from the kitchen and McCloskey pointed to his glass. Eddie pulled him another pint.

"Can I get you anything, mister?"

Jigsaw turned slowly towards Eddie and bared his jagged yellow teeth. "Whisky."

Eddie stiffened. "You know we don't serve liquor here."

"Would you like to?"

Eddie just walked away. Jigsaw laughed and turned and fixed his gaze back on McCloskey. His eyes were dull, black, and bottomless.

"If I find you in the Border Cities tomorrow, you're fair game."

"You know you're the second person to sit in that stool and tell me that."

"Maybe you should try sitting somewhere else."

Jigsaw slid back off the barstool and adjusted his hat. His eyes swept the room and everyone looked away. He moved slowly across the floor, through the swinging doors, and into the lobby of the hotel. Conversation didn't resume in the bar until he was seen to make the street where, despite the heat and the sun, he still appeared as dark and cold as the river in February.

McCloskey looked down at the greasy chicken and frog leg bones on his plate. The last meal he had was at one of Lieutenant Brown's clubs in Hamilton. New York steak. Whisky. Cigars. What was he doing here? A girl came out of the kitchen and picked up his plate, exposing another section of the sports pages. McCloskey looked down and saw the listings for Kenilworth. He noticed the name of Green's foal, Contender.

"Welcome back, Jack."

"Thanks, Annie."

"Checking the want ads?"

"Picking a horse. Heard anything?"

She rounded the bar and paused behind him. "Yeah — all bets are off."

"Thanks."

McCloskey left some silver on the bar, tucked the rolled up newspaper under his arm, and headed out. He had parked the

Light Six over on Goyeau Street, away from the pool hall. He had no idea what he'd do if he ran into the Lieutenant, or for that matter what the Lieutenant might do if he ran into him, so he thought he'd steer clear for the time being. He opened the car door and climbed in. The Light Six was reassuring and familiar. Everything fit just right.

Heading up Goyeau he considered the homes that lined the street. They looked safe, quiet, and predictable, nothing like his home growing up. Maybe they were more like his home on the inside. Somehow he doubted it. He couldn't imagine the police stopping by to settle a domestic dispute or drop off children that were picked up for stealing from the general store.

Had he not seen their bodies with his own eyes he probably wouldn't have believed it. His pa and Billy had lived through so much, it seemed as though they'd be alive forever. It had been a family of men, much like his pa's. His mother, however, came from a family of women — a pious, Irish Catholic family that she escaped by marrying a city boy. Frank McCloskey was the youngest son of a Scottish merchant. He was rebellious and out to make a name for himself as a contraband smuggler. Mary Callaghan loved the idea of Frank McCloskey but not the man. She gave him sons, did the chores, and attended church alone on Sundays. Her dying wish was for her husband to let a priest into the house. The moment she died, Frank McCloskey threw the priest, his manual, and his holy water across the front porch.

McCloskey was still trying to get past the idea that if he had he arrived in Ojibway only minutes earlier he could have saved them. If he had got out of the train station quicker, if he got Sophie there sooner, if they hadn't messed around, if they hadn't met, if he hadn't let himself get sent to Hamilton in the first place, if he hadn't taken up with the Lieutenant, if he had just stayed home after the war and worked things out with his pa and Billy. If only he could learn to stop torturing himself.

He paused for traffic at Park and looked over at the new police headquarters. He had to wonder what their orders were. Again he got the feeling that he was exactly where someone wanted him and he hated it. He didn't believe what Jigsaw said about the Lieutenant. He remembered the day he got shipped off to Hamilton and the look in the Lieutenant's eyes. Was his old boss being pushed aside? Was it Jigsaw's play or was the Captain playing Jigsaw off the Lieutenant? A long time ago the Lieutenant had asked for McCloskey's help in building an empire. Was he really all business? McCloskey had to find out for himself and there was no better place to confront the situation than at a crowded racetrack.

He'd go see Clara, beg her to put him in touch with Henry again, get the lowdown on Gabrese, and then plan to run into the Lieutenant at Kenilworth.

Chapter 16

POISON IVY

Vera Maude was flipping through an old copy of the *Star* in the ladies' room when something on *The Women's Page* caught her eye. It was an article describing a garden party she had attended earlier in the summer.

> … held by the Music, Literature, and Art Club of Windsor at the lovely home of Dr. and Mrs. Raymond D. Menard, Riverside, on Saturday. From the time it was announced last month it had been arousing no little interest in local

social circles. Plans were extensive and many
of the details were kept secret until the last
moment. The event was well-attended and
according to reports it was one of the most
delightful of M., L., and A. affairs.

It was amusing to read the *Star*'s version of the event. The
writer made it sound so charming and convivial. Vera Maude
remembered it being anything but.

Most of the fifty-odd club members and their guests spent the
afternoon playing bridge on the lawn behind the house. Vera Maude
didn't like her odds against these teetotalling cardsharps so instead
she lingered in the sunroom, sipped lemonade, and pondered the
garden — a nightmare of allergic proportions. When the afternoon
tea was served she was waved outside. She had taken a seat at a table
under the willow tree, just a stone's throw from the water's edge.
Daphne and another one of the Daughters of the Empire joined her.

'Maudie, I'd like you to meet Isabelle.'

Isabelle handed Vera Maude four clammy fingers.

'Pleased to meet you, Isabelle.'

'Likewise.'

(Vera Maude remembered hating her instantly.)

'I'll pour,' said Daphne.

Isabelle passed the sugar to Vera Maude.

'No thanks,' she said. 'May I have the lemon instead?'

'Certainly.'

'Maudie works at the library too,' said Daphne.

'Really?'

'Really,' said Vera Maude. 'Do you work, Isabelle?'

'No,' replied Isabelle. 'Daddy won't have it.'

No, of course not.

'I don't plan on staying on at the library forever.'

Thanks, Daphne.

'As soon as I've married I plan to leave. Who knows, maybe

Clive will be the one to rescue me.'

This was news to Vera Maude.

'What about you, Maudie?' asked Isabelle.

'Yes, Maudie, what are your plans?'

They were both staring at her.

You bitch, Daphne.

'Oh, I don't know. I was thinking of becoming an opium addict. Or maybe a switchboard operator. I haven't decided.'

Vera Maude always hated going to those things but she knew if she stopped getting invited it would be a sign of worse things to come. The library would eventually let her go and then the doors in the cultural community would start closing. And then what? It wasn't a big city. Teach? Go to business college? Become a sales clerk at Bartlet, Macdonald, & Gow? Daphne on the other hand was a full member of the club. Whenever Vera Maude got to go to an M.L. & A. event it was as her invited guest and with the approval of Miss Lancefield, who was on the club executive. Vera Maude figured the only reason Daphne kept inviting her was to help her feel superior among the other members. Why else would someone like Daphne have anything to do with someone like her?

It occurred to Vera Maude that she still hadn't received her formal invitation to the next meeting. Perhaps the garden party had been the last straw. Maybe the first door had already closed. She folded up the paper and tossed it on the floor.

"Maudie, are you in there?"

"Yeah, what is it?"

"Do you mind if I go for lunch first?"

"Knock yourself out."

"Goody — Clive is here and he's taking me to the Prince Eddie."

"Tell everybody I said hi."

"Okay," said Daphne with no sense of irony.

She listened to Daphne march away in her size fives.

"I hope you choke on a cucumber seed."

Vera Maude adjusted her accoutrements and went back to work.

— *Chapter 17* —

CURTAINS

Henry Fields was recovering in a hospital bed at St. Joseph's. A bullet had grazed the side of his head in the shootout and nearly taken off his ear. In the bed next to him was a man in much worse shape. Clara thought he looked as if he had fallen down a flight of stairs. She got up to check the cloth on her brother's forehead. It was as warm as his cheek and the pitcher at his bedside was empty. There had to be a utility room on the floor somewhere.

"Henry," she whispered in his ear, "I'll be right back."

She glanced over at the other bed. The man seemed harmless enough, sawing away like some big ugly baby. She set out in search of an oasis. Clara had done some volunteer work after the war, light duty looking after soldiers like Henry who needed some fine-tuning before they finally got to sleep in their own beds. It had started with one of the nurses asking if while she sat there she could roll some bandages. Next thing she knew she was serving lunch. So today while she was at St. Joe's, Clara thought she would look in on the veterans' ward.

It wasn't what she expected. These weren't outpatients coming back for follow-up treatment. Three years later these soldiers were still waiting to complete their journey home. There were more than a dozen of them; pale, thin bodies dressed in bandages with red, yellow, and purple stains. Broken and disfigured, they were held together with steel plates, tubes, and wire. In their wheelchairs and prosthetics they looked half man, half machine. Several of the sisters were ministering to their hearts and souls. Clara paused at the door at the other end and gazed back across this white linen wasteland. She could not imagine a worse existence, but there was. Upstairs were the soldiers with the invisible wounds, the shell-shocked and sick of mind that had yet to wake from their nightmare. These boys' introduction to the modern age came in the form of gas grenades, flamethrowers, armoured tanks, and bombs dropping out of airplanes. Where others worked to keep the memory of the war alive, these men spent every minute of every day trying to forget.

Clara stepped backwards through the swinging door and was almost knocked down by a doctor in a hospital robe and mask.

"Pardon me," she said.

He didn't even look at her, just continued on his way, turned a corner, and disappeared.

The utility room was at the end of the hall. She set the pitcher down in the sink and let the water run. When it was full she poured herself a glass, downed it in three long gulps, and then headed back to the ward.

The swinging doors were closed. She pushed one open. It looked as if the other patients had been taken into the garden already. After a restless night under the sheets they usually got wheeled outside, where they could sit in the shade and drag some lemonade through a straw. The curtains were drawn around Henry's and the other patient's bed. Clara figured the nurses were trying to give them some peace while they moved the other patients out.

Clara gently pulled the curtain back and found Henry fast asleep. The other patient was stirring. She set the pitcher down on the table and went around to his bed.

There was a pillow over the man's face. She yanked it off. She'd seen dead before and this guy was it. A shadow caught her eye. She jumped around, pulled the curtain back, and saw the doctor from the hallway holding a pillow over Henry's face. He grabbed her mouth before she could scream. Soon Henry was awake and struggling. The doctor pushed Clara down on the bed and was trying to pinch her nose with his thumb. Unless she did something quick he'd finish them both off. Her hand fell on the pitcher. She swung at his head and with a thud and a splash he dropped to the floor. Henry pulled the pillow off his face, gasping for air.

Clara cursed McCloskey out loud. She knew he had to have something to do with all of this, and if she never saw him again it would be too soon.

Over at the *Border Cities Star,* the final edition was being proofed. There was a new headline: WELLINGTON'S DEFEAT. All told, three men died at the shootout at the Elliott — one constable, a motorcycle cop, and some nameless gangland thug. The paper called it "Wellington's Defeat" because the police had originally gone to the Wellington Hotel at the corner of Elliott and Wellington instead of the Elliott Hotel a few blocks south on Wellington. That mix-up gave most of the gang time to escape or at least prepare for a confrontation with police. No one knew how it happened. There was talk of an investigation.

Chapter 18

THE METROPOLE

The staff was testy. The air was stifling. Her new shoes were attempting to assassinate her feet from blind corners. Vera Maude moved slowly from room to room, assuming up discarded magazines and shelving abandoned books. The day couldn't end soon enough for her.

And the rumours were piling up about the shootout this morning, blocking her path to the truth. What she needed was facts. Her problem was she didn't know where to look for them. There was no card catalogue indexing clues, no place to look up *bootleggers*: see *Braverman*. When Daphne came back it was Vera Maude's turn for lunch.

"Tag — you're it."

"Abyssinia."

Vera Maude passed through the outer doors of the library and walked straight into a wall of hot, humid air. There was some relief as she made her way across the lawn, but when she reached the sidewalk she felt like she was standing on a hot plate. Tonight she would say a little prayer to her gods again for rain.

She stopped to wriggle her sunglasses out of her purse. They were the best investment she ever made: thirty-five cents, and she could give any guy the once-over without looking like she was coming on to him.

The streets were filling up with the usual lunchtime cast of characters: professionals from London Street; students and instructors from the School of Business; stenographers, secretaries, and the grand old ladies from west of the Avenue that took their lunch at the Prince Edward Hotel. There were dark suits with long faces going in and out of the Licence Inspector's office, the crusader's chief bureaucrat and red tape dispenser.

In quiet moments did he reflect on the futility of his work? Or was he all about the revenue from the fines?

Vera Maude briefly toyed with the idea of taking a detour around the Curtis offices and accidentally running into Braverman.

And then what? Ask him for directions? Tell him what I really think about his tie?

With each step Vera Maude became more irritated by the layers of clothing that clung to her body. Her cami-knickers and stockings were starting to feel like a wool sweater and a pair of hip-waders.

She cut over to Ferry and continued north to Pitt. She thought of this section of downtown as the Wrench Quarter, since it was home to Bowman Auto Supplies, Drouillard Gasoline, Riverdale Tire, Ferry Car Storage, Thompson Auto, just to name a few, and the Industrial Café where the motorheads that worked these joints fuelled up every morning. Vera Maude often ate lunch across the street at the Metropole.

It was one of those new self-serve lunch bars that got its start catering to moviegoers.

It was a long, narrow space with an open kitchen in the back corner. The self-serve counter ran along the wall away from the kitchen to the cashier at the front. Tables covered in red and white gingham and chairs with curved cane backs were arranged about the floor. The walls were decorated with scenes from the great European cities: the grand architecture of London, the boulevards of Paris, and the ruins of ancient Rome. These images contrasted sharply with the fishing and hunting postcards from Niagara Falls, Grand Rapids, and Thunder Bay that adorned the cash register. Vera Maude picked up a cheese sandwich and poured herself some lemonade. She found a table near the front window.

Lurking in the back of her mind was the possibility that Braverman was just a middleman, procuring liquor for his clients and co-workers. It didn't sound very interesting but it was probably closer to the truth. Vera Maude pressed her glass against her cheek. On days like this she was tempted to bob her hair like so many girls suggested.

— I'm telling you, you would be so much more comfortable if you cut it all off.
— But it's grown quite attached to me.

And the more traditional folks would inevitably complain that she had gone flapper. There was just no pleasing anyone. Vera Maude wondered what Braverman would prefer and then she admonished herself for thinking she ought to tailor herself to please a man, a complete stranger no less. Anyway, she was supposed to be gathering intelligence on Braverman.

But shouldn't a girl use all the weapons at her disposal?

Her mental landscape was all quicksand: thoughts moved slowly, then sank and disappeared. She looked back at the diner. The woman leaning over the register was reading a detective magazine. Two men each sat at their own table. One was sipping coffee and the other smoking a cigarette. The coffee sipper looked up and Vera Maude turned her gaze back towards the window, where a fly was repeatedly bashing its head against the glass. She finished her lemonade and abandoned the rest of her sandwich.

She decided to take the Avenue back to the library to see what was what. First she crossed the street to have a look at the new movie stills posted outside the Empire.

Nell Shipman in
"The Girl From God's Country"
and Wanda Hawley in
"Too Much Wife."
It is a breezy comedy of married life, a bride's
noble resolutions, and how living up to what
she considered her duty nearly wrecked her
husband's happiness.

She had to roll her eyes at that one. People started coming out of the theatre, squinting at the daylight and still chuckling at the Harold Lloyd two-reeler. Since the heat wave the theatres were open almost continuously so people could take advantage of the air conditioning.

Jackie Coogan in
"My Boy"
"I'm starting a riot at the Empire.
Wanna join us?"

Vera Maude decided that was what she needed: a little silver screen mayhem. She'd make a date this weekend with Jackie.

She continued walking and caught a whiff of tobacco. The cigar shop was up ahead and she was once again in the mood for adventure. She tweaked the wooden Indian's nose and stepped inside.

The humid air was laced with cigar smoke. It was almost overwhelming. She wondered how men could huddle together in their clubs and roadhouses and suck on these brown, leathery sticks and come out alive, especially if they happened to be spending the day in a factory. And it seemed like since the war all of the rest of them were smoking cigarettes. They all had their favourite brand and wore it like a badge. Vera Maude studied the displays in the showcases.

Player's Navy Cut — *Greatest Value in the World!*

Macdonald's Cigarettes — *The Tobacco with Heart!*

Wilson's Bachelor — *The National Smoke!*

She wondered if there really was a difference between any of them.

"Maybe you'd prefer a good old-fashioned cigar?" said the man behind the counter. "*For the Sunday Smoke* — Haig Cigars — only five cents each, sir, as are the Peg Tops — *The Old Reliable.*"

The man behind the counter spoke in advertising copy.

"Do you have anything....?"

A man in a straw hat, leaning one hip against the counter, made a face that said *a little more subtle.*

"Of course, sir."

Vera Maude was throwing off the tobacconist's rhythm.

"I have the Jap. Manufactured from a native-grown Havana leaf. It has a true tropical flavor. Very exotic. Ten cents each."

The tobacconist turned, pulled down a box of Japs from the shelf, and set it down on the counter. He plucked out one of the cigars and handed it to Straw Hat, who dragged it across his upper lip and made a face.

"Awfully strong. Wife may not approve. Don't want to have to stand at the end of the walk to smoke it."

And Straw Hat spoke in telegraph.

"I understand, sir."

The Japs disappeared and the tobacconist pulled another box down from the shelf.

"How about White Owl, sir? Very smooth and a good price: three for twenty-five."

Vera Maude lingered around the conversation. She was curious. The tobacconist gave her a look. So did Straw Hat, but it was a different kind of look.

"Nice," he said.

Straw Hat slapped the quarter down on the glass counter and pulled another coin from his vest pocket. "Half-dozen," he said.

"Very good, sir."

The tobacconist pulled two more cigars from the box. "You wouldn't want to be caught short on Sunday."

"Come again?"

"The new law, sir — cigars can no longer be sold on Sundays unless served with a meal."

Vera Maude raised her eyebrows.

"Hmf," said Straw Hat. "I'll take a box."

The tobacconist turned around and Straw Hat gave Vera Maude the once-over while she wasn't looking.

Looks foreign. Big green eyes. Or are they brown? Real doll. Like to put her in my pocket and take her home.

The tobacconist held the lid of the box open. Straw Hat replaced his six stogies.

"Thank you, sir." He nodded, took one last long look at Vera Maude and went out the door. "May I help you, ma'am?"

The question was intended to shoo Vera Maude away, not to make her feel welcome.

"A pack of Macdonald's, please."

That caught the tobacconist by surprise. He had sold cigarettes to ladies before, but they were usually flappers or the sort that hung around bootleggers. This girl was neither.

"Fifteen cents?" asked Vera Maude.

The tobacconist pulled down a pack from the shelf. When he turned there were two dimes on the counter. Vera Maude picked up the pack of Macdonald's then helped herself to a box of matches from a display near the register.

"Keep the change."

She smiled to herself when she walked out and then looked around to see if anyone saw her leave the shop. It would be just her luck to run into her father or someone from the library. She counted it a good day when she was able to open the door a little further to vice. This one would be tough, though. Booze was easy. It could be consumed and concealed with relative ease and little chance of discovery. Cigarettes were different: the matches, the smoke, the smell on your clothes and in your hair, and the tobacco stains on your teeth and fingers.

But what to do with the butts? Details, details.

She paused at a newsstand on the Avenue and scanned the magazine covers. She had an idea. Once in a while periodicals meant for a home delivery got mixed up with the library's delivery. She could pretend to have received a magazine meant for Curtis and walk it over, *Business Methods* or *Graphic* or something like that. She could even make like the subscription appeared to be in his name.

I can't make out the name. Barterman? Is there a Barterman working here?

Chapter 19

LIKE A MOTH TO THE FLAME

She wanted to kill him when she saw him. Instead she fell into his arms. Once she pulled herself together she told him plainly and simply what happened at the hospital.

"And where is he now?"

"Sandwich — in county jail."

"Not downtown?"

"Locke has friends at county. He said he'd catch up with Henry at home after he finished his interrogation."

McCloskey knew what that meant. Locke always had his own way of doing things.

"So who is this guy?" asked Clara.

On his way to Clara's McCloskey had stopped by the garage to check in with Orval. One of Orval's regulars, one of the more reliable big mouths, had told him that Gabrese was dead, found hanging from the bars in his cell this morning. So much for getting a first-hand account of events at Ojibway.

"He's somebody's housekeeper."

"Do you think whoever killed your father and Billy were behind it?"

"I'm not sure."

McCloskey was holding his cards close; he really didn't want Clara getting tangled in this.

"Jack, if I arrived any later that man might have killed Henry too."

McCloskey wasn't in the mood to listen to any mental hand-wringing. "It's pointless to talk like that."

"I know but —"

"But what?"

"Henry's all I got left."

McCloskey was thrown back to a summer afternoon several years ago. He had wandered by the Fields' house looking for Billy and found Clara alone on the veranda, crying. She said Billy went with some friends to enlist.

The war in Europe had been raging for almost two years at that point and this latest wave of volunteers knew exactly what they were getting themselves into. McCloskey jumped over the side of the veranda and hit the ground running. He caught up with Billy just as he was leaving the enlistment centre. His brother was wearing that stupid grin that made him look ripe for a beating. He asked Billy if their pa knew. Billy said no, not yet. Jack creased him with a right to his gut and then walked into the office and signed himself up.

Some said he didn't want to get outdone by his younger brother. Others spoke of a promise Jack had made to his father.

Frank McCloskey took ill once when the boys were very young and made Jack promise to look after Billy. Jack never forgot that and so there was nothing for him to do but follow Billy all the way to the Western Front. And now Billy was gone, having survived the Great War only to get killed in a gang fight over some bootleg liquor.

"Henry'll be okay."

"I hope you're right," she said. "You want a drink?"

"Yeah."

She went to the kitchen. He heard the icebox open and then a glass shatter on the floor. He found Clara standing with her eyes closed, gripping the edge of the counter. When he approached her she moved away. It was embarrassing for her to be like this. She felt like she had used up the last of her strength and courage at the hospital.

"It slipped out of my hand."

She dropped a few shards of ice into tumblers and poured some rye. The ice popped. She handed one of the tumblers to McCloskey.

"Cheers."

The rye went down nice. It warmed you when you needed warming and cooled you when you needed cooling. It also listened to you when you had something to say and talked to you when no one else would. It was the drink and the drinking companion all rolled in one. Possibly the only thing you couldn't do with a bottle of rye was make love to it.

"Tell me," he said, "did you see much of Billy after I left town?"

She was already walking to the window.

"No," she said without turning. "They contacted me when he was admitted to hospital. The doctors said he'd probably pull through. After that I just followed his progress in the papers."

McCloskey swirled the ice around in his tumbler. "Did you ever believe what you read about me?"

"What? That you had shot him?" Clara let McCloskey hang for a moment. "No. It never sounded right. I know the both of you too well. Unless —"

"Unless it was an accident — which it wasn't. I didn't even have my finger on the trigger. I was just trying to give Billy a scare."

She turned to McCloskey. "Then who did it?"

McCloskey was still trying to piece together what happened in the alleyway behind the Crawford.

"The only other weapons I remember seeing were in the hands of the cops. But there was so much going on, and it happened so fast."

McCloskey finished his glass and Clara refilled it.

"Henry still thinks it was you that shot him."

"I've never said anything that would make people want to think otherwise. You'd be surprised what it does to your reputation when people believe you're capable of gunning down your own brother. In my line of work, it can really open doors for you. Does Henry ever talk shop with you?"

"Not really. Why?"

"Just wondering. Hey — you want to go to the track?"

"What?"

"Kenilworth. You wanna go?"

"Is this another Irish tradition I didn't know about — placing a bet on your dead brother's favourite horse?"

"You can wear black if you want."

Clara gave him a look. "Is this business or pleasure?"

She knew that, as always, Jack was up to something.

"A little of both."

"Why do I have to go?"

McCloskey paused. "I'd like to keep an eye on you right now."

It hadn't occurred to Clara that she might be in some kind of danger.

She wanted to laugh, but she didn't dare. "But why would I be —"

"We don't know how far they're willing to take this, Clara."

She rubbed her temple with her free hand. She was exhausted, confused. She sat down.

"Have you eaten?"

"No," she said, "not really."

"I'll make you something."

McCloskey went into the kitchen and started rummaging through the cupboards. He really had no idea what he was doing. "And I should probably stay here tonight," he said.

"Okay."

Neighbours would talk but she didn't care. She'd stopped caring the third or fourth time she brought a man home. How could she expect them to understand? She kept Billy's name on the register at the front of the building and still referred to herself as Mrs. William McCloskey. Had she hopes of her and Billy getting back together again? Maybe. Or perhaps like McCloskey she just enjoyed living outside of society's boundaries, an exile in her hometown.

McCloskey leaned through the kitchen doorway holding a tin of corned beef. "Got a can opener?"

Clara sighed and got up. "Look," she said as she took the can from McCloskey. "It's got this little key on it, see? The little key is what you use to open the can."

The kitchen was tiny. McCloskey stood close to Clara, almost on top of her as she twisted the key slowly around the edge of the can. She could feel his breath on the back of her neck. She stopped moving, sensing the inevitable, waiting for the wolf to pounce. McCloskey grabbed her shoulders, spun her around, and forced his mouth on hers. She dropped the can on his foot and he bit her lip. He kicked the can and broken glass out of the way and lifted Clara onto the counter. She hit her head on the cupboard.

"You still like to play rough, don't you, Jack?"

He slid Clara's skirt up her thighs, exposing the bare flesh above her stockings. He tucked the fabric under her hips and started working his hands up inside her blouse. Clara was already massaging him through his pants.

"You gonna use that? Or are you just trying to give me a scare?"

"Shut up."

He closed her mouth with his. Clara stretched her arms out along the cupboards and McCloskey hungrily kissed her neck. When he got close to her ear he pinned her wrists against the cupboard doors and asked her who she was waiting for last night.

"C'mon, you can tell me. I need to know what I'm up against here." McCloskey pulled her legs further apart. They were both feeling the rye.

"Actually, I was waiting for one of the boys from the department," she grinned. "That's how I watch Henry's back for him."

McCloskey leaned into her and held his mouth against hers until she almost lost her breath and had to pull away.

"What is it about me and you, huh, Jack?"

"I don't know. I guess we both just bring out the worst in each other."

They were lying on her bed with the little electric fan whirring next to them on the floor. They decided to take a quick siesta before heading out to the track.

Clara fell right asleep but McCloskey couldn't stop turning things over in his mind. She had asked him whether he was settling in Border Cities. He didn't have an answer. What could he tell her? That there was nothing for him here, nothing but bad memories? That the city felt like a prison to him now and all he could think about was going to look for Sophie? Depending on how things played out this afternoon with the Lieutenant, he might just leave town right away and try and pick up her trail.

He reached down and grabbed the bottle of rye, lifting it to his lips. Clara rolled off him and onto her back. He gazed at her and wondered about the love she shared with her husband, his brother, or the love that any two people shared for that matter.

He was convinced that love, if there even was such thing, was in the moment. How can anyone in their right mind promise love? There were no promises, not anymore at least.

He took another swig from the bottle then climbed on top of Clara. Half asleep, she resisted at first but then instinctively grabbed the headboard. The bed shook and there was a clatter. McCloskey leaned over and saw a pair of handcuffs dangling from the frame. He remembered what Clara had said about watching Henry's back for him.

Sweat was glistening on her chest and she was breathing heavily. Sensing he was about to finish, she wrapped her legs around his waist, squeezed him closer, and bit his neck. McCloskey groaned and drove himself so deep inside her, she had to curl her body sideways to keep from being crushed against the headboard.

He rolled off her and collapsed. They lay there panting, too drunk and too spent to say anything. *Relationships like this never end good*, McCloskey thought.

Chapter 20

WE HAVE MET TOO LATE

"Are you reading *Alice Adams*?" Daphne asked.

"You mean in the *Star*? No. I read the book a while ago. Where are they?"

"The apparition in the mirror."

Vera Maude remembered the passage *"who in the world are you?"* Alice looks in the mirror and her image transforms into that of the creature she feels is responsible for the lies she tells, lies meant to make her seem like she is someone other than who she is, someone of a higher social class. But at the end of the day, she is who she is and nothing can change that.

Let that be a lesson to you: to thine own self be true.

Daphne and Vera Maude were cataloguing newly arrived fiction titles. Daphne was seated at the desk behind the counter and Vera Maude was leaning over the counter with her back to Daphne. They each had a pile of books in front of them. Daphne just finished the card for Tarkington's *Gentle Julia* and was reaching for the next book on the pile.

"Ooh — here's one," said Vera Maude.

Daphne looked up from the desk. "One of my favourites?"

"Yep. Guess which one."

"Hutchinson?"

Vera Maude shook her head.

"Rinehart?"

"Nope."

Vera Maude flashed the book at Daphne. "Haggard," she said in a deep, dramatic voice, "*Virgin of the Sun*."

Daphne made a face.

"Shipwrecked sailor lands on Peruvian virgins, becomes white god of the Aztecs. Look — pictures."

"I'll tell my brother," said Daphne.

"How many more have you got?"

Daphne checked her pile. "Not many," she said. "Eight or nine. How about you?"

"The same," said Vera Maude.

"Anything good?"

Vera Maude tipped her pile and scanned the spines. "Chambers, *The Flaming Jewel*; Deeping, *Orchards*…"

"I loved *Lantern Lane*."

"…Marsh, *Trailer of Toils*; Robinson, *Mustered Men*; Van Vorst, *Queen of Carpathia*…."

"You're making those up, aren't you?"

"Let's take a break," said Vera Maude. "Feel like running over to Lanspeary's? I'd love a Vernor's."

"There's an idea."

Daphne stuck her pencil in her hair and got up from the desk. Vera Maude flipped up a section of the counter and saluted her as she passed through the checkpoint.

"Cover me," said Daphne.

She could be okay, thought Vera Maude, when they were by themselves. It was really only when they were around other people that Daphne became an absolute cow.

The library settled lazily into the afternoon. A table of veterans was reading Westerns. Some girls were thumbing through fashion magazines. There was a woman trying to corral a small group in the children's room. Vera Maude shifted her pile of books, stretched her arms up over her head, and yawned.

"Excuse me; do you keep back issues of the *New York Times Book Review*?"

Vera Maude went to answer but lost her capacity for speech. It was Braverman.

"Ah — yes, yes we do. I mean we generally, we usually —"

"I'm looking for the June 11 issue. Would you have it?"

He had his artist's case with him.

"Wait here a minute, I'll go check."

She returned momentarily with it.

"Thanks."

He found an empty table and sat down. Vera Maude watched him flip through it. He smiled when he found what he was looking for. She casually walked around the counter and began to straighten chairs in the general vicinity. Out of the corner of her eye she could see the page he was reading. It had a small headline and an illustration.

"Excuse me, Miss."

Vera Maude turned to find a young girl standing behind her with an armful of books.

"Do you have any books about fairies?"

"Ferries?"

"No — *fairies*."

Vera Maude glanced back at Braverman. He was engrossed in the article and looked like he might be a while.

"I'll show you where they are. Let me help you with those."

Vera Maude bent down, scooped up the little girl's books, and brought her back to the children's room. When she returned a few minutes later Braverman was gone.

Damn.

"Where's the copy of the *Book Review* that man was reading?"

"Behind the counter."

Vera Maude pounced on it.

"Don't worry; it's all in one piece. And your Vernor's is on the desk." Daphne paused. "You're welcome."

Vera Maude was already riffling through the *Review*, looking for a page that resembled the one Braverman was reading. Nothing looked familiar. Then she turned it upside down and flipped through it again.

On the right — my right.

Then she stopped flipping.

'*With James Joyce in Ireland.*'

She had this article in her scrapbook. She skimmed it, looking for some sort of connection. A man who knew Joyce in his youth wrote it. He was trying to reconcile the young man he knew then with the author of the now infamous *Ulysses.*

Colossal parody … Homer … Divine Comedy … "I'm afraid you have not enough chaos in you to make a world" … he talked about walking the streets of Paris … his ideal in literature is that which is simple and free … He was glad he had left Dublin.

She looked at the caption below the illustration.

Did not this youth say to Yeats, "We have met too late; you are too old to be influenced by me."?

"We have met too late," muttered Vera Maude.

"Reading with your lips again?"

Vera Maude folded up the paper. "That man that was just in here, the one reading the *Book Review*, have you ever seen him in here before?"

"Sure," said Daphne. "He's been in here looking for copies of a Toronto paper. I forget which one. He told me he has a friend that's a foreign correspondent. He was probably just trying to impress me." Daphne stopped and grinned. "Are you interested? You go for Yanks?"

"No, and not particularly. Have you ever talked to him?"

"He never has much to say. Why? What's up?"

"I don't know. I think he might be a bootlegger. Don't act so surprised. There are more bootleggers than mechanics in this city and you know it."

"That's not true."

Daphne lived somewhere just this side of Deep Denial. She also had a big mouth. It was time to change the subject.

"Come on, let's finish before Miss Lancefield gets back."

After two minutes of pencil pushing Vera Maude lifted hers and started drumming her cheek with it.

"Daphne?"

"Hm?"

"Are you familiar with *Ulysses*?"

"The Tennyson poem?"

"No, the novel, Joyce's Irish novel."

"I've heard of it. Why? Was someone looking for it?"

"Not exactly."

Vera Maude let her mind wander over some rocky terrain inhabited by bootleggers, Greek gods, and Irish poets. She imagined Braverman slaying the Cyclops with a giant corkscrew then he and Joyce pouring libations of whisky over Tennyson's grave. Yeats fired a lightning bolt at them from the heavens and Vera Maude knocked over her Vernor's.

"Futz!"

She tipped it up before it spilled onto her file cards.

"Oh, Maudie, you're hopeless."

Chapter 21

KENILWORTH

The first event is for Canadian foals at seven furlongs. Azrael looked the best on one race that he ran with American breeds. War Tank, always there or thereabouts, should prove the contender. Somme a morning glory that has worked well, but seems to fade away in real contests for money may take a notion on this outing to shake the glory off.

Sword ran a remarkably good race only a day or so ago, and may be a little better than

rated. Dorius' last race was a real good one,
and should be tabbed. Ultimata is going to
step to the front when the starter says come
on, and will set a dizzy pace for the first three
quarters of a mile, and might want to curl up
the last eighth of a mile.

"Don't believe everything you read in the papers, especially
if it involves horses."

Clara folded the *Star* back up and tucked it under her seat.
"You would know."

People were arriving at Kenilworth from every direction and
by every mode of transportation imaginable. McCloskey parked
the Light Six on the shoulder of the road, under the big wall
behind the grandstand.

"Hang on — slide over and come out my side before you
land yourself in the ditch."

McCloskey helped her out while cars were whizzing by.
They joined a group walking single file along the shoulder
towards the gate.

The track was still buzzing from the events of the past
weekend. Things hadn't looked this lively since Man O' War ran
his last race here two years ago.

"C'mon," said McCloskey, "business first."

He led her up to the deck. The Lieutenant always had a table
in one of the corners overlooking the track. McCloskey let his
eyes wander but he saw no one from the outfit.

"Jack?"

"Yeah?"

"Isn't that your neighbour from Ojibway?"

When Billy and Clara were courting, Billy used to borrow
Lesperance's car to pick her up so she could come swimming in
the river. McCloskey caught a glimpse of the old man through
the bodies milling about.

"Yeah, it is."

It was unusual for Lesperance to be upstairs. Whenever McCloskey saw him he was at the front of the grandstands or hanging over the guardrail, shouting at the horses.

"Let's go see what he's up to."

Lesperance was heading towards a table near the front.

"Whoa." McCloskey grabbed Clara's arm.

"What? Oh." She moved closer to McCloskey. "Is that your old outfit?"

He surveyed the table. "Some of it."

"Is the Lieutenant there?"

McCloskey barely recognized him. He was a shadow of his former self, gaunt, pale, and worn-out looking. McCloskey just stared at him. He was having trouble reconciling this image with his memory of the burly gangster that had propositioned him in the pool hall over a year ago.

"Yeah."

Clara could easily imagine McCloskey seated with these men. At the same time it made her think it was a miracle Billy managed to survive as long as he did. These men looked seasoned, hard, and fearless. It gave her a chill to see them gathered like this. She noticed others looking at them and wondered if her face held the same expression theirs did, a combination of anger, unease, and morbid curiosity. Who were they and how did they come to own the Border Cities the way they did?

One of them got up to intercept Lesperance, and Lesperance started shouting. The Lieutenant looked embarrassed and appeared to be making excuses to a distinguished-looking man seated next to him.

McCloskey had been focusing on the Lieutenant so he hadn't noticed the other man until now. McCloskey realized it was this man holding court and not the Lieutenant. He wore a white linen suit and a matching wide-brimmed hat. He had thick ginger moustaches and moved with grace and precision.

He ignored the Lieutenant and looked away, casually puffing at his cigar.

"What's going on, Jack?"

"I'm not sure."

The Lieutenant got up and went over to Lesperance, presumably to tell him to get the fuck back home to his pigs and chickens. Then, right out of the blue, Lesperance swung his fist into the Lieutenant's gut and doubled him over.

McCloskey was shocked. The old farmer from Ojibway had just creased the man that was supposedly running the Border Cities. While the Lieutenant tried to recover some of his dignity, Lesperance made for the table. A wall of thugs went up instantly and two of them dragged him away.

"Do you recognize him?"

"Who — the guy in the suit? No."

A minute later it was like nothing happened; the man in the white linen suit went back to telling his story and the boys at the table hung on his every word.

"Maybe he's an owner."

"Maybe."

McCloskey looked around for someone that might be on the same footing as this man. A gentleman with his nose buried in the racing form walked by.

"Pardon me," said McCloskey, "do you know who that guy is over there?"

"Where?"

"The fellow in the corner with the hairy lip who looks like a plantation owner."

The man squinted at the table and then made a face. "That's Davies, Richard Davies."

"Should I know him?"

"You may have seen his face in the papers."

"What's he into?"

"Everything," the man snorted and walked away.

McCloskey turned to Clara. She was fanning herself with her hat.

"Ever heard of Richard Davies?"

"Yeah, rumours mostly."

"What have you heard?"

"Well, when the Prince Edward opened I heard his name a lot. And he's always being linked with business types from Detroit. What do you suppose Lesperance wanted with a guy like Davies?"

"I was asking myself the same question. Maybe his horse didn't come in and he wanted to lodge a complaint."

"C'mon, Jack, they've got lemonade over there."

Clara was pointing to the concession stands along the back of the deck.

"We're leaving."

"But we just got here!"

McCloskey tugged his hat further down over his brow and the two went arm in arm down the stairs.

"Where we going?" asked Clara.

"To find Lesperance. He was at Ojibway last night and he knows something."

McCloskey stopped a couple of steps from the bottom to take a look over the crowds. Lesperance was nowhere in sight.

"What now?" Clara asked.

"I'll drop you off at Henry's and catch Lesperance at home."

"You at least owe me a drink."

There were a lot of cars parked along the road now. He manoeuvred out of his space then did a U-turn and took the county road back into the city. Clara slung her arm across the seat behind McCloskey.

"Is anything wrong, Jack?"

"The Lieutenant didn't kill Billy and pa."

"Did you ever think he did?"

"Not really, but seeing him like this ..."

It got quiet in the car. Clara watched McCloskey's expression. He had a faraway look in his eyes and he was twisting the steering wheel in his grip. He cruised right through an intersection without slowing down.

"You should have seen him before. He was a force to be reckoned with. I'll wager he tried to save Billy and Pa."

Clara put her hand on McCloskey's thigh. "Slow down, Jack. You're making me nervous."

Jack remembered the expression of fear in the Lieutenant's eyes when he sent him off to Hamilton.

"He knew something was going to happen in the Border Cities, something bad."

"You're not going to do anything crazy, are you, Jack?"

"No. I'm through with all that stuff. Trust me."

"I want to, Jack. I really do."

It fell quiet in the car again and McCloskey could feel the tension building. There was nothing he could say to Clara right now that wouldn't sound like so much bullshit.

"If you want I'll buy you that drink after you check on Henry."

"Sure," said Clara. "Whatever."

She slumped down in her seat. It suddenly occurred to McCloskey why he'd wanted so much to remove Sophie from that scene in Hamilton. It was because he didn't want her to end up like Clara.

— *Chapter 22* —

FLAPPERS

Hazel Short was wearing a red waist, black shirt, and yellow stockings. She thought people were staring at her because her outfit was daring and modern. Actually, they were staring because she looked like she was wrapped in the German flag. Her sister Lillian was wearing the same kind of attire but in a different colour scheme: white, pink, and brown. With her ample proportions she resembled a scoop of Neapolitan ice cream.

Vera Maude was sitting across from her cousins in a booth at Lanspeary's. They had caught Vera Maude as she was heading out the door for her afternoon break and asked if she wanted to go for a soda. Vera Maude was suspicious but went along anyway.

Daughters don't always like to open up to their fathers, even in these modern times, so Robert Maguire had asked his sister to ask Vera Maude out for lunch so they might find out why she'd been acting so peculiar lately. Aunt Gertie said the job was better suited to her daughters. She said she didn't understand young people today. In her words, they were "an altogether different animal."

By the time they were finished their first Vernor's, Hazel and Lillian had exhausted their favorite subjects — boys, clothes, movie stars, dance music — and were starting to make attempts at a heart-to-heart. This took Vera Maude by surprise; it wasn't like Hazel and Lillian at all. But rather than fight it, she thought she'd take advantage of the opportunity to pick their brains about a few things.

The first thing she had to do was gain control of the conversation. She started with flattery.

"You're liberated, women of the world...."

And finished with intrigue.

"...can I tell you something in confidence?"

And when she knew she had them she outlined the scenario. It had to do with a good-looking bootlegger, his curious adventures, and whether or not to get involved.

Hazel jumped in first. "You mean romantically?"

"Well, no. I mean —"

"You thinking of ratting him out, then?" said Lillian.

"No," said Vera Maude, "of course not."

The sisters were confused. Then a dim light went on in Hazel's head.

"Aah — you want in!" she said.

"Whisky, right?" asked Lillian.

"I can't blame you."

"And if there's a cutie in the mix, all the better."

Whoa, thought Vera Maude, *shallow waters. Maybe try a different tack.* She started working up the courage to ask.

"Tell me, girls," she said, "are you both happy?"

The sisters looked at each other. This seemed to them like a stupid question.

"Well ... of course," Lillian chimed. "Sure."

Vera Maude continued to struggle to find the words.

"So much has changed, you know, since we were kids. It's funny, I mean, sometimes I feel overwhelmed at all the possibilities and other times I ask myself *is this it? Is this all there is?* War is over. Women get the vote. We all move out of the house, go to business college, and get jobs. I know it's not perfect but compared to what our mothers had, well, it's pretty good, isn't it?"

What she wanted was someone to tell her that yes, she should be happy; that she was lucky to be a young person in this day and age, and that everything was going to be all right.

"Yeah, sure, Maudie," said Hazel.

She was just thinking out loud, throwing these words out, feeling them roll off her tongue, seeing what kind of reaction they got. She decided to go for broke.

"Then how come I feel so ... empty?"

Now there was a question. Hazel had the answer.

"Maudie, honey, you need a man."

Her sister agreed. "A man'll cure what ails you," said Lillian.

"Yeah, that's all it is," said Hazel, looking as if she had just solved the mystery of Vera Maude Maguire.

No one could understand why Vera Maude didn't have a steady boyfriend. Aunt Gertie said she was too wild and unrefined. Hazel said Vera Maude was too smart for her own good. Her sister Lillian agreed. "Boys," she said, "don't go for those intellectual types. I should know."

Vera Maude still thought of herself as that gangly, awkward schoolgirl holed up in her bedroom with her books and daydreams, wondering when adulthood, and freedom, would come. And as for being smart, she thought the smart folks were the ones travelling the world, writing books, starting revolutions, and challenging our perceptions through art. They weren't working as assistant librarians in factory towns.

"Look at us," said Hazel.

"We've each got a steady boyfriend," said Lillian. "We go dancing and to the track, to clubs in Detroit, speakeasies...."

"All the stuff our moms wanted to do," said Hazel, nodding to her sister.

"But couldn't," said Lillian.

"Like you said."

Vera Maude wanted to scream. She fended off the urge with an image of her Aunt Gertie dancing on a table at a speakeasy.

"See? We got plenty to be happy about," said Hazel.

I've embarrassed myself enough for one day, thought Vera Maude. Time to end the discussion.

"Yeah, I guess you're right."

"Now, about this bootlegger," said Hazel.

"Does he have a friend?" asked Lillian.

"Lillian," gasped Hazel, "what about Andy?"

"A girl should keep her options open."

When the sisters stopped giggling Hazel asked Vera Maude if her bootlegger had reasonable terms.

"Maybe we could come to some sort of an arrangement."

"Well, I'm not sure — I mean I've never actually —"

Vera Maude glanced out the window at the people walking up and down the street. "Sure, I'll talk to him," she said.

"Great. Let's plan something for Friday night then. It'll do you a world of good. And if your bootlegger doesn't want to come along, then I'll set you up with someone."

"Sure," said Vera Maude. "It sounds like a plan."

"See, I knew we could sort this out," said Lillian.

"Say, you won't..."

"Don't worry, Maudie. You're secret's safe with us."

"Girl stuff, Maudie, just girl stuff," said Lillian.

"Well, I have to get back to the library."

Vera Maude slipped out of the booth.

"We'll talk soon," said Hazel.

"Yeah," said Lillian, "your boyfriend will probably want a deposit."

"Uh, right."

"See ya."

"Bye."

Vera Maude forced a smile and waved as she walked past the drugstore window. She prayed the earth would open up sometime real soon and swallow the Dreaded Sisters Short. A falling piano would be too good for them.

The streets were quieter now. Anyone who wasn't working was probably looking for a cool spot to while away the rest of the afternoon.

She waited for a break in the traffic along Park Street. Engine exhaust sputtered out of automobile tail pipes and hung heavy in the air, mingling with the heat and humidity. She looked up and noticed that the sky was buried under a thick, colourless haze.

Rain, rain come today.

A little girl was perched at the top corner of the steps into the library, reading. She reminded Vera Maude of herself way back when the biggest decisions she had to make were which book to sign out and whether to have her ice cream straight up or in a float.

Chapter 23

TWO COPS:
ONE FAT, ONE THIN

A shadow swept across the yard. McCloskey looked up in time to see a turkey vulture light upon a branch in the black oak. The sight of it made the hair on the back of his neck stand on end. He picked up a charred piece of wood frame from the burned cabin and hurled it at the creature. It hissed and flew off, wobbling through the haze like a falling angel.

The trap door in the floor was open and there were footprints everywhere. On top of the footprints were tracks where the coroner had pulled up his wagon to collect the bodies. The shadows were dull but McCloskey could still feel the sun beating down hard. He slowly made his way across the little radish field that divided the two properties.

There were no signs of life outside Lesperance's house and not a sound came from within. He opened the screen door and let it slam shut behind him.

"Well, well, well," said Jigsaw. "I knew if I stayed in one place long enough, et cetera, et cetera."

He was sitting at the kitchen table, tipping a bottle into a tumbler. Off to the side were two cops, one fat, one thin. They were standing shoulder to shoulder with stupid grins on their faces. The thin one looked drunk. The fat one was eating sliced peaches out of a jar.

"If it ishn't young McCloshkey," said the thin one.

"Spitting image, isn't he?"

"Na. His da was better lookin'."

McCloskey could feel his blood beginning to boil. "Where's Lesperance?"

Jigsaw gave the two cops a look and they each took a single step in opposite directions. Behind them in a chair was Lesperance, or what was left of him. With his beaten and bloodied head thrown back, McCloskey figured he had to be either dead or very nearly so. The two cops then took up strategic positions in the room, one back at the screen door and the other at the way to the front of the house.

"Have a seat," said Jigsaw and McCloskey parked himself. "I saw you at the track. You should have stopped by and said hello."

"I got a good look at the Lieutenant."

"So you did."

"And you're trying to tell me he's still running things? He couldn't run a hot dog stand."

Jigsaw pushed the tumbler of whisky towards McCloskey. McCloskey ignored it.

"Suit yourself." Jigsaw downed the whisky and then refilled the tumbler. "Where's your friend, Killer? You two make a cute couple."

"Let's get to the point."

"All right, this is it: Jack McCloskey's brother and their old man were spoiling his bootlegging career and making his bosses very angry, and so he came home and dealt with it. He iced them both and as compensation he helped himself to their working capital and liquor stash."

Jigsaw took a sip from his glass before he continued.

"Then there's Jack's sister-in-law, a real hottie and awful lonely these days. Jack's always been sweet on her but that pesky brother of his kept getting in the way. Now Jack can move right in."

Jigsaw filled the tumbler again and once more pushed it towards McCloskey. McCloskey took it this time and poured the amber liquid down his throat. It was homemade. It burned.

"And here's the topper: the shootout at the Elliott. Jack then assessed the situation in the Border Cities and felt things were in a state of flux. An opportunity for a power play comes up at the Elliott where he takes out a couple of pretenders, retires a few cops, and sends a Yankee home with the message that Killer McCloskey is back in town.

"The way I see it, you got three choices: spend the rest of your life behind bars, on the run, or dead. And no matter what you choose out of that hand, your sweetheart and her do-good brother are left, shall we say, vulnerable."

McCloskey pushed the tumbler back towards Jigsaw. Jigsaw refilled it and McCloskey drained it.

"As bad as it looks, Killer, there are steps you can take."

"Like what?"

"For starters you can off the Lieutenant."

McCloskey blinked. "What?"

"He hasn't got it anymore. He let the good life dull his edge. I shared my concerns with the boss. The incident at the track was the last straw. That pathetic display will cost him his life."

"Why don't you do it?"

"Two reasons. First: the Lieutenant still has allies and we don't want to start a war. We're trying to stay the course in the day-to-day. Second: I've consulted with local law enforcement and, not to put too fine a point on it, they prefer it this way. You've got to admit there's a certain symmetry to you offing the man that pushed the button on your father and brother."

Jigsaw sat back and delivered his summation. "It's your life or Green's."

"You're singing a different tune than you were this morning."

"It's all about survival."

"I'll think about it."

"There's nothing to think about. I've got a bead on your girlfriend, Killer, so you better not disappoint me."

The room fell silent except for the sound of the flies buzzing around Lesperance.

"What is it you want me to do?"

"Be at the pool hall at midnight. Green will be there, alone. I told him there were some things he and I needed to discuss."

"Only it won't be you — it'll be me."

"I shouldn't have to tell you he'll be expecting the worst. He's been a bit jittery lately."

"I'll bet. And what'll you be doing?"

"I got other more pressing matters. I'll meet you at the British-American shortly after midnight. You can deliver me the good news and we can say our goodbyes."

"Was that the boss at the table at Kenilworth?"

"Yep."

"He looks like he knows his way around the playground."

"Ex-British Army. Blue blood. Very connected. His type knows how to get things done. If anyone can bring an end to the coal strike and get things back on track, it's him."

Jigsaw stood up. "Now scram. We gotta perform a burial at sea."

"He's the one that gave the order, isn't he?"

Jigsaw grinned. "His clean-up crew is rolling across the Border Cities right now. It was one of his boys that hired those three goons to take care of you, your father, and your brother. They were supposed to wait until you got home but somebody jumped the gun. When the Lieutenant found out you were still alive he bought you some time. Now he's out of time."

This was a lot for McCloskey to think about. He got up and made for the screen door. The thin cop stepped aside.

"Take care o' yourshelf, Jack."

McCloskey hauled off and belted him one, right on the chops. It felt good. The cop staggered backed and bounced off the wall, coughing up blood and broken teeth.

"Take care of yourself, pig."

Jigsaw let out a laugh that brought the temperature in the room down several degrees. "You got off lucky, copper. Killer just tickled your jaw."

The turkey vulture was picking through the rubble of the cabin. McCloskey climbed into his car.

The steering wheel was too hot to touch and the seat was too hot to lean back on. For a moment he considered returning to the house with his revolver and doing what really needed to be done. Instead he started the engine and took it in reverse all the way up the path.

— *Chapter 24* —

"HOW ROTTEN THEY WERE UNDERNEATH"

Vera Maude took one look at the streetcar packed with elbows, long faces, and crying babies and decided it would be a good day to walk home. She watched it pull away.

Standing alone on the curb she suddenly felt cut loose, set adrift. She became anxious and was overcome by a powerful urge to smoke.

The impulse passed through her like an electrical charge. She looked around before taking the pack out of her purse. When she popped it open the odour of the tobacco wafted out. She breathed it in.

Here goes nothing.

The filter was hard and dry on her lips. She struck a match on the side of the box and held the flame to the tip.

She had to yank the cigarette out of her mouth so she could cough without swallowing it or spitting it onto the sidewalk. When she caught her breath she replaced it and continued walking up Dougall Road.

She held it the way she had seen men hold it. The first time she exhaled she walked into her own cloud of smoke and started coughing again. The second time she turned her head and made like she was blowing out birthday candles — not particularly graceful, but very effective.

When she finished it she took a moment to gauge its side effects.

Dizziness: only slightly more than usual.

Shortness of breath: no worse than the experience of riding in a hot, cramped streetcar.

Lingering tobacco odour: a little perfume can fix that.

Dry mouth: So? It's a hot day.

She pulled a fresh cigarette from the pack and got it going without missing a beat. She was developing a rhythm. Now she could call herself a modern woman.

Yeah, like that's all it took: a pack of Macdonald's.

She was reminded of the first truly modern woman she ever met. It was at a Club meeting.

> Following a dinner in her honour at the Elmcourt Country Club at which 32 members and friends of the Music, Literature, and Art Club were entertained, Miss Grace Blackburn, assistant editor of the *London Free Press*, London, Ont., and a Canadian writer of merit, gave a program at the Y.W.C.A., last evening.

Vera Maude felt that it probably took more courage to be a modern woman than it did to be a soldier in the Great War.

Where the doughboy ran away with his buddies to take pot shots at strangers huddled in trenches, women were facing violence and injustice on a daily basis, oftentimes in their own homes.

Maudie, honey, you need a man.

Vera Maude hated hearing that all the time, especially from Hazel and Lillian. She'd met some of the boys they went out with and in her humble opinion they were all duds.

At Erie Street she dropped the butt and mashed it under her heel. So far there was nothing about this smoking business she didn't like. She drew another cigarette out of the pack and got it going. She stood there with it sticking straight out of her mouth, waiting for a break in the traffic. A few heads turned, particularly among the men folk.

They were noticing how her body forced that demure library attire down some dangerous curves; how her wild and wavy hair was struggling to break free from a battery of clips and pins; and how her dark-rimmed cheaters barely hid her wide, girlish eyes.

"Zowie," exclaimed a fellow in a passing car.

Euh.

There were two kinds of guys, according to Vera Maude: guys that were all talk and guys that were all hands.

And never the twain shall meet. Oh to meet a guy that can woo me with fine words while groping me in his roadster.

Vera Maude's mind was like a needle skipping across a gramophone record.

> Miss Blackburn, who is a most interesting and vivid personality, as well as the composer of many delightful poems and plays, was introduced by Miss Hazel Scott, president of the M., L., and A Club, who presided for the evening.
>
> Each of Miss Blackburn's contributions was made even more delightful by a short preface. Her first number was a charming little play,

entitled "The Little Grey," given with a wealth
of dramatic expression and atmospheric charm.

Vera Maude regretted opening up to Hazel and Lillian the way
she had. She let her guard down. And it was such a stupid thing to say.
Then how come I feel so … empty?

Her angst probably didn't even register with them. She hoped
that was the case; the last thing she wanted was for them to report
the whole thing to her father.

She froze for a moment on the sidewalk.

Shit — that's what it was all about.

The other day her father asked her why she was acting so
peculiar. She got defensive. Was she acting peculiar? She wasn't
sure. At any rate, she should have let it go, or told him something so
personal, so *girlie* it would have scared him and sent him running.
He would probably have gone straight to the family doctor.

Is there anything you can prescribe for her modern ills?

A woman glared at Vera Maude and her cigarette, and Vera
Maude glared right back. She was getting herself worked up. She
thought about taking a break and counting to ten, like her father
always told her to do.

"Futz that." She dropped another shell and reloaded. "I got
me some butts to smoke."

Miss Blackburn also gave a stirring war poem, and
another play, this a tragedy of a French murder,
depicting dramatically the self renunciation of a
simple old French priest, who, absolving his servant
and housekeeper from the murder of her lover,
receives with silent lips her accusation of the crime,
and goes wordless to his doom on the scaffold. Miss
Blackburn here presented a charming picture of
the lovely Breton country, its continual sunshine,
gorgeous vegetation, and charm of landscape. Not

long ago she spent considerable time among the
French peasants there.

Vera Maude wondered if romance was restricted to people
who lived in lovely places like Brittany. Was there no possibility
of romance among the automobile factories and distilleries along
the Detroit River? Her mind skipped over to Braverman.

*Nice girls who fall for bad boys fall for nice girls like me. I've
never fallen, not really.*

She added nausea to her list of side effects from tobacco-smoking.

> She has a very forceful and interesting personality,
> and a keen appreciation of the dramatic and the
> ideal. Asked her opinion on the flapper, and the
> so-called outrages on convention perpetrated by
> modern young people, Miss Blackburn asserted
> her admiration of today's girl. "She is more
> sincere, more honest, infinitely more capable
> than her grandmother," said she. "Whenever
> I think of all this commotion in regard to the
> manners of the young people of today, I conjure
> up a vision of the lovely court ladies of the
> Louis periods, I see them pirouetting gracefully,
> bowing charmingly, curtseying, their manners,
> perfection, yet, ah! their morals. How rotten they
> were underneath. Do manners mean morals after
> all? If the young people of today have discarded
> this superficiality of mannerism, they are at least
> honest. I think if they haven't manners, they have
> the morals. Indeed, I love them."

To top it all off, or bottom it all out, Vera Maude's feet were
getting worse. She took off her shoes and walked in her stocking
feet for a while.

We have met too late for you to be influenced by me.

So what was with Braverman and the *Book Review*? She would have to look for that article in her scrapbook and check it again for clues. She was on her block now.

Not a moment too soon.

She dropped her butt in the gutter and pinched her feet back into her shoes.

Sweat was rolling down her back and behind her knees. She managed to get in the house before vomiting all over the front steps. Inside it was quiet and relatively cool. She used the handrail to pull herself up the stairs. Once in her room she unhooked her dress, let it fall to the floor, and collapsed on her bed.

> Miss Blackburn composed the following poem
> especially for the club:
> A scowling softly scudding sky
> Green as the mist on the lagged sward
> Grey boughs the brave buds glorify
> Brown earth the tulip's lance has bored.
>
> A waft of wings and a shiver of song,
> Rain, and at heart, lain of the sun
> For you who have wearied and waited long,
> April is won.

"Maudie? Is that you?"

Futz.

Vera Maude lifted her head and hollered back. "Yes, Mrs. Richardson."

"I was wondering about you, dear."

Vera Maude groaned.

"Better wash up; your supper's ready."

Vera Maude let out another groan and rolled over onto her back. She could smell the cigarettes in her hair.

— *Chapter 25* —

THE PRINCE EDWARD HOTEL

At sunrise one morning earlier in the summer, Hiram H. Walker, president of the Border Cities Hotel Company and heir to the Walker distillery empire, christened the Prince Edward Hotel with a bottle of champagne on the roof mast. Walker, with the assistance of the hotel manager and a Royal Navy officer, then raised the Union Jack.

Later that day the hotel was open to the public for inspection. The city had never seen anything like it. People marvelled at the size of the pile and the richness of its décor: a lower lobby with a barbershop, tailoring department, and a bar room; a main lobby with a clerk's desk in marble and a dining room done all in white with marble flooring; a mezzanine with a beauty parlor, flappers' barbershop, miniature balconies overlooking the lobby, and a ballroom with a ceiling dripping with chandeliers. The townsfolk were mightily impressed.

Evening ceremonies began with dinner in the main banquet hall. Afterwards, everyone congregated in the ballroom to hear the speeches.

> The answer, no doubt, to those who may marvel at the fact that so little difficulty was experienced in raising the one and three-quarters of a million dollars that was necessary for the construction of the hotel may be in the Board of Directors. The most conservative businessmen in the Border Cities and in the city of Detroit have purchased preferred stock in this company, and the influence of all-important local business and social organizations has been behind the enterprise and assures its success. I have the distinct pleasure of introducing one of these businessmen. Ladies and gentleman, please welcome Mr. Richard Bathgate Davies....

The tailor, holding the jacket by its hanger, woke the bellhop from his reverie with a gentle squeeze of the elbow.

"Oh — looks good. I'll grab his shoes."

When they got to the elevator the bellhop poked the button. One of the cars started making its way down from the third floor. It paused for a moment before a slender, gloved hand pulled the doors back.

"Hey, Olive."

"Gerry, Horace. Where to?"

"Can't you guess?"

The elevator lurched, Olive jiggled, and the car began its ascent. The three stared at the numbers on the dial above the door. The bell went and Olive stopped at the seventh floor. A chambermaid walked in with an armful of linen.

"Ten please, honey."

When Olive pulled the doors open again the chambermaid got out and led the way. By the time the others caught up she was already knocking. Nobody one wanted to be late.

"Housekeeping."

Charlie Baxter checked the peephole then swung the door open and stepped aside. Richard Davies was standing at the window, talking on the telephone and gazing at the street below. Pearl Shipley was sitting in a big, winged-back chair with her legs hanging over the side, reading a movie magazine. Davies finished his conversation then set the telephone back on his desk.

"Emma, after you've put those things away I need you to tidy up the place. Charlie had some friends over for poker this afternoon and they're still learning to pick up after themselves."

"Yes, Mr. Davies."

Davies sat in a chair and let Horace detail his shoes. "Excellent."

Gerry handed Horace the jacket. Horace slipped it over Davies's arms and then pulled it over his shoulders. Davies buttoned it himself and Horace smoothed the lapels.

"Very nice, Mr. Davies," said Gerry.

Davies looked down at Pearl. She flipped a page in her magazine.

"I still want you to join us for dinner. Then if you like you can take your sister to the movies."

"I'm ready when you are," she muttered as she continued to thumb through her *Photoplay*.

Davies glared at her. The room fell silent. "You're not wearing that."

Pearl put her free hand on her hip. "What's the matter with this?"

"I've an important guest this evening. Do you think you could play the part of a lady for me? Now go to your room and find something decent to wear."

Davies gestured to the chambermaid, who hustled Pearl down the hall. These modern American girls were so smart-mouthed, undisciplined, and fearless, a completely different animal than what he was used to back home. Pearl was a gift from an auto executive in Detroit who liked his girls a little wild. Davies was thinking what he needed was a more traditional girl, a girl who knew her place, a Canadian girl.

"Gerry, I'd like to go down and inspect the dining room. Have the wait staff meet me there in five minutes."

"Yes, sir."

Charlie got the door and Horace followed Gerry out.

It fell dead quiet in the suite. Davies let the silence hang for a minute. Charlie waited. Then the words came in hushed tones.

"Charlie."

"Sir?"

"Pearl's getting careless. She's talking to the wrong people and drawing too much attention. Keep an eye on her for me and let me know by the end of the week what you think we should do about it."

Davies circled Charlie and then stopped to look him straight in the eye. "Understand?"

Davies' gaze was hot and penetrating. Charlie prided himself on being able to withstand anything his boss served up. Charlie was going to be his Number One.

"Yes, sir."

Davies walked over to the cigarette case by the telephone. He squeezed it and it popped open. There was a photo of Pearl on the table.

"But honestly, Charlie, can you blame me?"

Charlie suppressed a smile. "No, sir."

"Cigarette?"

"No, thank you."

Davies eyed Charlie as he placed the cigarette in his mouth and lit it with a fancy tabletop lighter. The chambermaid reappeared from the hall.

"Will that be all, Mr. Davies?"

"Yes, Emma. Thank you."

The chambermaid showed herself out and they were alone again.

"I can trust you, can't I, Charlie?"

Charlie looked at his boss. He wondered where all this was coming from and where it was going. He knew Davies was putting together a big deal and things have been a bit tense lately, what with rumours of Jack McCloskey being back in town. But considering the small army that Davies was now able to command, there should be no worries.

"Of course, sir."

Davies smiled. "Right."

He walked over to the mirror and checked his tie. If this deal went through tonight, it would be the first step towards something truly great, something he couldn't accomplish back in England or in Montreal. It was a way into America, and America was ready for him.

"I'm going downstairs to inspect the dining room. Order yourself some room service while I'm gone."

Charlie nodded.

"And later on what would you say to the night off?"

"I wouldn't say no, sir."

"Jigsaw will be around, so will most of the others. And our friend from Detroit's bringing his own people. Just make sure you're back here by o-seven-hundred tomorrow. It'll be a new day, Charlie."

Davies closed the door behind him and Charlie stood there motionless for a couple minutes. Then he pressed his ear against the door and opened it slowly. He could see the dial above the

elevator door counting down. Gerry and Olive would warn him
if Davies was on his way back up.

"Yoo-hoo ... Charlie!"

He walked over to the gramophone and dropped the needle
on Club Royal Orchestra's rendition of "The Sheik" and stopped
at the credenza before heading down the hall. There was a bottle
that still had a little brandy in it. He poured the liquor into him.
It went down good.

"Where's my desert flower?"

Pearl Shipley was writhing under the sheets of her canopy bed.
She just loved the feeling of silk on her skin. When Charlie swung
open the door she let out a gale of giggles. There were candles
everywhere. It was all very romantic and inspired by the latest
cinematic marvel, *The Sheik's Wife*. Pearl had a mania for Arabia
ever since Valentino rode onto the screen last year. She was always
trying to get Charlie to participate in one of her little fantasies.

"Thought you could escape me, didn't you?"

"Nope," she said, "just playing hard to get."

"Aw, Pearl, you ain't that hard."

"I ain't easy, neither!"

When the music stopped she could hear her heart beating.
Pearl watched his shadow move across the bed curtain. Then he
pulled the curtain apart.

"Ah-hah!"

Pearl let out a yelp. The sheer size of Charlie always surprised
her. He filled doorways.

He crept slowly across the massive bed, leaned over, and
pinned her legs under his ribs. Pearl held the sheet up to her
chin and trembled in an exaggerated way. They played a tug of
war with it until she couldn't grip it any longer and let it snap
out of her fingers.

Pearl covered her eyes with the backs of her hands and
pretended to faint. Charlie pulled the sheet down slowly,
watching intently as Pearl's body revealed itself — the soft,

rounded belly and the smooth white thighs. The sight of Pearl's nakedness never ceased to amaze him. He thought she looked perfect, "more perfect than the girls in the movies," he liked to say. Pearl loved hearing that.

When the sheet reached her knees he yanked it off with the flourish of a vaudeville magician. He drank in her beauty and then picked up one of her tiny feet. It wasn't much larger than his hand. He kissed it. She wiggled her toes but still kept quiet. When he tickled the bottom she burst out laughing and tossed a pillow at his head. Looking down at her again he saw her biting her lip and fluttering her eyelids.

Charlie slid his braces off his shoulders and let his trousers drop. He almost fell over trying to kick his shorts off.

"Why don't you blow out those candles before we burn the place down?"

Tiny plumes of smoke rose from each extinguished flame. Pearl sunk back and soaked it all in — the warm, fuzzy feeling from the champagne, the hot humid air, the smell of the candles, and the tingling between her thighs. She purred like a kitten, Charlie's kitten.

He didn't feel as guilty now that he knew his boss wanted to dump her. But how could he make Pearl his without rubbing the boss the wrong way? And more importantly, could he ever afford to keep a girl like Pearl?

— *Chapter 26* —

COMING AND GOING

Clara opened the door for McCloskey and he pushed right past her to get to Fields.

"Why didn't you tell me?"

"Tell you what?"

Fields was collapsed on the chesterfield. McCloskey didn't wait for him to get up.

"Last night you told me the Lieutenant's boss was operating out of the Border Cities. What you forgot to mention was that he was Richard Davies."

Clara turned to her brother. "You knew? Why didn't —"

McCloskey wasn't finished. "I thought you were letting me wander into the lion's den, and I didn't care. But now I'm thinking it was more like you were sending me in do your dirty work for you."

That got Fields' blood moving. "Hey, I fight my —"

"You don't want to go up against that kind of power, the kind of power a crusader cop and upstanding citizen like yourself bows down to every day."

Fields tried to get up but then sat back down before he fell down. For as alive as he was right now, he felt like that bullet might as well have gone straight through his head. McCloskey continued kicking.

"You were counting on me to quickly make the connection and take out Davies, and why not? I got nothing to lose, not like you. You're on the right side of the law, the right side of the tracks, the right side of everything, aren't you, Henry? Davies' cleanup crew has been tearing through the city ever since he arrived. You turned a blind eye at first because they were only killing their own — people like my pa, Billy, and Mo Lesperance."

Clara let out a little gasp. "Lesperance is dead?"

McCloskey turned to Clara. "Yeah, and with the full cooperation of Ojibway's finest."

The stench of corruption. McCloskey held it right under Fields' nose.

"So has your opinion changed now that you've seen how easily you and Clara can be targeted, now that there is no right or wrong side? Honestly, Henry, I can't figure out if you're naïve or just plain stupid."

Clara kept eyeing her brother. She knew she shouldn't be surprised at his behaviour any more, but she was. To naïve and stupid she would add conniving and two-faced. McCloskey started pacing the room. Fields sat with his eyes closed and his hand bracing the side of his head.

"No," confessed Fields, "I didn't tell you everything. Neither did I have a plan. I just knew that if I added you to the mix, something was bound to happen, and it might lead to an opportunity for me and the other boys."

He gave a heavy sigh and then spilled. He explained how Davies had wasted no time establishing himself in the city, winning over the chief of police, a good portion of city council, and a number of key businessmen. Old allegiances broke down and new ones were forming. Cops were talking about left and right, black and white, red and Richard Davies. He said that for Davies bootlegging was a means to an end rather than an end in itself, though Fields wasn't exactly sure what exactly that end might be. McCloskey told Fields what Jigsaw said about the coal strike. Fields' eyes went wide.

A knock at the door cut the conversation. McCloskey instinctively receded into the room.

"Are you expecting someone?" he said.

Fields straightened up. "It's Locke."

"What?"

"He's in the pro-Davies camp, so don't even mention his name, all right?"

"Jesus, Henry."

"Trust me."

Clara answered the door. Locke was in uniform. He almost drew his weapon when he saw McCloskey.

"Whoa," said Fields and raised a hand.

"What's he doing here?" asked Locke.

"It seems we have a common enemy," said Fields and then he looked to McCloskey to jump in.

McCloskey felt like Fields had just pushed him into a corner. He had to think fast, and he had to make this work.

"The Lieutenant," he said. "He had my father and brother taken out last night. Apparently I was supposed to be part of that takedown, but something somewhere went wrong for them."

Locke must have felt the same. He was clearly uncertain. McCloskey continued to improvise.

"They know I'm not going to walk away without a fight. But when it's over I'll leave the Border Cities for good, peacefully."

"We're laying old grievances to rest, Tom," said Fields. "We need to work together if we're going to get through this."

Locke was still hesitating. Fields asked McCloskey to excuse them and then led Locke into the dining room for a heart to heart. He would have to leave out mention of Davies. That was okay; Fields knew what angle to play.

"Look at this as an opportunity for us to change things, Tom. We help McCloskey take down his old outfit and there's a good chance they'll take down the dirt we have on the force with them."

Locke liked the idea but felt there was still a lot at stake. He would agree only if they'd make McCloskey the fall guy should anything go wrong.

"Okay," said Fields. He was expecting that. He wanted Locke to make the demand so that he felt like he was getting something for his troubles. The two cops went back into the front room. Fields gave McCloskey the nod.

"Now," said Fields, "what did you learn from the good doctor?"

"He's not a real doctor."

"My aunt could have told you that."

"I know. His lawyer stopped his mouth before I could get anything else out of him."

"Lawyer?"

"Arrived minutes after we did. Somebody must have called from the jail."

"So we've got nothing."

"Not quite."

Locke pulled a photo from his breast pocket and handed it to Fields. "This him?"

"Look familiar?"

"I think so."

"He was at the Elliott."

Fields was still trying to sort out the morning's events. It was coming back to him slowly, one piece at a time and in no particular order. "Yeah, he ran right past me."

"Was he the one that shot you?" asked Clara.

"I'm not sure."

"Do you remember the photo I showed you last week?" asked Locke.

"The guy you followed from the Prince Edward?" said Fields.

"Yeah."

"It's the same guy."

Fields studied the photo a little closer. Locke filled in McCloskey, gave him the nickel version.

"A bootlegger I was shadowing met up with this guy in the picture a few days ago and passed him a thick envelope. I followed him to the Prince Edward. He resurfaced about an hour later, got back in his car and headed out to Riverside. He pulled into a waterfront property, opposite Belle Isle."

"Whose?"

"Belongs to a businessman from Detroit. He rents it out in the summer months. That's all I've been able to gather."

"We should check it out," said McCloskey.

"*We?*" said Locke.

"Yeah, me and you."

"This is a police matter, McCloskey."

McCloskey knew how Locke operated. "Will you be wearing your uniform? Carrying a badge?"

All eyes went to Locke, who swallowed bitterly.

"I thought as much," said McCloskey. "Meet me outside the British-American at ten tonight. We'll take my car."

Fields slumped back in the chesterfield. He needed to get some rest. And McCloskey needed to get away from Locke. Clara came to the rescue.

"Jack, don't you owe me dinner?"

"There's an idea," said Fields. "Tom can stay with me."

Fields hated the idea of his sister going around with McCloskey. He told himself that after tonight there would be no need for him, that if everything worked out the way he envisioned, McCloskey and his kin would soon be a distant memory and he could have his life and his city back.

"We'll see you later then," said McCloskey.

"Right," said Locke.

Clara kissed her brother's cheek. "Take it easy, Henry."

McCloskey walked Clara to a speakeasy over on Wyandotte. It was in the basement of a tailor's shop and the entrance was off the alley. The owner knew McCloskey from way back and sat them at a good table.

"I think Henry's warming up to you."

McCloskey took a sip from his teacup. "Don't be fooled. Politics makes strange bedfellows. I know he's just using me to get what he wants."

"Does it matter if you both want the same thing?"

"Maybe we don't."

"You mean you're not going after Davies?"

McCloskey set down his cup. "Last night you were telling me that I'd already lost the battle and should just leave town with my tail between my legs. What gives?"

Bodies were crammed in the speakeasy. The humid air was thickened with cigar smoke. Clara downed her whisky.

"Nothing."

"No, you've seen the man that gave the order. Now an eye for any eye doesn't seem like such a crazy idea."

Clara tapped her spoon on the side of her teacup and a man wandering among the tables with a porcelain teapot came over and filled it. McCloskey dropped some more change on a saucer.

"What would you be avenging?" asked McCloskey. "It wouldn't be Billy. And what would Davies' death mean to you?"

Clara took a sip from her cup. "You wouldn't understand."

"Try me."

She sighed. "I've never had Billy or you all to myself. You arrived at my door with all your baggage, which included Billy, the war, bootlegging, and the law. You both disappear, leaving me at the side of the curb, and then you reappear with, well, whatever all this is."

She took another drag on her cigarette. "A girl can't hardly have a life of her own; she has to find a man to have it with, and you men got these crazy lives and everything always has to be so goddamn complicated."

"You're drunk."

"No, I'm not."

"Well, you're not making any sense. You want me to hunt down Davies because you can't find a man that can hold a regular job, sit by the radio with you at night, and take you and your mother out for brunch on Sundays."

"That's not what I said."

"That's what I heard."

They cooled for a moment.

"Well?" Clara said. "Are you going after Davies or aren't you?"

McCloskey glanced over Clara's shoulder at the happy faces swilling rye. As far as blind pigs go, it was one of the better ones in town.

"No."

That was only sort of a lie.

"Why not?"

"Because I'm supposed to be going after the Lieutenant."

"Huh?"

"There's this guy in the outfit, and he's got ambitions. He wants me to meet up with the Lieutenant tonight at the pool hall and ice him."

"What do you get out of it?"

"I don't have to go to jail; I don't have to spend my life on the run; I don't have to die."

McCloskey left out the part about how Clara and Henry would be spared. He also left out the part about how he thought it was a set-up and Jigsaw was probably counting on him and the Lieutenant taking each other out. He was starting to feel like everybody's all-purpose, unwitting, and disposable assassin. They had him coming and going.

This was too much for Clara to take in, especially as lit as she was. Sadly, her years with the McCloskeys had left her no wiser or better prepared.

"We're burying your pa and Billy tomorrow, you know."

"Thanks for taking care of all that for me."

"I'm not going alone, Jack. If you get killed and can't make it to your father's funeral, I'll never forgive you."

"Now I know you're drunk. C'mon, let's go."

McCloskey got up and led her out the door and into the street. It was still just as hot as it had been in the afternoon. In the distant sky they saw lightning flashes but heard no thunder.

"Oh, Jack, maybe you should forget about Davies."

"You don't know what you want, do you?"

"Do you?"

McCloskey stopped to watch the lightning flash. Clara moved in front of him.

"Davies isn't some bootlegging yokel or gangster like the Lieutenant. He's bigger than that. He's all that and —"

"You're wrong, Clara. He's a gangster like all the rest."

They turned back down Glengarry.

"Please don't do this, Jack. Nothing good'll come of it. You're just going to get yourself killed."

The porch light at Fields' house came on. They stood together on the sidewalk for a moment. She knew this might be the last time she would get to see McCloskey. He could break a girl's heart a hundred different ways. She was trying hard not to cry. What she really wanted to do was hit him, make him feel a fraction of the pain she was feeling.

"I'll come for you when it's over."

"I won't wait up."

Chapter 27

PRINTED MATTER

IMPROPER NOVEL COSTS WOMEN $100

Greenwich Village Publisher and Her Editor Fined for Producing "Ulysses."

WOMEN'S DRESS DESCRIBED

Prosecution, on Anti-Vice Society Complaint, Said Description Was Too Frank.

February 22, 1921 — Margaret C. Anderson and Jane Heap, publisher and editor respectively of the Little Review, at 27 West

Eighth Street, each paid a fine of $50 imposed by Justices McInerney, Kernochan and Moss in Special Sessions yesterday, for publishing an improper novel in the July and August, 1920, issues of the magazine. John S. Sumner, Secretary of the New York Society for the Prevention of Vice, was the complainant. The defendants were accompanied to court by several Greenwich Village artists and writers.

John Quinn, counsel for the women, told the court that the alleged objectionable story, entitled "Ulysses," was the product of one Joyce, author, playwright and graduate of Dublin University, whose work had been praised by noted critics. "I think that this novel is unintelligible," said Justice McInerney.

Mr. Quinn admitted that it was cast in a curious style, but contended that it was in similar vein to the work of an American author with which no fault was found, and he thought it was principally a matter of punctuation marks. Joyce, he said, didn't use punctuation marks in this story, probably on account of his eyesight. "There may be found more impropriety in the displays in some Fifth Avenue show windows or in a theatrical show than is contained in this novel," protested the attorney,

Assistant District Attorney Joseph Forrester said that some of the chief objections had to do with a too frank expression concerning a woman's dress when the woman was in the clothes described. The court held that parts of the story seemed to be harmful to the morals of the community.

Vera Maude was a voracious reader, and there was evidence of that in her room: newspapers strewn about the floor, volumes of Shakespeare alongside detective stories and romances, a pile of magazines on her night table. When she read it was never as simple as opening a book and reading it through. One idea always led to another. A history might lead to a memoir, which in turn might lead to a novel, then *Scribner's*, *Black Mask*, or last Sunday's *Times*.

She was lying diagonally across her bed, facing the window, with her scrapbook opened up next to her. Feeling a little light-headed, she set her cigarette down on a saucer on the windowsill and took a deep breath.

She loved how the streetlights lit the humid air that hung from the trees. It was picture-still. At the core of this quietude she felt anticipation, of what she couldn't say. She noticed Braverman's light was on.

The bohemian toiling away in his garret, or the gentleman bootlegger waiting for nightfall?

> Who's this Mister Braverman?
> Smuggler, spy, or lover-man?
> Why, he crosses the border
> To fill your special order.
> But what's he brought Vera Maude?
> Not trouble, I hope — dear God!
> Don't you worry 'cause Maudie
> Hasn't time for anybody.

It occurred to her that while she did select every picture and article in her scrapbook, none of it was by or about her. And while she knew this wasn't all that unusual for a scrapbook, she suddenly felt that it was evidence of a life being lived somewhat vicariously, and she closed it up.

People were often telling Vera Maude that she had a smart mouth. She'd met enough smart people that never spoke up and dumb people that never shut their mouths to know she should take that as a compliment. She learned at a young age how to turn her thoughts into words. What she was having trouble with now was turning her words into actions. She was twenty-two years old, as old as the century, but by her own accounts she hadn't really lived.

Braverman is living. What am I doing? Watching from across the street, like Mrs. Richardson staring through the curtains at the neighbours. Maybe I really am all talk.

She rolled over and listened to the crickets for a while. Then, on impulse, she sat up and looked out the window. The light was out in Braverman's room.

Gone to bed or just plain gone?

Vera Maude knew that day would come soon. He'll catch up with his friends in Paris while she would have resigned herself to an unhappy, unfulfilled life in a booze-soaked, car factory of a town, bitter, smart-mouthed, and hateful with no one to blame but herself.

That's the gin talking.

It was just her and the night now, two stragglers left alone in a bar. Night had its charms but clearly had no intention of going all the way. Night seemed to listen; night was easy on the eyes; night even seemed to understand the needs of a girl like Vera Maude. But night was non-committal. Night wanted to be able to trade up in the event that a certain someone's moon was on the rise. And this time Vera Maude was looking for more than just a "one night stand."

She had drunk Mrs. Richardson's gin, hoping it would settle the riot in her head. It was crowded with people these days: her father, Mrs. Richardson, Mrs. Cousineau, Hazel and Lillian, streetcar passengers, Miss Lancefield, library patrons and society matrons, Daphne, Clive, Isabelle, and the woman with the big hat that always seemed to sit in front of her at the cinema, just to name a few. It was getting to be a bit much. Something or someone had to go.

Me, I have to leave this party before I get cornered and talked at by some horrible relative or stupid boy or silly girl. While you're all punching back the hors d'oevres; when you're not looking and raising your glasses and congratulating yourselves, I'll be slipping quietly out the back door.

The to-ing and fro-ing of boxcars could be heard in the distance. She imagined them, boxcars from western New York and southern Ontario, getting strung together and pulled through the tunnel up into the rail yards of Detroit.

I just don't want to get switched to the wrong track or hitched to a bunch of clunky boxcars.

She wondered how long it would take Mrs. Richardson to notice that her gin bottle was now full of nothing but water. Mrs. Richardson never seemed to take anything from it. Vera Maude always found it just the way she left it, level with the top of the label. Maybe it belonged to Mr. Richardson.

Pilfering a dead man's gin.

Vera Maude had seen him in photos, the sweet little gin blossom standing next to the droopy old sourpuss. The awkward body language of Mr. and Mrs. Ian Richardson: newlyweds outside the church; on their honeymoon in Niagara Falls; at family picnics; next to the Christmas tree; and during a surprise snowfall one day in May, the same expressions, year after year. Did the photographs tell any kind of a story? Did they do the marriage justice? One split second, several times in a lifetime. Unbeatable odds for a dime store Brownie. Vera Maude wondered if Mr. Richardson's tippling took the edge off. And now that death did them part, the bottle stood silent in the cupboard above the icebox. Did Mrs. Richardson keep it as a souvenir? Perhaps she drank from it on special occasions, like their anniversary.

Here's to old what's-his-name.

It was still dark over at Mrs. Cousineau's. Braverman had probably gone home or found some other place to hang his hat tonight — an all-night party, a brothel on Pitt Street, or a speakeasy, anything but the room he rented from an old widow at the bottom of Dougall Road. Vera Maude wondered what kind of room it was. She imagined it full of paints and varnishes from Paris, prints and sketches bought from street vendors, handmade paper and rolls of canvas, charcoal and oil pastels.

"Supplies for work … and he gets letters all the time."

Earlier, Vera Maude had found the *Book Review* article in her scrapbook. She read it over and over again, looking for clues. She found nothing but was amused again at the account of Joyce attempting to get into the cinema business.

> The Cinematograph had come in and an Italian
> company had theatres in many European cities.
> Joyce was over to open one in Dublin. That
> was in the foredawn of the movies. His "Volta"
> Theatre was opened, but I never heard that it
> was successful.

Vera Maude wondered how anyone could go wrong opening a cinema back then. It would have been like the early days of sliced bread.

More screens in this town than you can shake a dead stick at. Swing a dead cat from. Stick in a dead cat. Jesus, I'm drunk.

She had never heard Braverman speak until today. Until today he was nothing more than a moving picture show, a serial she caught between features.

Who does he look like? Sam De Grasse? Or maybe Elliott Dexter in The Affairs of Anatol. *Or younger, like Gaston Glass in* The Lost Battalion. *All the world's a silver screen.*

She opened her scrapbook again and flipped through it until she found the article from the *Review*. "He talked about walking the streets of Paris, poor and tormented, and about the peace that the repetition of his poems brought him."

She flopped back on her bed. The sheets were warm. She hated that. Some girls left them in the icebox all day. She'd have to remember that tomorrow.

Still no rain. Maybe I'm praying to the wrong gods.

Her hair was sticking to her. Her camisole was sticking to her. If only she could find the energy to strip down, turn out the light, and just go too sleep. She felt too drunk and too tired to perform either task.

Isn't that what boyfriends are for?

The bed wasn't spinning but it was definitely tilting a bit, and when Vera Maude leaned into it, trying to recover her balance like she was on the deck of a ship, it tilted the other way. She closed her eyes and waited for the ship to right itself. Her tiny ship, tossing back and forth, in between places, in the middle of the Detroit River.

French for strait. Strait of Calais. Dire straits. Strait jacket. I know into what straits of fortune she is driven. Because strait is the gate, and narrow is the way, which leadeth unto life, and few there be that find it. The water then flows down through Lake Erie, spilling over Niagara Falls into Lake Ontario, down the St. Lawrence and out into the estuary where it mingles with the salt water of the Atlantic. The place is too strait for me: give place to me that I might dwell. The ocean always looks so cold. And it's so hot here. Why does it have to be so hot? Could a ripple of fresh water make it all the way across the ocean? Into the Seine and the taps and toilets of the Left Bank? Drink a toast, Mr. Joyce, and drink Canada Dry! Stop! I won't listen. I was out last night on a yellow drunk with Horan and Goggins. Explain that to Mrs. Lancefield. Sleep, Maudie, sleep. I can't stand it. I can't face another day at the library. I can't go on. I'll go on. I could even get there early. Or at least on time. I can make a change. I can make it work. I can swallow my pride along with this gin and take the edge off. There is only one thing to do, boys, he said. Take them back to Terence Kelly. I hope I fall asleep before I tonight I hope —

— *Chapter 28* —

RECONNAISSANCE

Locke was walking up from the ferry dock with his hands in his pockets. He looked as if he had been pacing the downtown waterfront all evening. McCloskey pulled the Light Six up to the curb outside the British-American.

"Ready?"

"Yeah."

Locke climbed in and McCloskey turned around and headed east along the Drive. Most of the traffic was going in the opposite direction, pleasure-seekers from Michigan on their way back home.

McCloskey looked over at his passenger. "You okay?"

"I was just thinking."

McCloskey pulled a White Owl from his coat pocket, bit off the tip, and spat it on the road.

"Tell me, Locke, how do you like your chances of taking me down along with the rest of these chumps?"

"If Fields trusts you, then I trust you."

"You'll trust me as long as I'm helping you get what you want," said McCloskey. "What about after?"

"That's up to you, isn't it?" said Locke. "You choose your own path."

A long time ago the Lieutenant had told his men to beware of a cop named Locke who had ties to militant temperance factions. Locke and his crusader friends were into smashing stills, harassing roadhouse proprietors, running bootleggers off the road, and destroying any bottle they could get their hands on. The Lieutenant said he was a necessary evil: Locke discouraged small-time operators and in his overzealousness created more demand for the product. The chief left Locke to his devices because Locke had no problem enforcing unpopular laws and made the Methodist do-gooders feel like they had an insider. Locke had little idea what a fine line he was walking.

"Slow down," he said. "This is it."

McCloskey hung a right and parked the car on Esdras, the nearest side street. The two of them hustled across the road and took cover behind a line of parked cars leading up to the house.

This was more than your usual summer rental. It looked like something from a movie magazine, like one of those places in the hills outside Los Angeles. Its single storey was long and symmetrical in design and covered in white stucco. There was a big oak door at the centre and a bay window at either end looking over the expanse of lawn. The front was dimly lit with decorative floodlighting. It was noticeably brighter towards the back. McCloskey scrambled up to a side window. Locke crouched behind him.

"See anything?"

It looked part hunting lodge and part war room. In the middle was a massive desk covered with maps and papers. A Union Jack hung on the wall to the right and to the left was a window that faced the river. A buck's head was mounted over the fireplace and there were photos of athletes and men in uniform arranged along the mantle.

"Three of them, all with their backs to me. Hold on." McCloskey shifted along the window ledge. "Okay, come here and tell me if you know this guy." He traded positions with Locke.

"With the suspenders?"

"Yeah."

"He's the one I followed here the other night."

They traded positions again.

"Here come a couple more. Well, well, well."

"What?"

McCloskey waited for a cloud of cigar smoke to dissipate before he was certain whom he was staring at. "There's something I neglected to tell you about the Lieutenant's boss."

"What's that?"

McCloskey turned to Locke and told him that the Lieutenant's boss, the man at top of their syndicate's food chain, was none other than Richard Davies. Locke blinked a few times, like a light bulb shorting out.

"What?"

"Richard Davies is in there right now talking shop with a few of the most dangerous men in the Border Cities."

"I don't believe it."

"See for yourself."

McCloskey shifted over.

"But how —"

"Shh."

There were voices coming from behind the house. Two men carrying what looked to be cases of liquor were making their way down towards a luxury vessel tied to the dock. It went by the name *Strait Shooter* and it was flying the Stars and Stripes. McCloskey wanted a closer look at the back of the house, so while the two men were busy loading their cargo on the boat, he made his move.

"Watch my back."

The property sloped down to the river so there were two full storeys at the back. The two men had come out of a basement-level storage facility full of military surplus, bottles, boating gear, crates, and containers.

"Seen enough?"

A man with the weight and precision of a pile driver held McCloskey down and was preparing to strike.

Thud.

Then he collapsed. Locke was standing over the two of them gripping a rock the size of a grapefruit. McCloskey rolled the man off him.

"I thought I told you to keep watch."

"I was watching the boat — this guy came from the front of the house. I didn't see him until he —"

"Let's get the hell out of here," said McCloskey.

They made their way back along the line of cars. When they reached the Light Six, McCloskey told Locke what he saw at the back of the house. He speculated that Davies was diversifying his smuggling operation and might even be preparing to do battle with the coal strikers in Michigan.

"So what do you think? Could you get some uniforms together and raid the place tonight?"

"I don't know, McCloskey."

McCloskey's couldn't believe it. "What do you mean? You saw the cases of liquor; you saw the boat. There were cars in the driveway that belonged to guys from my old outfit. What do you need? A written invitation? Permission from your mother?"

Locke just sat there shaking his head, muttering Richard

Davies' name over and over again. McCloskey would continue poking until he hit the right nerve.

"You're telling me that since he has money, flies the flag, and looks good in a tux he should get off? What's the matter, Locke? You only go after low-lifes like me? Does a little polish scare you?"

The truth was that Locke was having difficulty reconciling these two sides of Richard Davies.

"I'll handle it myself," said McCloskey.

Locke snapped out of it. He wasn't going to let McCloskey take control of this. "I'm going with you."

"All right, but don't forget your badge and uniform. You're going to need them this time."

Chapter 29

GET A WIGGLE ON

Enjoy Some Hot Jazz Tonight

Music! Oh, boy, hear the harmony when Johnnie Smith's jazzy melody men play — you just have to dance — no resisting. Come on — bring your partner.

There's only one place to really enjoy dancing these summer evenings — that's out in the cool lake breezes. You'll feel you made a real discovery after one evening on the S.S. *Rapids King*.

Charlie, Pearl, Pearl's girlfriend Daisy, and Dexter, her blind date, arrived early so they could get seats on the top deck. Daisy and Dexter sat in the bench behind Pearl and Charlie. The girls were hanging over the side, cracking jokes and behaving like a couple of genuine jazz babies. Dexter pulled a flask out of his hip pocket.

"Let's get bent."

He unscrewed the cap, took a swig, and passed it to Charlie. Charlie almost choked.

"Jesus, Dex, this is hooch."

"You're spoiled, Charlie. You've been sampling too much of your boss's liquor cabinet."

"Seriously, Dex, you don't need to be drinking that stuff."

"As a matter of fact, I'm meeting somebody on the boat tonight that's going to fix me up nice."

Charlie shook his head. Dexter was always trying to look like he knew his way around the block.

"Hey, what's all the boy talk? Ooh, can I have some?"

Charlie handed Pearl the flask. She tilted it against her lips and made a face.

"Euh — where'd you get the paint?"

"All hail!" someone shouted.

They were coming up on the corporate headquarters of Walker's distillery empire. Everyone raised their arms and then lowered them toward the south shore. It was sacred ground over there.

"God Save the King!"

"The Maple Leaf Forever!"

"Drink Canada Dry!"

"Daisy, would you like a swig?"

"No, thanks, Dex."

"She doesn't touch the stuff," said Pearl.

Dexter's face fell. The petals had just fallen off his precious flower.

"She prefers her noodle juice."

Daisy nodded. Dexter shot Charlie a look. Charlie shrugged. Half a nautical mile into the journey and the evening was already a disaster. But Daisy sensed Dexter's disappointment.

"There's other stuff I like," she said.

"Yeah, like what?"

"Well," said Daisy, "on hot, sunny days I like to sunbathe on the roof of my building and smoke reefer."

Dexter's drink almost shot out of his nose. Good thing it didn't; it would have killed his chances with Daisy. She had no time for men that couldn't hold their liquor.

Pearl could feel the music before she heard it. "The band's started! Honey, I gotta dance."

"Then let's go."

Charlie got up and everyone got out of his way.

"Daisy?"

"Sure, Dex. Let's went."

Pearl led them down the stairs. "Get a wiggle on, sister!"

There was a crush of bodies at the bottom of the stairs and then everyone paired off on the dance floor. It was a foxtrot, a fast one.

"Check out those two leading the struggle."

"Yeah, he's a regular Oliver Twist."

Bodies were writhing and kicking to the rhythm. The brass in the band was ear-splitting at times and the drum beat hard in your chest. The crowd worked itself into a frenzy and every once in a while the girls would spontaneously start screaming. It was sheer joy and nobody wanted it to end. At the end of the first set there was a roar of applause.

"Charlie, it's time I go see a man about a horse."

Charlie rolled his eyes. "I'm telling you, Dex."

"Come along and you can be my spotter."

"Okay."

Charlie thought that was big of Dexter. He informed the girls they had a rendezvous.

"Don't be too long," smiled Pearl.

The girls watched them walk away.

"So, Pearl, where'd you find this one?"

"He's the boss's new Big Six."

Daisy's eyes went big. "Messing around behind the boss's back is one thing, Pearl, but with his number one guy?"

Pearl's smile turned upside down and she shifted her gaze to the kids on the dance floor.

"You can't expect to be able to get away with this for very long. Someone's going to find out. And then what?"

"Oh, Daisy, why do you have to be so reasonable?"

"Reason has nothing to do with it. What goes around comes around, honey."

Daisy watched her girlfriend's face get longer and longer. She was getting tired of being Pearl's conscience all the time. She was obviously smitten by this guy. Daisy decided to play along.

"So, is he from around here?"

"No — he's from up north somewheres. Okay, so I love telling this story: the boss was visiting one of his lumber mills and happened to be in the local watering hole when a fight broke out between Charlie and a lumberjack and Charlie wiped the floor with him and when he went to throw the bum out Charlie missed the door and threw him through a wall."

"Goodness," gasped Daisy.

"Yeah, the boss admired his skill and technique so he brought him down a couple weeks ago to add a bit of muscle to his front line."

"Sounds like his boss thinks very highly of him."

Pearl smiled. She thought highly of him too.

"Oh, Jesus, don't look now."

Pearl grabbed Daisy's arm but it was too late.

"How's tricks, Pearl?"

"Everything's Jake, Petey. You?"

"Just swell."

"Go figure."

Daisy looked to Pearl for an explanation. Pearl turned around, stuck two fingers down her throat, and crossed her eyes.

"What are the odds, eh?" said Petey.

"Not high enough, I'd say."

"You alone?"

"No, Petey, I'm here with someone."

"Oh, yeah? Who?"

"You don't know him. Look, I think you oughtta just scram, Petey. My new beau's very large and very jealous, like Montana but with a temper."

"But Pearl ..."

Petey couldn't take a hint. Pearl was losing it.

"But nothing! I gave you the icy mitt months ago, so why don't you just drop your torch and go chase yourself."

"Aw, Pearl."

"I mean it, Petey, or me and my date here are going to toss you in the river."

"Your date?"

"Yeah. I was just kidding about Montana. I got me a Northern Belle."

Pearl grabbed Daisy's face, pushed her mouth against hers, and proceeded to perform a tonsillectomy. Someone nearby dropped a glass on the floor.

"Ain't she the bee's knees?" said Pearl and she slapped Daisy on the bum. Daisy giggled.

"You're crazy, Pearl."

"Don't knock it if you ain't tried it, Petey."

The two girls went away arm in arm and nearly bust a seam laughing.

"Take it or leave it," the man said to Dexter.

"Jeez, that's a lot of mazuma."

"This isn't a one-off, pal. I'm selling you a way in."

Charlie didn't like the sounds of that. Dexter's pleasure craft was drifting into some rough waters.

"I just didn't see it that way," Dexter said.

"I think we should forget it," said Charlie.

"Hey, why don't you go take a flying leap?"

"Let's go, Dex," said Charlie. He was trying not to embarrass his friend.

"We're not through negotiating," said the dealer, grabbing Dexter's arm.

In a flash, Charlie grabbed the dealer firmly by the throat and threw him to the floor.

"Yes, we are," said Charlie.

When Charlie saw him reach into his jacket, he grabbed the dealer's wrist with one hand and the pistol with the other.

"When you go back to Detroit, tell your boss he better ask for Jigsaw next time he wants to do business in the Border Cities."

Charlie threw the gun into the river and then he and Dexter calmly walked away. Pearl and Daisy found them stewing near the bow.

"What's eating you two?"

"Nothing," said Charlie.

"C'mon, Daisy, let's dance," said Dexter.

"Sure, sweetie."

"How about you, Sheba?"

Pearl looked across the water at the Canadian shore. "I want to stay out here for a while." She snuggled up against Charlie. "Isn't that the boss's place over there?"

Charlie looked around and got his bearings. "Yeah."

Pearl ducked under one of Charlie's arms and Charlie squeezed Pearl between himself and the rail. They gazed out at the big, sprawling house.

"We could spend a weekend there next time he's away on business. I get so bored at the Prince Eddie," said Pearl.

It was cool on the lake, so Charlie gave Pearl his coat. It was a small gesture but she was really touched by it. Fellows were always doing big things for her — whisking her away at the spur of the moment to exotic places, buying her jewellery, taking her to private clubs. It was fun and all, but these fellows seemed to forget how much a girl enjoyed the little things too, like holding hands, dancing on a river boat, or going out for Chinese food.

"Charlie?" said Pearl, all teary-eyed.

"Yeah?"

"I think I'm starting to fall for you. Real hard."

Charlie gave Pearl a squeeze. He had been thinking about what Davies said to him earlier. Charlie felt that he himself was partly to blame for Pearl becoming a liability. He'd take her to his place tonight without letting on that there was trouble. Maybe by morning he would have a solution to their predicament. Right now all he wanted was this moment, the two of them adrift under the stars.

"You ever heard the expression what goes around comes around, Charlie?"

"Yeah, it means we all get a turn."

"Or people get what's coming to them."

"That too. But I'm not worried."

"That means someone's going down, though, doesn't it?"

Charlie knew where Pearl was going with that.

"Baby, as long as you're with me everything's Jake."

"If you say so, Charlie."

"I say so."

— *Chapter 30* —

RECRUITING DRIVE

10:28 p.m.

McCloskey locked the door behind him and pulled out his revolver. The stairwell was pitch dark except for a tall sliver of light coming from the open door above. He ascended cautiously, listening. At the landing he eased open the door with his free hand.

The light was coming from the windows facing the street, and the only sound he could hear was the drone of the ceiling fans. He made his way over to the Lieutenant's office. The place had been frisked. There were papers everywhere, drawers pulled, pictures smashed on the floor, but no sign of Green. There was a noise on the roof.

McCloskey ran out and stood motionless between two pool tables, waiting to hear it again. He noticed the door to the roof was also open a crack. He checked the windows along the alley and saw that one of them was propped open with a broken pool cue. He went over and lifted the windowpane just enough to free the stick then waved it around to see if he'd get a reaction. He didn't.

He slipped out the window onto the fire escape and then climbed the ladder attached to the side of the building to get a view of the roof. Green was standing behind a chimney, holding a gun and watching the door that led down to the pool hall. McCloskey threw the broken pool stick to the right of Green, who pivoted and fired. He looked nervous, dishevelled, possibly even drunk.

"That you, Killer? I didn't do it ... it wasn't me."

Green fired another shot. This time the bullet whistled right over McCloskey's head. He needed to find a better way to get a read on Green. He made himself a moving target, travelling back and forth along the length of the fire escape.

"Did what, boss?"

"I didn't give the order," said Green.

"I know. And this, tonight, Jigsaw set it all up."

Green popped his head over the edge of the building, gun in hand. McCloskey threw himself crashing through the nearest window and fell tumbling onto the pool hall floor. More shots were fired and plaster started raining down. McCloskey looked up and saw Green occupied with trying to spy him through the skylight, so he took the opportunity to run up the stairs to the roof.

"Hey, boss."

Green jerked around. McCloskey already had his revolver fixed on him.

"Whoa — you still got those quick hands, don't you, Killer?" Green steadied himself. "So ... how much?"

"How much what?"

"How much do you get for bumping me off?"

McCloskey took a small step closer. "I'm not here to take you down, boss."

"What am I worth? C'mon, what's Davies paying you?"

Green pulled a handful of loose cash out of his pocket. It fell on the roof and some of it blew away. McCloskey took another step closer.

"You must have the right blood flowing through your veins, Killer. Not like me. Though frankly I can't see it. What are you? Half Irish and half … what?" Green laughed. "Polish? That won't do. I'd watch my back if I were you."

Green rubbed his eyes and stumbled a bit. He looked like he hadn't slept in days. He was starting to fade.

"Let's you and me go have a drink downstairs, boss, just like old times."

"There ain't no more old times, Killer."

"I know you tried to save Billy and my pa. And I know why you sent me to Hamilton."

"Didn't do any good. When you came to the house after Billy got shot, Davies telephoned to say he was coming. He told me there were going to be some changes. He told me he was going to clean things up. I knew what he meant."

"We could go into business together, boss, buy another couple of pool halls, maybe a hotel. We could build that oasis you used to talk about."

McCloskey inched closer and Green sprang to attention.

"Not so fast, Killer."

"Boss, I'm only trying to —"

"You're not taking me without a fight. I'm gonna do something I was supposed to do a long time ago."

In the split second before the hammer hit the shell, McCloskey reacted and fired his own gun, grazing Green's hand. Green's gun went off and he stumbled backwards into the skylight, shattering it, and landing with a great deal of commotion onto the pool table directly below. Feeling a sudden chill in the air, McCloskey looked around the rooftops. He guessed Jigsaw had made arrangements for the cops to pick up whoever was left standing at the pool hall. He threw himself down the fire escape and hit the alley running.

When he reached the British-American he telephoned Locke and told him he had no choice but to organize a raid on Davies and his black-tie bootleggers. In turn, McCloskey said, he would assemble a team to take down Jigsaw and his gang.

"Meet me here in an hour."

McCloskey started his recruiting drive at the British-American. He cornered some fellows in the bar and knocked on a few doors upstairs but had no luck. Anyone that was willing to talk claimed loyalty to Jigsaw. That included Twitch, an old infantry buddy.

"Otherwise, you're nuts."

"That so?"

"Yeah. Jigsaw's tight with the Captain. If you were smart you would be too."

"Guess I ain't so smart."

McCloskey went over to the Crawford, where he heard the same line from a variety of other characters. Ditto at the Imperial and the International. He had shown his hand. There was no turning back now. Not knowing exactly why, he returned to the pool hall.

He was surprised to see Green's body still lying on the blood-soaked table. The framework of the skylight was twisted under his body, forcing it into a hideous contortion. McCloskey heard shoe leather on broken glass and swung his revolver towards a shadow in the corner.

"Take it easy, Killer. It's me."

McCloskey lowered his gun and took a deep breath. "Jesus, Shorty, I thought it was Jigsaw."

"Jigsaw's already been through here with a couple of uniforms. I was at the Imperial when you came by."

"Why didn't you say something?"

"How could I?" Shorty gestured at the pool table and the body. "This your handiwork?"

"It was an accident."

"That's a terrible thing."

"You don't have to tell me."

"I think he liked me. So what're you up to, Killer?"

"Would you believe I've teamed up with a bunch of crusader cops?"

"What the hell for?"

"To ruin Jigsaw's plans and undermine the Captain."

"I still don't get it."

"I'm staying in the Border Cities."

"So?"

"So as much as Jigsaw would love me to stay, it would be conditional on my being dead. And even if I survive Jigsaw, that would mean life in a town run by Richard Davies."

"I got you. They're quite a pair, aren't they? They even speak the same language."

"What language is that?"

"They talk about blood — good blood and bad blood. They talk about the bolshies and the unions, and the old days, before the war, when people knew their place and the Empire ruled. They say it's all gone to the mongrel races and the socialists, whatever the hell that means."

Shorty leaned back on one of the pool tables.

"I heard Davies came back from the war with a head full of ideas and fell in with some like-minded folk who enjoyed making lots of noise about what's right for England. When it got embarrassing for his old man — who was a lord by some accounts — he sent his son packing to the colonies. Lucky us."

"I thought he came from Montreal," said Shorty.

"That's where he got started. At one time he was our biggest customer. Then he got the notion of becoming a partner. He didn't square right with the bosses; he came off a bit fancy and they were all from the street. That's when he started throwing around his big ideas. Apparently he hit the right note with some people, because in a matter of weeks he had the organization turned inside out and he moved right in."

He glanced over at the Lieutenant's body and lowered his voice.

"First thing Davies did was kick out the Jews and the Irish. It was over for the Lieutenant when the Captain found out he was a Hebe. And you should hear him go on about the coloureds. Did you know Smoke Jackson's been missing for weeks? I don't even want to think."

"Jesus."

"Davies is winning a lot of friends in high places. He could wind up bag man for the next mayor, or end up sending someone to Ottawa to do his talking for him."

"I got that beat: he's putting together a small arsenal so he can take on the coal strikers in Michigan. He'll have Henry Ford eating out of his hand. How you enjoying peacetime so far, Shorty?"

"We're going to need some help."

"Any suggestions? I'm supposed to meet my cop friends over at the B-A in about fifteen minutes."

"There's a card game going on over at the Imperial. It wouldn't take much to convince those guys to join us."

"How many?"

"Three or four."

"Hardly an army. Anybody I know?"

"Mud Thomson, Stitch Gorski, and Three Fingers."

"That's quite a cast."

"Just a few of the guys that didn't make the Captain's A-list. I'll see what I can do and meet you back at the B-A."

When McCloskey got to the British-American, Locke was standing on the corner with a couple of uniforms.

"McCloskey," said Locke, "this is Bickerstaff and Corbishdale."

"Here comes the rest of the team," said McCloskey.

Shorty was walking towards them with his one recruit.

"Jack, you know Mud."

"Thanks for coming out, Mud. And the rest?"

"Stitch took his winnings to another card game and Three Fingers is jackin' the ball with some girl on Pitt Street."

"More glory for us," said McCloskey. "Boys, these are officers Locke, Corbishdale, Bickerstaff."

There were some awkward nods. Their paths had already crossed at one time or another. It was agreed that Locke should be squad leader.

"McCloskey, you move in with your team first. When you've subdued Jigsaw and his group, my team will move in for Davies."

While they cruised down Riverside Drive in their separate vehicles Shorty took the opportunity to try and gain a perspective on things.

"What's in it for the cops if we walk away scot-free?"

"Yeah," said Mud.

"A shake-up in the department."

"You mean our cop friends are gonna get tossed out?"

"No, I'm going to make sure that doesn't happen."

"You saying you want to run things?" asked Mud.

"Have I said as much?"

McCloskey couldn't bring himself to think like that. But maybe he had to. His life always had a momentum of its own but seemed to be suddenly slowing down. A little ambition right now might not be a bad thing.

"It's just that we'd feel a whole lot better if it was your hand on the tap and not somebody else's."

Chapter 31

THE GOOD STUFF

Situated on the north side of Wyandotte Street, Star Meat Market occupied part of a two-storey building that had alleyways running along either side and behind it. Montroy had been watching the butcher's for close to an hour from an alcove across the street, but so far saw nothing suspicious. Maybe he was wasting his time. He thought back to how this adventure started.

Last week one of his men purchased a bottle of full-strength beer at Star Meat. It was wrapped in a couple pounds of ground chuck. "Look," Bickerstaff had said as he held the opened package under Montroy's nose. Montroy remembered telling

Bickerstaff that he should try opening the bottle if he wished to enjoy the full effect of the marinade. Bickerstaff didn't even crack a smile. *Boy's a wet towel*, thought Montroy. "All right," he said to Bickerstaff, "where'd you get it?"

The whole thing came about quite innocently: while waiting to be served, a gentleman started up a conversation with Bickerstaff, and when Bickerstaff got a sense of where the conversation was going, he decided to play along. "The gentleman told me all I had to do was ask the butcher for four pounds, four ounces of the good stuff," he explained. When they called Bickerstaff's number he gave his order. The butcher nodded, went into the cooler in the back room, and returned with a package wrapped in brown paper. After completing the transaction, Bickerstaff marched the evidence straight to police headquarters.

"Good job," Montroy had said. He then told Bickerstaff to go back to Star the next day and perform the exercise again. "It's just a little weed popped up in our backyard. And it's easy to get rid of a weed: all one has to do is make sure to pull its root out. Now go home and make your supper." Bickerstaff gripped the brown wrapper, twisted the greasy bottle out of the meat, and placed it on his sergeant's desk. It had immediately started attracting flies.

This afternoon when Bickerstaff went back for a third time, the butcher told him that he was sold out of that particular cut but was expecting a shipment overnight. Bickerstaff reported this to Montroy. Montroy's plan was to intercept the delivery, but so far things were looking d —

Hello.

A pale yellow light from a window in a neighbouring apartment betrayed the figure's movements. Montroy watched the shadow dissolve behind the building. When a cat jumped out of a nearby ashcan, the figure surfaced and was caught in the light. Seeing Montroy poised, it bolted around the corner, crossed the street, and continued up the alleyway that ran down the middle of the next block.

"Stop! Police!"

Still running, Montroy pulled out his revolver. A few back porch lights from surrounding houses threw light on his path but he saw nothing. He did a slow about face and thought he saw someone crouched beside a storage crate.

"You — step in the light."

The figure didn't move. It held something in its right hand that looked like a knife. Montroy raised his revolver, making sure it was visible.

"There's no need for that; put it down."

The figure made a sudden movement and Montroy instinctively lunged and brought the butt of his gun down on the offender's wrist, knocking the object out of his hand.

"Ow!"

He couldn't believe it. What he thought was a knife was a piece of broken pipe and what he thought was a hardened criminal was a boy of no more than thirteen years of age. Relieved but still angry, he replaced the gun in his holster.

"I didn't do anything, you know."

The boy was rubbing his wrist but trying to look tough.

"What're you up to?"

"Nothing."

"You had some business at the butcher's? I think he's closed for the day. Turn around and put your hands on the wall where I can see them — now."

The boy obliged and Montroy frisked him.

"Hello."

In each of his hip pockets was a bottle of beer.

"What's this?"

"Hair tonic."

Montroy swatted the back of his head. "You got a smart mouth, kid. Where'd you get the beer?"

"I stole it."

"Where from?"

"I didn't get his name."

"Maybe if we went to see your pa he might do some remembering for you, eh? This your old man's?"

Montroy held up a bottle. It was the same brand as that purchased by Bickerstaff at the butcher shop.

"Well, it's mine now."

"Enjoy it," said the boy.

Montroy resisted the urge to take another swipe at the kid. Instead asked him how old he was.

"Eleven and a half."

"A boy your age has nothing better to do than risk his neck selling off his father's beer?"

"He won't miss it. He's back to his whisky again. Says the beer gives him a headache."

Montroy popped the caps on a doorframe and started pouring. The boy watched the puddles foam at his feet.

"A fella's gotta make a living, you know," said the boy. "I used to make good coin selling papers."

"So now you're selling beer to butchers in back alleys? In case you hadn't heard, that's against the law too."

"Yeah, but nobody I know's busting laws so they can sell three-cent newspapers."

Montroy was silent for a moment. "Does your pa stay out of trouble?"

The boy was calming down. "Yeah."

"It's his beer and his whisky? Legally obtained and with supporting documents?"

"Yeah."

Montroy let the kid dangle then told him to go home.

"You're not going to arrest me?"

"No, not tonight. What's your name?"

"Mailloux. Joe Mailloux."

"Where you live, Joe?"

"Over on Aylmer."

Montroy made a mental note. He felt sorry for the kid. He reminded him a bit of himself when he was that age.

"You'll be looking for new work now. Come by the station Saturday and I'll let you wash the police flyer."

The kid ruminated. "How much?"

"Two bits," said Montroy.

"Fifty cents."

"Jesus, kid, I thought the thrill of working over a brand new Studebaker would have been compensation enough."

"I'm supporting some habits."

"All right, fifty cents. Now go home."

The boy walked away slowly at first but then sprinted off, disappearing into the night. When Montroy couldn't hear his feet any longer, he picked up the empty bottles and hurled them against a brick wall. Dogs started barking and more porch lights came on.

"Hey — keep it down!" shouted a voice from a second-floor window.

"Shut your face or I'll cuff you!"

Montroy stepped over the puddle of beer and headed back down the alleyway towards the station. The boy's father would have questions. The boy would swear that he was staying out of trouble. He'd remember what the cop in the alleyway said and remind his dad to stay out of trouble, too. Hopefully his father would be sober enough to know better than to smack his boy for making such a smart remark and send him off to bed.

Bed sounded like a good idea to Montroy. But he knew he would just toss around. Sleep hasn't been coming easily lately: shift changes, working late but rising early and letting daytime activities spill over into night, to the point where there was little or no difference between day and night, up and down, black or white.

Chapter 32

SWOLLEN RIVER BLUES

The rain started falling hard on Riverside Drive. Steam was coming off the pavement.

"We're not just going to let McCloskey and his friends walk away at the end of this, are we?" asked Bickerstaff.

"Yes we are."

"Then we'll only be doing half the job."

"McCloskey would deny it, but he wants to take control of the bootlegging activity in the Border Cities. It won't be easy for him; there's too much infighting among the gangs right now. So while he's busy trying to get his unruly mob to fall into formation, we'll be exposing the corrupt elements in the department and setting them back on the right path. Once we've done that, we will then all of us turn our sights on McCloskey."

"Does Fields know about your plan?"

"Not exactly," said Locke.

"I'm wondering if we shouldn't be approaching the situation a little differently," said Bickerstaff. "McCloskey could end up holding the balance of power in the Border Cities."

"All the more reason."

"But if you take down McCloskey, won't someone else just come along and replace him? It might be better if we came to some sort of mutual understanding."

Locke didn't respond. He wasn't going to get into a debate with Bickerstaff and divide the group. Besides, what Bickerstaff was talking about was politics, and politics was the devil. Fortunately, they reached their destination before Bickerstaff could ask any more questions.

They parked their cars on Esdras, ran out, and got into a huddle beneath a willow tree. The rain was coming in gales off the river. McCloskey had to shout over the din.

"We're small but we've got the element of surprise. Don't take stupid chances; stick it to them before they stick it to you. What you don't want is to give them time to call for reinforcements."

They checked their weapons. In the wind and rain the clatter and click-clack of ammo dropping in chambers and revolvers snapping into place was still sharp and clear. Locke took his group to the end of the line of cars in the drive and McCloskey led his to the window of Davies' war room.

The rain was streaming down the glass, making it impossible to see details. McCloskey told Shorty to stay and keep watch. He and Mud were going to take the path down to the dock.

The dock was shaped like an "L," with *Strait Shooter* tied inside the angle. Jigsaw was standing at the point, looking down river.

McCloskey told Mud to open fire on anything that moved on the decks of *Strait Shooter* then made his way slowly towards Jigsaw.

The rain was coming down in sheets. There was a lightning flash and a thunderclap that reverberated between the shores. McCloskey blinked and was suddenly staring down Jigsaw's .44. He rolled into the tall grass and Jigsaw unloaded his weapon on the shadows.

McCloskey went around to the left and climbed onto the dock. He caught Jigsaw trying to reload. Jigsaw dropped the gun and went for his bayonet, but McCloskey was already on him. He delivered a blow to Jigsaw's face.

Jigsaw staggered back and spat two broken teeth onto the dock. When he straightened himself he took a swipe at McCloskey with his knife. McCloskey threw his hips back, thereby avoiding getting sliced in half.

McCloskey delivered a kidney punch with his left then grabbed Jigsaw's wrist with both hands and bent his arm until his elbow snapped. Jigsaw dropped his blade, swivelled his body, and sent a powerful left hook into McCloskey's face.

While McCloskey stumbled on the wet dock, Jigsaw pulled a pistol from his ankle holster. McCloskey wasn't ready for that. Fortunately, Mud was; he buried one in Jigsaw's back. Jigsaw stumbled but managed to fix his aim back on McCloskey. McCloskey was ready this time with his own revolver and put one in Jigsaw's chest.

Jigsaw dropped the pistol but still refused to go down. He just grinned his hideous, bloody grin and walked stiffly towards *Strait Shooter*, his right arm dangling and a dark stain growing on his jacket.

A man in a slicker appeared on the deck of the boat. He and Mud exchanged fire until McCloskey pulled a second revolver out of his belt, stepped wide of Jigsaw, and answered with some lead of his own. The man tumbled off the deck into the river. The motor revved up.

Jigsaw continued to stagger towards the boat, trying to hold his ribs together. McCloskey buried another one in his back. His body slumped but his legs continued to carry him. *Strait Shooter* pulled away but not without some difficulty, and Jigsaw dropped to his knees.

"You missed your ferry, Jigsaw. You won't even make it to hell now."

Jigsaw looked up at McCloskey with his cold, black eyes. "Ain't you gonna finish me off, Killer?"

It was almost a dare. McCloskey held his revolver to Jigsaw's head then lowered it again.

"How about a burial at sea?"

McCloskey gave him the boot and he hit the river with a splash and a gulp and disappeared. McCloskey looked down and noticed the river was rising.

Two men came running out of the back of the house with guns blazing, and Shorty dropped them both.

Mud and McCloskey joined Shorty and informed him that Jigsaw was dead. McCloskey told Mud to make some noise if *Strait Shooter* tried to dock again; he and Shorty were going inside.

They climbed the stairs up to a deck behind the house. Rain battered the canvas awning. A table and chairs had toppled over and were in a heap in the corner. McCloskey opened the screen door.

All they could hear was the water from their wet clothes dripping on the tile floor. They made their way slowly down a hall. McCloskey tested doors to his left and Shorty tested doors to his right. All were locked. They kept moving. When they reached the end of the hall they paused to take a breath before entering the front room.

It looked like a cocktail party gone bad. Davies was standing in the middle of the room holding a gun to Locke's head. Bickerstaff was leaning against the front door gripping his wounded arm and Corbishdale looked confused and panicky, aiming his gun at Davies. There was a cop standing to the right of Davies and a sharp-dressed man on his left. They had their revolvers fixed on Corbishdale and Bickerstaff.

"You must be that pitiful mongrel Jack McCloskey that I keep hearing about," said Davies.

McCloskey sized him up. He looked confident and capable. And it wasn't all polish either; there was a well-oiled machine under the tux, one that got used to executing orders long before it started giving them.

"These officers came in here shouting something about a raid. Was this your idea, McCloskey? It couldn't have been the police depart-ment's because they know better — just ask Officer Wallace here."

McCloskey could feel his knees getting weak. It was as if Davies was sapping the energy out of everyone in the room. The weapon McCloskey was holding suddenly felt like it weighed ten pounds. He steadied it with his left hand and tried to keep it fixed on Davies.

"Wallace, I want you to arrest these intruders and take these misguided police officers with you."

Locke's expression seemed to be imploring McCloskey to act. Bickerstaff looked like he would faint from pain or shock at any moment. Corbishdale shifted his revolver towards McCloskey and Shorty. McCloskey could see Shorty's revolver shifting towards Corbishdale.

"Hold it, Shorty," whispered McCloskey.

"Don't even think about it," said Davies, "not if you want to get out of here alive."

"C'mon, put those weapons down, boys," said Wallace to McCloskey and Shorty. "Your little street fight is over."

"Yeah," piped in Corbishdale, "put them down."

"I knew this would happen," said Shorty.

Bickerstaff collapsed. McCloskey flinched and Wallace took a shot at him. He missed McCloskey but grazed Shorty's arm. Shorty managed to put one into Wallace before stumbling back into a curio cabinet.

"Dogs like you need to be put down."

There was a gunshot from outside followed by a ship's horn. *Strait Shooter* was attempting to dock, probably with Davies' reinforcements. More gunfire.

Wallace was on the floor but still armed and Corbishdale was moving his revolver back and forth between McCloskey and Shorty. At the moment they were all about to open fire, the big picture window shattered and Davies' body was propelled backwards, hitting the wall then slumping to the floor. The shot echoed throughout the big house.

The world stopped moving for a second or two and then Montroy came in through the front door. There was glass everywhere and rain blowing in. He calmly walked over to Corbishdale and pried the revolver out of his trembling hand.

"Locke, go look at Bickerstaff. We'll talk later, you and me. And how about you, young man?"

"I can still hold a gun," said Shorty.

"Good."

McCloskey stood up.

"You're Jack McCloskey."

"That's right."

Wallace was whimpering in the corner. Montroy walked over to him and kicked him in the ribs.

"Shut up, you disgraceful little ... if you're wanting some attention you can walk yourself down to St. Joe's. If you're lucky, you won't bleed to death before you get there."

"But sergeant —"

"Don't you *sergeant* me, you two-faced son of a bitch, or I'll ask everyone in this room to look the other way while I plug you myself. Now where was I? McCloskey —"

"Yes, sir."

"Introduce this fellow to a chair."

McCloskey picked up one of the wooden chairs near the fireplace and pushed the sharp-dressed man into it.

"Now, what's your name?" Montroy asked with a smile.

The man didn't answer. He was trembling like a leaf and there were cuts on his face from the flying glass.

"Mr. McCloskey, would you be so kind as to show this fellow your calling card?"

McCloskey belted the man with a right so powerful it threw

him against the wall, where Davies was collapsed in a bloody heap. Montroy walked over to him, grabbed him by the collar, and pushed his nose against Davies' cold, dead face.

"If you're worried about jeopardizing your relationship with your partner, then maybe you should check with him."

"Is he…?"

"I'd say he was dead and a half."

McCloskey was liking Montroy's style.

"Everything square now with you and Mr. Davies?"

The man nodded.

"Good. Now, what's your name?"

"Jones," cried the man, "Henry Jones."

Jones had connected with Davies at a political rally in Detroit. Jones had friends in the auto industry who needed help. Davies had resources and men and lots of ideas. Jones explained how he and Davies had begun to organize a campaign to purify the labour force in Detroit and end the coal strike in Michigan.

It sounded like a job for the RCMP, but the last thing Montroy wanted was the Mounties poking around. They'd upset the balance of things.

"So how's Bickerstaff?"

"He's all right, sir," said Locke. "I've tied up his arm."

"Good. Now, we don't have time for introductions. Everybody reload. We got Yankee pirates trying to establish a beachhead. My boys along with your Mud Thomson are trying to beat them off, but they could use some help. Follow me."

Montroy led McCloskey, Locke, and Shorty back down the hall to one of the locked doors. He kicked it in. It was a bedroom with big windows in two sides overlooking the river and the property between the house and the dock.

The beach was underwater. A car had been pulled up to within twenty yards of the dock and was being used for cover.

"The Pig's Knuckles," said McCloskey, surprised.

"Those are my boys," said Montroy. The Pig's Knuckles were

a gang of about a half dozen teenagers that Montroy kept on a long leash, allowing them to police their own kind in the streets of downtown. In return, they would occasionally provide him with useful information. "They prevented the boat from docking but she's putting up a fight. Whatever Davies has, those guys aboard *Strait Shooter* want it real bad."

"I say we sink her," said Shorty.

"We don't want an international incident," said Montroy. "This is our battle. We have to drive her off ourselves somehow."

"We could destroy the dock," said McCloskey. "I'll go see what Davies has in his armory. Maybe we can blow it up."

"Oh, that's discreet," said Montroy.

"We're in the middle of a thunderstorm."

"True enough."

McCloskey ran back into the house and found the stairs to the basement. There was a crate of grenades and McCloskey pulled three out and tucked them in his belt.

When he returned, the Pig's Knuckles were falling back closer to the house and *Strait Shooter* was navigating her way carefully back inside the dock.

"Now how are you going to go about this? You're still in their line of fire. And if you lob a live grenade out there, it's liable to blow back at your feet."

"I could drive it onto the dock."

"What?"

"The floodwater's not too deep for me to drive through it and onto the dock. I could detonate the grenades, jump out, and wade back to the shore."

"That's crazy," said Montroy. Then he said, "Grease — I'm commandeering your vehicle."

Grease, one of the Pig's Knuckles, brought his Packard down from the road. McCloskey climbed in and made for the dock, but with his head just below the dash. He could barely see where he was going and ended up driving the right side of the car off the dock, almost tipping it into the drink.

He quickly detonated the grenades and jumped into the river. Now all he had to do was get away from the dock without getting caught in the current.

They saw him struggling when the explosions came: three in quick succession along with the Packard's fuel tank. Pieces of the dock and the car showered the property. When the smoke cleared they could see *Strait Shooter*'s windows blown out and there were no hands on deck. She was bobbing slowly back to Detroit.

Shorty waded into the river and started sifting though the floating debris looking for McCloskey.

"There he is!" shouted Montroy.

McCloskey was walking towards them from about a hundred feet down the shore. At the last second he had taken a chance and let the current carry him away from the dock. Luckily it took him to a marshy little cove in the next property, where he was able to pull himself up onto the shore.

Satisfied that *Strait Shooter* had been driven back to wherever it was she came from, the Pig's Knuckles disappeared and the others returned to the house.

Montroy looked around and sighed his world-weary sigh. "What a fucking mess." And then he turned to Locke. "Interesting group you've assembled here."

He pulled a pack of cigarettes out of his shirt pocket. It was soaking wet. He squeezed the water out of it and threw it on the floor. He pulled a flask from his hip and drained it.

"Sir … how did you…?"

"You think I don't know what's going on in this city? What the fuck do you think I'm doing prowling around these streets every night?"

Montroy's face was beet red as he tore into Locke. "I'm trying to keep the fucking peace, which ain't easy with crusading assholes like you running around trying to start shit you can't finish."

He paced around for a bit. No one uttered a word. It was

time to break up the party and start to somehow sort things out. Another sleepless night.

"If anyone asks, this was my idea. You can tell the chief I got tired fending off Cossacks and chasing newsies down dark alleys for the price of a bottle of beer. And these three mugs," he said pointing to McCloskey, Shorty, and Mud, "they've got their own reasons for being here and I don't need to know what they are."

Montroy approached McCloskey. "I'd appreciate it if you didn't leave town. We need to get our stories straight but we haven't got time for a rehearsal."

McCloskey nodded.

"Where will you be if I need you?"

"Ojibway."

"Fair enough. Now scram, the three of yous."

Parts of the Drive were flooded out and McCloskey had to cruise slowly though the deluge. He dropped off Shorty and Mud at the roadhouse just down the way then headed south on Lauzon Road.

His mind was still reeling. What just happened? Where was he going? He started thinking about his father and Billy. Then he started thinking about Clara. Then he thought about Sophie. Then he stopped thinking.

When he reached the junction at Highway 2 he kind of surprised himself when he didn't hesitate. He turned and headed straight to Ojibway.

He took it easy, listening to the rhythm of the engine and the sound of the wheels on the wet road. It lulled him. When he got home he parked behind the house.

The place had been ransacked again. He was relieved when he found a bottle of brandy underneath a floorboard in the kitchen. He carried it up to bed with him.

The breeze off the river was stirring the curtains in the window. He took a drink from the bottle and let his head settle into the pillow. The last thing he remembered was the feel of the bottle in his hand and the moonlight reflecting off the wall.

THIRD GEAR

(TUESDAY, JULY 25)

Chapter 33

YOU KNOW WHERE THE LIBRARY IS, DON'T YOU?

She was convinced now that Braverman didn't spend the night at Mrs. Cousineau's. She checked the clock in the foyer. Her moment of truth was going to have to wait.

"Bye, Mrs. Richardson."

"Goodbye, dear, and have a lovely day."

When she got to Tecumseh Road she didn't see any of the usual suspects. She figured she missed the streetcar. Sure enough, when she got to the Avenue she could see it rolling towards the downtown, too far away to catch on foot.

Futz.

Vera Maude was already walking on thin ice with Miss Lancefield; it would be unacceptable for her to be late again. She looked around. She remembered the cabstand at the motel on the corner and ran over. As luck would have it, there was a Yellow Cab waiting in the parking lot. The driver was slouched sideways in his seat with his size twelves hanging out the passenger window, reading the morning paper.

"Excuse me, mister. Can I get a ride?"

He was about to tell the body attached to the voice to scram, that is, until he saw the body. It made him forget about the old man in Room 3 he was supposed to take to the train station.

"Yeah, sure, honey. Where you headed?"

"Downtown — to the library."

He straightened up, folded his paper, and tossed it on the passenger seat.

"The library?"

"Yeah, you know where the library is, don't you?"

"Sure, sure."

He leaned over and popped the door open.

"Thanks. I'm in an awful hurry."

This was a new one. He'd heard of people being in a rush to get to the ferry dock, the train station, the racetrack, even a poker game, but never the library.

"That must be some book," he said as he wheeled the cab around.

"Actually, I work there."

"That so?"

He took another look at Vera Maude in his rear view mirror. She looked nothing like the librarians he remembered. And in his book, she didn't act like one either. Vera Maude was watching the traffic while bouncing up and down in her seat.

"Here's your chance. Go! Go!"

He crossed Tecumseh Road and shot up Pelissier Street. Pelissier was the first street west of the Avenue; it was one way almost all the way to the river and you never had to worry about getting stuck behind a streetcar.

"We'll be there in a flash, honey."

Every time another vehicle got in the driver's way he swerved around it without even slowing down. Vera Maude didn't even notice. She was stewing over Braverman, behaving like a housewife whose husband failed to come home after a night on the town.

Not terribly Maudern of me.

"Ah, honey — the library?"

"Huh? Oh — Park Street is fine."

"I'll just make a left here and drop you off at the front door. Is that okay?"

"Sure, thanks."

Vera Maude started digging in her purse for some change. She had never taken a taxi before. "Is this enough?" she asked.

"That's fine, honey."

He took the money, hopped out, and opened the door for Vera Maude.

"Gee thanks, mister," she said with a wink.

He nearly melted in his boots. "Call me anytime," he said and he watched her walk up the steps of the library.

"Gotta get me a library card."

Vera Maude couldn't remember the last time she was early for work. When she got to the top of the steps she could see some of the girls staring through the windows with their *ooh, isn't that interesting?* faces on.

"Buzz, buzz, buzz," said Vera Maude as she passed through the inner doors.

"Good morning, Maudie," said Daphne with a smirk.

"Shoo, fly."

Chapter 34

MARBLE CITY

When McCloskey sat up, the bottle he was sleeping with rolled onto the floor. It felt like it landed on his head. He checked his watch. There was still time.

He pivoted off the bed, walked stiffly over to the wardrobe, and picked out a dark suit and a clean white shirt. He peeled off his damp clothes and then went down into the kitchen to wash up.

He forgot what a mess the place was. A fly was buzzing around his ears. He looked up; the strip hanging from the ceiling was encrusted with insects. He pumped some water into the sink and found a razor and bar of soap on the windowsill. He shaved carefully around his cuts and bruises, and when he was finished he made himself an Irish coffee and went back upstairs to get dressed.

He was starting to feel better. Then he started to remember things and didn't feel so good anymore. The first thing he remembered was the Lieutenant's body on a pool table, then a shotgun blast, and Jigsaw falling into the river. He wasn't sure if that was the right order or if any of it was even true. The more he tried to remember, the more it seemed to fade away as if it were a dream.

He made his way back downstairs and with the bottle of whisky in one hand and his coffee mug in the other he elbowed his way through the kitchen door to drink his breakfast in the shade of the black oak.

He didn't want to go to church. He didn't want to hear the priest and he didn't want to see the pine boxes. The pine boxes would make them seem small, like everybody else, and that was the saddest thing, especially since they were both so much larger-than-life.

McCloskey walked over to the ruins of the cabin. Should have thrown dirt on them both right then and there, he thought, like in the battlefield. He noticed how their bodies left a reverse shadow on the floorboards. He topped up his coffee then poured libations on the spot where their souls were parted from their bodies.

"Here's to you, Pa and to you, Billy."

He dragged himself over to the Light Six and found his sunglasses in the glove box. He glanced over at Lesperance's house. Did the old man get his burial at sea? His mind flashed to Jigsaw. No, it wasn't a dream. They were both at the bottom of the river now. He started the engine, spun around, and headed up the path.

He took the bend at the old fish hatchery then slowed to turn left onto the highway. He hit the gas and felt the wheels grab the road. He was retracing his steps again. Around, around, and around. When he was doing shift work he seemed to be living the same week over and over again. As an infantryman in France it was a hundred yards forward and a hundred yards back. When he returned home after the war it was the fight circuit. Then he was a cog in a crime machine.

He heard the bell of a locomotive in the distance, or so he thought. He might have imagined it, an echo in his mind from the other night, or past fights.

He relaxed his grip on the wheel, sat back, and fumbled a cigar from the box on the seat next to him. He bit the tip off the end and spat it onto the road. He struck a match on the dashboard, held the flame to the end of the cigar and puffed away at it until there was a nice orange glow. The aroma quickly filled the car. When he was a boy his father was his hero, a giant of a man, and so handsome with his jet-black hair and broad shoulders.

But Frank McCloskey cried like a baby when his sons returned home from the war. And his sons hardly recognized him.

McCloskey rolled to a stop in front of the church. He had heard it all before and he couldn't bear to hear it again, though he knew there would be a few new twists, just to keep it current, and some custom fittings. He pulled around the corner and parked next to the cemetery.

"We have come to pay our respects to Francis John McCloskey and his son William Peter. Francis John's eldest son, John Stephen, and William's wife, Clara, survive them."

The priest nodded to Clara and to Henry, who was standing at her side.

"They shall hunger no more, neither thirst any more; neither shall the sun light on them, nor any heat."

There were vets from the old battalion, a few crusty bootleggers, and a host of other characters from the county.

"But though our outward man perish, yet the inward man is renewed day by day. For our light affliction, which is but for a moment, worketh for us a far more exceeding and eternal weight of glory."

Clara was quietly cursing Jack, wondering where the hell he was.

"For what is a man profited, if he shall gain the whole world, and lose his own soul?"

There were some clumsy segues into the virtues of temperance that made Clara roll her eyes.

"Woe unto him that giveth his neighbour drink, that puttest thy bottle to him, and makest him drunken also, that thou mayest look on their nakedness!"

The priest was whipping himself into froth now. His face was red, his chin flecked with spittle, and when he waved his arms his robe billowed like a ship's sail. He glared at the brother by his side and the layman seated across from him. No one was safe from his fire and brimstone.

Clara looked over at Henry. She could tell his head was pounding.

"Know ye not that the unrighteous shall not inherit the kingdom of God? Be not deceived: neither fornicators, nor idolaters, nor adulterers, nor effeminate, nor abusers of themselves with mankind, nor thieves, nor covetous, nor drunkards, nor revilers, nor extortioners, shall inherit the kingdom of God."

Clara wondered who that left. She looked up and the priest's eyes met hers.

"Let us hear the conclusion of the whole matter: Fear God, and keep his commandments, for this is the whole duty of man. For God shall bring every work into judgment, with every secret thing, whether it be good, or whether it be evil."

McCloskey watched the procession file out of the church and weave through the cemetery. He spotted Bernie Lesperance. He wondered if Bernie knew his cousin was dead. He probably came looking for him.

The procession stopped in front of two fresh piles of earth and the priest signalled the pallbearers to lower the coffins.

"... return unto the ground; for out of it wast thou taken: for dust thou art, and unto dust shalt thou return."

There were a few final words for the congregation. Clara looked down at the mud and rainwater streaming onto Billy's coffin. She tried to imagine him buried in that trench in France. Now he was finally past rescuing.

"Choose you this day whom ye will serve; whether the gods which your fathers served that were on the other side of the flood, or the gods of the Amorites, in whose land ye dwell: but as for me and my house, we will serve the Lord."

The priest walked back to the church. The little group of mourners shared a few words and broke up, heading out in different directions. Henry walked away with the vets. The yolks from the county piled back into their trucks.

McCloskey waited until people were well on their way before he moved in on Clara. She didn't stop walking or turn to face him.

"You should have come, Jack."

"You saw me?"

"Yeah — hiding in your car. Why didn't you come?"

"What for?"

"Oh, I don't know — out of respect maybe?"

"You like what the priest had to say? You all prepared to hop on the wagon, sing a few hymns, and love thy neighbour?"

"No. We're going to Chappell House to get drunk."

"What about the cops?"

"They're bringing the ice."

She noticed how beat up he was but resisted saying anything.

"We'll either end up bawling our eyes out or throwing furniture at each other, or both."

"Typical Irish wake."

They stopped at a street corner. The sun was blazing but the humidity was gone. The lawns looked lush and green

"What are you going to do now, Jack?"

"I don't know."

"Oh, come on, Jack, you've been waiting for this moment all your life. Running the Border Cities is what you were born to do."

Clara looked down the street.

"I'm the one that needs a new life. I'm tired of this one."

She read his expression.

"Don't worry," she said. "I'm not going to do anything rash. Though I am thinking about becoming a respectable member of society, maybe getting a steady job and doing some more volunteer work at the hospital."

"How's Henry? He okay?"

"Yeah, he's going to be fine."

"He didn't say anything about last night?" said McCloskey.

"I didn't ask and he didn't tell. Was it everything you hoped it would be?"

"It's too early to say. You might want to wait for the late edition."

"Somebody told me not to believe everything I read in the papers. You're lucky, Jack. You always have been. One day, though, your luck's going to run out."

"What's that supposed to mean?"

Clara kissed him on the cheek and looked into his eyes. "See you later, Jack."

She turned and ran across the street towards the waiting streetcar.

— *Chapter 35* —

CANADA CUSTOMS

)

"Mr. Braverman is with a client right now. He'll be finishing soon but then he has to leave for an appointment. Would you like me to take a message, Miss —?"

"Uh — no, thanks. I'll catch up with him later."

Click.

Vera Maude ran out the front door of the library and raced down to Chatham Street. When she didn't see Braverman right away, she thought she missed him, but then he stepped out of the building, case in hand.

At Pitt he stopped to let a truck pass and she came up right behind him. She looked down at his fingers wrapped tightly around the handle of his case. It looked heavy. They cut over to Ferry Street.

I could tell him that I'm on to him. Then I could say I only want to talk, maybe go for a coffee.

They were near the top of the hill. She never hated being five-foot-three more than she did right now. This was supposed to be her moment of truth, her opportunity to turn her words into actions. It was no time to be petite.

She lost sight of him in the crowd, panicked, and blurted out his name. "Braverman!"

He turned and walked straight into a group of businessmen making their way up the hill, and his case got lodged between them. He gave it a tug and it popped open. Out spilled brushes, tins, bottles, and a package loosely wrapped in brown paper.

"Shit!"

He quickly rescued his oils before turning his attention to the package. He saw Vera Maude peeling the paper away and his face went white.

It was a book, bound in blue leather, with a single word embossed on the cover.

Ulysses.

"Thanks," said Braverman.

He grabbed it, wrapped it up again, and shoved it back in his case.

"How did you … where did you…?"

"It isn't any of your concern."

He was trying to close the latch on the case.

"I've been reading about *Ulysses* for a long time, and about New York and Paris, and Mr. Joyce and Miss Beach."

Braverman checked his watch. "Look, doll, it's been fun but I've got a ferry to catch."

"I work at the library. I helped you today with your *Book Review.*"

That stopped Braverman. He smiled. "Yeah, yeah, I remember."

He knew he had seen her somewhere before.

"I'm planning a trip to Paris." She surprised herself with that one. "And I'd love to meet Miss Beach."

Braverman was noticing the line of commuters at the ferry dock. She had to make her move now.

"Maybe you could come by the library tomorrow and we could go for a coffee."

"Sorry, I'd really love to, but it's bon voyage for me."

"Bon voyage?"

"Yeah — my work here is done. Time for me to get back to the real world. Nice meeting you, though. If I'm ever in the Border Cities again I'll look you up."

"What? What do you mean? Aren't you —"

She couldn't believe what had just happened. What *did* just happen? She saw him disappear into the crowd funnelling through Canada Customs and suddenly felt ill.

"Too late," she said, "we met too late."

She stood there until the ferry slipped away and the dock was deserted.

Braverman was glad it was finally over. Several weeks ago when he first laid eyes on the crate at the post office, he wondered what he had got himself into.

The first thing he did was negotiate a better duty rate. He did this by convincing customs the books were cheap dime store novels. Next he had to get the crate up to his room at Mrs. Cousineau's. He paid the courier a mickey of rye to help him get it up the stairs.

The next day he wrapped a copy of the book in brown paper, packed it in his artist's case and rode the streetcar down to the ferry dock. He remembered the journey across the river being the longest ten minutes of his life. If anyone recognized the book at U.S. Customs he was finished; it would be time and money wasted and *Ulysses* would be stranded on the shores of the Border Cities.

The official opened it to make sure there wasn't a whisky bottle hidden in hollowed-out pages. Satisfied the book posed no threat, the official instructed him to move along. He thanked the official, gathered his things, and walked up to Jefferson Avenue. When he got home he tied up the package, addressed it, and sent it on its way through the United States postal service to the first subscriber on Miss Beach's list: Washington Square Press.

He would repeat the process thirty-nine times.

Braverman shifted his gaze over the bow of the ferry. The city of Detroit was looming in the near distance. Soon this city would be an old memory, too. He couldn't wait to tell his compatriots in Paris how he pulled one over on the Republic and its Methodist smut-hounds.

Surprise, disappointment, frustration, heartbreak: just a few of the emotions Vera Maude was experiencing right now. She was standing outside the British-American, wondering what her next move should be. There was no point in going back to the library. She was officially AWOL.

She looked up the Avenue and down the Drive. The Border Cities were a great, sprawling machine, constantly evolving, always re-inventing itself. Would it ever become the kind of place she could truly be happy? She couldn't wait to find out. Life was too short. Maybe she could become a catalyst for change. She could become active, work outside the Music, Literature, and Arts Club. Maybe she could teach.

Be a Maudern missionary?

It was true what she said, she had been reading about Joyce's novel for a long time. She even tried to procure copies of the *Dial* issues that contained excerpts. It had come to mean more than the words on the page. And Braverman had come to mean more than just a bootlegger, more than an interesting neighbour. There was something romantic about him, something ideal. There was life in him.

She wandered over to the Michigan Central Railway ticket office and read the fares posted in the window. She stepped inside. There were maps and posters on the walls and postcards for sale. A clerk was sitting in the ticket wicket eating a sandwich.

"May I help you, ma'am?"

"Have you travelled much?"

"Beg pardon?"

"Have you been to any of these cities?"

Vera Maude pointed to a poster advertising Chicago.

"I been to our regional office."

"But you must be tempted to buy a ticket yourself some days."

"No, not really."

McCloskey asked Fields to meet him at the British-American so he could hear the police department's version of last night's events. Fields found McCloskey seated at the bar.

"You're looking better, Henry."

"I feel like hell."

"Eddie — a couple of Vernor's. And a clean glass for my friend here."

Fields told McCloskey that the Mounties had been watching Davies for some time and were just waiting for the right moment to come charging over the wall.

"You beat them to it and ruined their investigation."

"Do I have anything to worry about?"

"No one's quite sure what to do with you. Locke was the sacrificial lamb. He was dismissed this morning." Fields took a sip of his ginger ale. "He didn't take it well. I'm expecting Wallace to be let go this afternoon. They're being a bit more careful with him since he was in so deep with Davies. The Mounties want to use him to mop up some of the mess."

"And Montroy?"

"Early retirement. He's going to spend the rest of the summer fishing on Lake Erie."

"You seem to have been left out of the dance."

"Not quite. I'm going to be made detective." Fields seemed a little embarrassed. "Sure, it's what I wanted but it's not the way I wanted to get it."

"I know what you mean."

Fields was working around to something. "Jack, the city's pretty shell-shocked and most don't even know the half of it. Can we call a truce?"

It was the first acknowledgement of McCloskey as the new boss.

"Yeah," he grinned, "but only for a little while."

There was some small talk, but no mention of Clara. After Fields finished his ginger ale he was on his way.

"See you in the streets."

McCloskey was undecided about what he was going to do next. He had a feeling the gangs were waiting to hear from him. He dropped some coin on the bar and surveyed the room. The handful of patrons averted their gaze.

The king is dead. Long live the king.

He stepped out of the British-American and down to the lane that ran behind the docks. Boats were bobbing in the water. Beyond them was the Detroit skyline: the Ford Building, the Buhl Building, and some new pile that looked like it was going to dwarf them all.

A girl was walking towards him, taking in the same view. She was attractive, with wild waves of chestnut hair and an unusual style of dress, a style he'd heard others refer to as bohemian. She had on a man's shirt, a few long strands of beads, a skirt that stopped just below her knees, and shoes with chunky heels, all in black. She walked behind him then stopped a few feet away to watch the ferries pass each other.

McCloskey was in the mood to talk to someone who knew nothing about him and his world. He made furtive glances. She had a foreign look. Her skin tone suggested a Mediterranean background. And those eyes; even behind the cheaters they were captivating. She pulled a pack of smokes out of her handbag. As soon as the cigarette touched her lips McCloskey had a flame on the tip.

"Going somewhere?"

She looked up at him with her big green-brown eyes and he could feel his tongue begin to swell and the hairs on his neck stand on end.

"Sorry?"

"That's a train ticket."

"Oh — yeah."

"Where to?"

"New York City."

"Really?" McCloskey looked over at Detroit. "That's got to be one of my favourite places."

She leaned back against the fence and sighed.

"You're not in any kind of trouble, are you?" he asked.

She chuckled and said, "No."

"Good. My name's Jack."

"Vera Maude."

"Nice to meet you, Vera Maude."

"You from around here?"

"More or less."

"I'd give anything to get out of this place."

"I thought you were going to New York."

"Here — take it," she said and she handed him the ticket.

"What?"

"It was too impulsive of me. I got commitments here in town, family, a job."

McCloskey had to find out what this girl was all about. "Can I buy you a drink?" he asked. "I know a little place around the corner."

Vera Maude looked at him sideways. "C'mon. I'll tell you about all the things you have to do while you're in New York."

"So you've been there before?"

"A couple of times. And I'm always looking for an excuse to go back. When does your train leave?"

"Around five."

"We got time. You ever been to an Irish wake, Vera Maude?"

"Does that line usually work for you?"

"I don't know. I never used it before."

Vera Maude crushed her cigarette under her heel and they started walking together up Ferry Hill. "Can I ask where you got the black eye?"

McCloskey had forgotten how beat up he was. He touched the cut over his brow. "You wouldn't believe me if I told you."

"Try me."

"It's complicated."

McCloskey watched her wiggle all the way up the hill.

"You're gonna need a bodyguard in New York."

"That's cute. You learn all these lines hanging around in hotel bars all day?"

"As a matter of fact —"

She turned to face him.

"Look, you're sweet and everything but I'm not looking for romance. I'm just getting over a really bad relationship."

"Okay, okay." McCloskey held his hands up in mock defense.

"I just thought it would be nice to talk, and you look like the kind of guy that might know a few things."

"Like what?"

"Who do you have to know in this town to get a decent bottle of whisky?"

Chapter 36

CROSSROADS

Jack and Vera Maude were sitting at a little table in a speakeasy near the bus station on Chatham Street. He was listening to her every word, and she was filled with them. At first he listened because he was tired and just wanted to hear a friendly voice, but before long he was captivated. After an hour he felt like he was in love.

She told him about her experience with Braverman at the dock, the episodes leading up to that fateful moment, and the significance, for her at least, of Joyce's novel. He knew nothing of the book but her passion got to him. Then she told him about her father and her brothers and sisters and what it might mean if she left town. She was torn, she said. She loved her father but couldn't stand most of her siblings. They were strangers to her in so many ways and there was really no hope of them ever coming to any kind of terms. Why shouldn't she be able to live her life the way she wanted? There was a life for her out there somewhere, of that she was certain. But could she go it alone? And what if she failed? Wouldn't there just be more heartbreak and disappointment? Probably. But better to go through all that while you were actually living your life rather than avoiding it. You don't regret the things you've done only the things you haven't. She was philosophizing again, thinking out loud, reasoning with herself as she prepared to take her next big leap.

When it came McCloskey's turn to talk, he avoided reliving the events of the past twenty-four hours — or twenty-four months for that matter, the lost years of his life that left him spinning his wheels on county roads. Instead he recounted tales from what he could now call his youth, growing up on the banks of the Detroit River. Vera Maude liked his stories. McCloskey barely recognized himself in them. What ever became of that boy? The wake was going on right now over at Chappell House, but he couldn't bring himself to go. Actually, it was more like he couldn't pull himself away from Vera Maude. What was he doing? Only two days ago he had lived and breathed for a girl named Sophie. Then he was having rough sex with his brother's widow, a woman the two of them shared like a car. Just the thought of his brother could make his blood boil. It was a complicated web of self-loathing, bitterness, and revenge. Was that why he was always fooling around with Clara behind Billy's back? And she never said no. Misery loves company. And now was he blaming his brother for his father's death? Maybe.

And what was Sophie? An innocent girl, Clara before the McCloskeys got to her, a river in which he thought he could purify himself but ultimately would have poisoned and brought down to his level. Funny how he didn't miss Sophie, funny and sad. Something had happened to him in the last couple of days, something unexpected. A long time ago he had settled his mind, then realigned his body. What he had neglected was his heart. He never gave his heart much thought. He probably didn't know he had one until he met Sophie. And he didn't know how full it could be until just now, sitting here with Vera Maude. He already missed her, and they hadn't even said their goodbyes yet.

Someone once told him there were two kinds of people: question people and answer people. Vera Maude was the answer to his question. Now she was going off in search of herself. He was confident that Vera Maude would find what she was looking for. She had an inner strength that didn't come from a life in the street or from being smacked around by her husband or boyfriend. It didn't come from a bottle either; she wasn't bitter or angry. She was smart, genuine, the real deal, and fiercely independent. She was different from all the other girls. She talked about things like destiny, past lives, and other stuff he barely understood but wanted to hear more about.

He hung on her every word and loved watching her as she expressed these ideas and opinions for what seemed like the first time. He felt her loneliness. *But why me?* He didn't flatter himself. They were caught up in the moment. She recognized a kind of worldliness in him. She looked to him as someone who would understand and not laugh at her, someone who might even be able to explain what it was she was going through. Before he got to know her better, he would have to say goodbye. They have met too late. This girl sat her self down, opened up to him, and for the first time he was the one that was going to be left with a broken heart.

He studied her; he wanted to remember her face, everything about her. When she smiled she had dimples in her cheeks. He found it easy to turn that smile into laughter. Her laugh was natural, infectious, easy. Her eyes flickered between green and brown, depending on her expression and the light. He studied the curve of her brow, the shape of her nose. She kept pushing stray locks of hair away from her face, dark brown hair with the occasional chestnut streak. Pins held it off her slender neck. There was a smoky texture to her voice that contrasted with the sound of her s's — a tiny whistle from an imperfection in one of her teeth. She covered her mouth while she tried to get her food down faster and her words out quicker. She talked with her hands, her beautiful hands. She wore a fancy ring that was either a family heirloom or a piece of costume jewellery from a five and dime. He could never tell the difference. She wore her watch halfway up her arm. She probably couldn't get the band to go any smaller. Her left ear was double-pierced, with a little gold hoop through each hole.

Her mind went a mile a minute as she kept up the conversation and watched the door and the other customers. They weren't all heady thoughts; there were many asides about certain movie actors or what some boy had said to her once over a soda at the drugstore. She liked the movies, maybe just as much as she liked reading. She kept asking him if he had seen this movie or that. Half the time he had never even heard of the picture. She was encyclopedic, pages flipping all the time. She also liked to eat. He had to keep ordering more food and drinks. *Where did she put it?*

Vera Maude noticed that their waiter seemed nervous around Jack and that people would glance over at them and then exchange tense words in hushed tones. She studied Jack's busted-up face. Had she seen it somewhere before? She wasn't sure. Then, when he leaned over to grab an ashtray off the table next to them she noticed the shoulder harness inside his jacket. She nearly choked on her toast and tomato sandwich but managed to keep her cool. *Jack ... Jack ... who is this guy?* She casually took another look around the room as she polished off her glass of beer. Then it hit her.

"McCloskey! You're Jack McCloskey!"

She realized she was pointing at him with her finger like a gun barrel and relaxed her hand on the table.

McCloskey was a little embarrassed He wondered how much she knew. He tried to make a joke of it. "You're confusing me with a character I play in the movies. That happens all the time."

"No — I saw your name in the paper once, though I don't remember exactly what it was for." She lied.

"Don't believe everything you read in the papers."

She laughed. "So the bit about you organizing a rummage sale at Central Methodist wasn't true?"

"Except that — that was the absolute truth."

On top of everything else she had a sense of humour. It made him want to cry in his beer.

"What time did you say your train leaves?"

Vera Maude looked at her watch. "In about an hour."

Once again his timing was wrong. But he knew that had he met Vera Maude before today, he wouldn't be having the kind of conversation he was having with her right now, or feeling the things he was feeling. What sort of man had he become? Unfortunately, she wouldn't be around to show him.

There was another pause in the conversation. Whenever that happened, he knew they were thinking the same thing. He thought he knew what courage and sacrifice was until now.

"We should go soon. I need to pack a few things. And I should stop by the library."

A feeling of complete and utter loneliness washed over McCloskey, unlike anything he had ever experienced before. He buried it deep inside him.

"My car's parked around the corner; I'll give you a lift."

They walked out without paying and no one stopped them. Vera Maude briefly wondered what it would be like to be Jack McCloskey's girlfriend. Heads turned, girls giggled, and men got out of his way. She thought it was kind of fun. His vehicle was parked near Windsor Market. Bullet holes in the passenger door.

"Hop in."

She sat with his box of cigars in her lap.

"Where am I going?"

"Let's stop at the library first so I can pick up my things. The house I board at is on the way to the train station."

"Gotcha."

He parked in front of the library entrance. McCloskey followed her up the steps. He had never been inside the library before. When he came through the inner doors, the already quiet library fell dead silent. The vets reading the papers knew who he was and a few wanted to shake his hand. The children were a little frightened, but curious the way children always are. The librarians were at a loss for what to do until they saw he was with Vera Maude.

"Daphne, this is Jack McCloskey; Jack this is Daphne."

"Vera Maude's told me a lot about you, Daphne."

McCloskey turned on the charm, knowing full well that Daphne represented everything Vera Maude hated about this town. Daphne meanwhile took one look at this bruised, hulking gangster with the blood on his shirt, the bulge in his jacket, and the sway he held amongst the vets and was ready to be knocked over by the proverbial feather.

"Pleased to make your acquaintance, Mr. McCloskey."

"Is Miss Lancefield in?"

"Uh — no, she's chairing a club meeting."

"Oh, right. What's on the menu for this Saturday?"

"Miss Lancefield's lecture on modern sculpture."

"I'll have to miss it. Who's watching the store?"

"Peggy."

"Thanks. I'll just be a minute, Jack. I have to claim my belongings from the Properties Department."

"Sure."

Vera Maude disappeared behind the counter.

"So, Daphne, you read all these books yet?"

"Uh — no."

"Mm. You got Joyce's novel? I hear it's really good."

"No, we don't I'm afraid."

"You don't have to be afraid, Daphne." He took a step closer. "I don't bite."

"Jack!"

"What?"

"Let's went."

"Nice talking to you, Daphne."

"See you in the funny papers, Daphne."

Daphne finally snapped out of it. "Say — where you been, Maudie? And where you off to?"

"New York City. I'll send you a postcard."

McCloskey touched the brim of his hat. "I'll be back later for my library card, Daphne."

"Don't pay any attention to him," said Vera Maude. "He'd sell your mother out for a bottle of rye."

They galloped down the front steps.

"That was fun," said McCloskey.

"Yeah, a regular barrel of monkeys."

McCloskey headed straight up Victoria all the way to Tecumseh. He kept glancing over at Vera Maude. She had an elbow out the window. The wind was teasing her hair. She was smiling. McCloskey envied her. He couldn't imagine feeling as free as Vera Maude must have felt right now.

"Turn here."

McCloskey turned right at Hanna, left onto Dougall, and parked in front of Mrs. Richardson's.

"That's Mrs. Cousineau's house across the street." Mrs. Cousineau was looking out the window. "And that's Mrs. Cousineau." Vera Maude waved.

"C'mon," she said. "I'll introduce you to my parole officer."

Once again McCloskey followed Vera Maude into another corner of her world, the world she was saying her goodbyes to.

"Mrs. Richardson?"

McCloskey looked around the front room: an upright piano; old photos; furniture from the last century; lace everywhere. And cat hair.

Mrs. Richardson came out of the kitchen. She was drying something with a tea towel. "Vera Maude, dear, why aren't you at the library?"

When she saw McCloskey she almost dropped whatever it was on the floor.

"This is Mr. McCloskey. He's giving me a ride to the train station."

"The train station?"

"I'm leaving, Mrs. Richardson."

This was a lot for Mrs. Richardson to register. She needed to back up a bit. "Were you let go from the library?"

Vera Maude wondered what reason Mrs. Richardson had to think that.

"No, I quit."

"Oh, dear. Does your father know?"

"Not exactly."

"Vera Maude Maguire, what will I tell him?"

"You're not going to tell him anything. I am."

"And what's Mr. McCloskey's business?"

"Like I said, he's giving me a ride to the train station."

"Are you some sort of driver, Mr. McCloskey?"

"I guess you could say I was in the transport business, ma'am."

"Looks like you had a run-in recently."

"Someone refused to pay their fare, ma'am. Believe me, he looks a hell of a lot worse."

"Language, Mr. McCloskey."

"Sorry, ma'am."

"I'm here to pick up a few things, Mrs. Richardson."

Mrs. Richardson didn't miss a beat. "There's a small matter of the rent, Vera Maude."

There was a knock at the door. Vera Maude took the opportunity to scoot upstairs.

"Mrs. Cousineau."

"Mrs. Richardson — I saw our Vera Maude brought home by a strange man and I wondered if everything was all right."

They spoke in front of McCloskey like he wasn't even there, like he was the elephant in the room nobody wanted to mention.

"She's leaving us, Mrs. Cousineau."

"She isn't."

"She is."

"Who could she be leaving us for?"

"New York," said Vera Maude as she came down the stairs.

"Were you already packed?" asked McCloskey.

"Pretty much. That reminds me — Mrs. Richardson, those are my sheets in the ice box."

"I was going to ask you."

"A trip, is it?" said Mrs. Cousineau. "I hope you've remembered to bring something to read."

Vera Maude thought of the dozens of magazines she'd brought Mrs. Cousineau over the past several months. "As a matter of fact I —"

"You must stop by before you go." And with that Mrs. Cousineau was out the door and halfway across the street.

Mrs. Richardson brought up the subject of rent again.

"Let me take care of that." McCloskey reached in his coat pocket and pulled out a roll of bills as thick as his wrist. He proceeded to peel off a few layers. "Will this cover it?"

He handed Mrs. Richardson $80. Mrs. Richardson was looking for about $12. Vera Maude tried to contain her laughter. When Mrs. Richardson didn't respond, because she was nearly catatonic, McCloskey peeled off a couple more bills and handed them to her. When she didn't accept, he tossed them onto the piano.

"Well, Vera Maude's got a train to catch. It's been a pleasure, Mrs. Richardson. If we're not squared up then just send Vera Maude's bill to my attention at the British-American."

"Bye, Mrs. Richardson." Vera Maude gave her a kiss on the cheek. "I owe you a bottle of gin."

McCloskey followed Vera Maude out the door. Mrs. Cousineau was waiting for her on the sidewalk. She held something under her arm.

"Mr. Braverman gave me this but I have no use for it." It was a copy of *Ulysses*. "You've got a long trip ahead of you, dear. *Chatterbox* and *House Beautiful* simply won't do."

Vera Maude just stood there holding it, staring at it. She opened it up at the end — something she thought of doing only after her encounter with Braverman.

Yes.

She showed McCloskey.

"Yes," he said.

Vera Maude smiled and clutched it to her chest. McCloskey smiled back.

"We better get going," he said.

Vera Maude kissed Mrs. Cousineau goodbye and thanked her. McCloskey threw her bag in the back of the Light Six and Vera Maude climbed in. She flipped through Joyce's novel as they made their way along Tecumseh Road. She wondered aloud how she'd be able to get it across the border at Buffalo. McCloskey pulled something out of his coat pocket, something he had picked up in Riverside last night.

"What's this?" asked Vera Maude.

"A 'get out of jail free' card."

"*Richard Bathgate Davies, Esq., Riverside Drive*. Will it really work?"

"It's worth a try. Show it to the customs officer. If he gives you trouble, mail the book back to me and I'll hand deliver it to you in New York."

"Okay," said Vera Maude and she tucked it inside the book.

They passed the Elliott. McCloskey glanced across the rail yard. It appeared to be business as usual.

"What about your father?"

"I can't," said Vera Maude. "I know it sounds weak and stupid, but I just can't. I'll send him a long teary letter from the border."

McCloskey understood. Without saying a word he turned up McKay, dodged the puddles left by the deluge last night, and parked a ways from the main building. The locomotive engine was going through some routine maintenance and people were assembling on the platform.

"Come on. I'll walk you." McCloskey carried her bag. "I know it's gonna sound crazy," he said, "but I miss you already."

Vera Maude just smiled at him and that suited him just fine. He knew he couldn't ask her for anything more.

"Do you need anything? I mean —"

He went to reach in his coat pocket for that roll of bills but Vera Maude stopped him, gently touching his arm.

"No — thanks."

They looked into each other's eyes. There was an understanding, but no words, no interpretation of the last few hours. They would leave it a mystery.

"So if I address something to the British-American, you'll get it?" she asked.

"Yeah. It's my home away from home."

Another pause, then a powerful embrace.

"Bye, Jack. And thanks."

McCloskey could feel himself crumbling, his knees giving way. He felt like a schoolboy. He stopped himself, not wanting to embarrass or disappoint Vera Maude.

"Bye."

The porter helped Vera Maude board the car. McCloskey watched her stow her luggage and find her seat. This felt different than it did with Sophie two days ago. Two days ago it was "I'll catch up with you after I've rescued my father and brother, redeemed myself, and carved out a world for us to live in." Of course none of that happened. This time it was just "goodbye" and "I hope you find what you're looking for." Vera Maude waved through the window.

McCloskey waved back. He was tired, and a little drunk from the whisky and from Vera Maude. His mind wandered while he stood there on the platform and watched her through the glass. He imagined a life with Vera Maude.

He would catch up with her in New York, at the hotel-apartment in Greenwich Village she told him about. They had fertile common ground. They would plant the seeds of their future in it.

Eventually, Vera Maude got a job in a bookstore. She met up with some writers and showed them her work. They said it was good and they helped her get published by a small, local press. McCloskey worked in a gym, training young boxers. In the evenings he and Vera Maude hung out in the cafes. The poets liked McCloskey; they romanticized him way out of proportion. He got a kick out of it. Afterwards he and Vera Maude would walk hand in hand back to their apartment.

Life was good, but they were restless. Greenwich Village felt small after a while. Everyone told them to go to Paris. The next summer they did. McCloskey watched Vera Maude as she lived out her dreams, grew into the woman she imagined herself while she was boarding at Mrs. Richardson's. McCloskey saw a side of Paris he hadn't seen during the war. He opened himself up to the world. While other people were looking for answers he was still struggling to form the questions. But he wasn't afraid. He and Vera Maude were a great pair. They taught each other so much and they were still madly in love.

When Paris got too small, they could head east, far east. He had met British soldiers during the war that told him about places like Egypt and India. Vera Maude was keen too. Their life would be an adventure together.

McCloskey missed her like crazy already. He had discovered a huge piece to his life's puzzle, only to lose it again. He sat in the Light Six and watched the train pull out of the station. He had a clear view of the Elliott on the other side of the tracks. Yesterday morning seemed like a lifetime ago. He sat there, drumming his fingers on the steering wheel, thinking about Vera Maude, thinking about New York, looking at his fuel gauge.

A car pulled up at the edge of the lot. A big fellow stepped out and stood outside the vehicle, eyeing McCloskey in a way that suggested he wanted to be sure that he had the right man. He started walking slowly towards the Light-Six. McCloskey glanced down the track. Vera Maude's train was already out of sight, gone. He turned back to the fellow who was now stopped and standing about ten feet away from McCloskey.

"What's up, soldier?"

The fellow looked like he had been up all night.

"You Jack McCloskey?"

"Who's asking?"

The man came closer to the vehicle. He cast a cold shadow across the window and door.

"The name's Charlie Baxter. Richard Davies was my boss. I'm here to tell you —"

Baxter reached in his jacket for his weapon and aimed it at McCloskey.

" — what goes around comes around."

HE KNOWS THIS
FELLOW IN CHICAGO.

---

3 December, 1921
Chicago
Dear Mr. Joyce

I am writing this note to make you acquainted
with my friend Ernest Hemingway, who with Mrs.
Hemingway is going to Paris to live, and will ask
him to drop it in the mails when he arrives there.

Mr. Hemingway is an American writer
instinctively in touch with everything worth

while going on here, and I know you will find both Mr. and Mrs. Hemingway delightful people to know.

They will be at 74 Rue de Cardinal Lemoine.

Sincerely,
Sherwood Anderson

---

2 February, 1922
Paris

Dear Miss Beach

I cannot let today pass without thanking you for all the trouble and worry you have given yourself about my book during the last year. All I can hope is that the result of its publication may be some satisfaction to you.

Will you please telegraph to Darantiere (to whom I have already sent a message of thanks) telling him in my name also to get on with the covers otherwise we shall get only 20 copies?

Grazie di nuovo.

Sincerely yours,
James Joyce

7 February, 1922
Paris

Mr. B---

I was given your name by an acquaintance of yours. He suggested that you might be able to help me in my cause.

I have a book, or rather, I have published a book. My fear is that it will not be allowed to make its way to readers in your country. There are forces at work that are determined to keep it out of the United States. Authorities have unjustly labelled the book as obscene.

If I were to somehow get you copies of the book, would you be able to handle the distribution from your end? I must be honest: there will be risks involved. I will cover your expenses.

Please let me know at your earliest convenience if you are able to help. My author would be eternally grateful.

Sylvia Beach

9 March, 1922
Paris

Dear Sherwood

You sound like a man well beloved of Jesus.
Lots of things happen here. Gertrude Stein
and me are just like brothers and we see a
lot of her. Read the preface you wrote for her
knew book and like it very much. It made a
big hit with Gertrude. Hash says to tell you,
quotes, that things have come to a pretty pass
between her and Lewy — close quotes. My
operatives keep a pretty close eye on the pair
of them.

Joyce has a most god-damn wonderful
book. It'll probably reach you in time.
Meantime the report is that he and all his
family are starving but you can find the whole
celtic crew of them every night in Michaud's,
where Binney and I can only afford to go
about once a week.

I've been teaching Pound to box wit
little success. He habitually leads wit his
chin and has the general grace of the crayfish
or crawfish. He's willing but short winded.
Going over there this afternoon for another
session but there ain't much job in it as I have
to shadow box between rounds to get up a
sweat. Pound sweats well, though, I'll say that
for him. Besides it's pretty sporting of him to
risk his dignity and his critical reputation at
something that he don't know nothing about.
He's really a good guy, Pound, wit a fine bitter

tongue into him. He's written a good review
of Ulysses for the April Dial.

Ernest

CANADIAN NATIONAL TELEGRAM
WINDSOR ON
1922 MAR 21   PM 12 13

1625 DOUGALL AVE

MISS BEACH
SHOOT BOOKS PREPAID YOUR RES-
PONSIBILITY ADDRESSING SAME TO
ME CARE OF DOMINION EXPRESS
COMPANY

B

More Historical Crime Fiction from Dundurn

Fire on the Runway
by Mel Bradshaw
978-1459703353
$17.99

As Torontonians move to the beat of the Jazz Age, war is the furthest thing from their minds. Then a fatal grenade explosion outside a west-end hotel room breaks the rhythm. The room's registered occupant, a mysterious European woman calling herself Lucy, disappears before she can shed any light on the incident.

Police detective Paul Shenstone believes someone is trying to assassinate Lucy. Once he has found her, he will learn the reason: she has uncovered dangerous secrets that threaten world peace. Shenstone must protect Lucy and pursue her attackers. At the same time, his own experience as an infantry officer in Flanders compels him to go beyond his police function. He feels he must help Lucy get her message to the corridors of power, so that a new war may be prevented.

Trumpets Sound No More
by Jon Redfern
978-1894917407
$20.95

In 1840, the theatre world in London is shocked by the brutal killing of one of its youngest and most successful entrepreneurs, bludgeoned in his house. The discovery of a contentious theatre contract, a collection of promissory notes, and a walking stick, its bloodied ivory head in the shape of a dog, are the only leads. Inspector Owen Endersby, of the recently formed London Detective Police Force, is called upon to apprehend the culprit before Christmas Eve. The inspector has six days to chart the by-ways of the Criminal Mentality. The case soon involves street vendors, downstairs servants, money lenders, and the greatest performers of the stage. Who had motive to batter the young man to death? Without the techniques of the modern-day detective, Inspector Endersby must root out the villain any way he can — by disguise, break-and-enter, bribery, mail tampering, and physical force.

Winner of the Arthur Ellis Award for Best Canadian Crime Novel.